EVERYTHING IS BROKEN

John Shirley

EVERYTHING IS BROKEN

John Shirley

PRIME BOOKS

For
My
Sons

Special Thanks
to
Michelina Shirley
and
Paula Guran

AUTHOR'S NOTE

This novel's setting is purely imaginary. I made up my own "Freedom, California." There is, somewhere, a town called Freedom in California, but that is a different place. That "Freedom, California" is real—and mine is not. This novel's "Freedom, California" is quite dissimilar geographically and, doubtless, in every other respect, to any real-life town of that name. Nor should anyone suppose that any town anywhere called "Freedom" is in any way the model for my fictional town.

Also please note that this novel is set a short distance in the future . . . not too far but just far enough.

For everything born must truly die and truly out of death comes life. Facing what must be, cease from sorrow. All beings are invisible before birth and after death are once more invisible. They are seen between two unseens . . . There is no greater good for a warrior than to fight in a war of duty. There is a war whose fight opens the gates of heaven, Arjuna! Happy is the warrior who fights this war. Prepare for war with peace in thy soul . . .

—The Bhagavad Gita (circa 500 BCE)

PART ONE:

Welcome To Freedom

Streets are filled with broken hearts
Broken words never meant to be spoken—
Everything is broken
—Bob Dylan
"Everything Is Broken"

PROLOGUE

"My name is Dickie Rockwell and I fucking rule Freedom, California!"

He yelled it at the rising tide, the churning waves; yelled it so loud he was hoarse with shouting. "My name is Dickie Fucking Rockwell and I'm twenty-seven fucking years, two fucking months and three fucking days old, and I stand before you in Freedom, fucking California, in the fucking *U! . . . S! . . . A!*"

Gazing over the cold October sea, staring all the way to the horizon, the edge of reality, Dickie raised his arms like a prophet. The seagulls on the beach, big dirty-white birds squawking under the gunmetal sky, were his followers. "My name is Dickie Rockwell, and I will rule, *I do fucking rule! . . .* in Freedom, California!" When he raised his arms he could feel the 9mm Glock, moving against the small of his back, where the pistol was stuck in his belt under his fringed brown leather jacket.

Some of his followers—the Grummon brothers and Mike Sten and Nella—were forty yards behind him, getting impatient waiting on the asphalt walk next to the highway. But they weren't like real *followers*—not enough like that. They did what he said, most of the time, sure. Only, that wasn't good enough.

But still: Dickie knew how to make things happen. He declared what he wanted, declared it to the edge of the world, and when he did that his words went echoing out over the horizon to cook in the sun's rays out there . . . and then the declaration would come burning back—and make everything true. Sometimes it took awhile; sometimes he had to kick some ass to help it come true. *God helps him who helps himself.* But when he made these declarations, events seemed to line up with them, one way or the other.

He ran a few steps forward, splashing the foamy edge of the water, yelling again, "My name is Dickie Rockwell!" He turned and ran at the gulls, the leather fringe on his jacket whipping in the wind, the birds roistering around a big old log where someone had left a bag of chips half empty. "And I rule in Freedom, California!" The birds scattered before him, rising up to declare Dickie Rockwell the master of Freedom, California. He could hear it in the squawks of the seagulls. *He rules!*

Dickie raised his arms over his head and shouted, *"Freedom California, U! S! motherfuckin' A!"*

He closed his eyes and thought: *It's coming to me. Coming to me . . .*

And sure enough, just when the gulls were starting to settle down again, Dickie felt his declaration confirmed: it was coming back to him, bounced off the edge of the world. Like a vibration in the ground, a rumble, a small earthquake shiver under the balls of his booted feet. He could even *hear* the rumble. Saw the birds take off again—they felt it too.

Dickie rocked in the backwash from his declaration, taking deep breaths. The sea smelled good.

Then he dropped his arms and spun around, waited one beat—and raised a fist. And his peeps up there on the asphalt walk, above the line of busted-up boulders, knew enough to give him thumbs up and fists up and nods and grins. Except for Sten, of course, but Dickie understood that—Mike Sten had to stay in who he was, stay in the Cool Thing, or he'd just melt away. He wore those dark glasses and he kept that little amused smile on his hatchet face and he just waited for the right time. That was Mike Sten.

Dickie trudged back up to his boys, feeling the cold now, the rising late afternoon wind off the sea licking damply at his neck. Nella was standing with them: a girl he fucked sometimes. She always said she was one of his boys too.

"Gettin' cold out here," Liddy Grummon remarked, as Dickie walked up. Liddy was squinting, the sun was in his eyes. Like his brother Randle, Liddy had a drawn out, flexible face and it got all twisted up around the squint. He wore a long, dirty gray coat over a stained San Jose Sharks jersey.

"That a complaint? Poor Liddy gettin' cold? I was down there all of ten minutes."

"No, I wasn't complainin'. My ears is getting cold, but um . . . " Liddy had a funny way of flicking his hands, like he was trying to get something off them, to emphasize every phrase. "I was just thinkin' that with the sheriff being down at Buried Cove, this is the time to deal with Buff." Flick.

"Good fucking thing I've got you to advise me, Liddy," Dickie said, taking all intonation out of his voice as he said it.

Randle spoke up for his brother. "Dickie, come on, he just means sheriff's not gonna be busy with a burning trailer forever . . . " Randle was a plumper version of his younger brother; same crooked teeth and long, lank brown hair and little sharp blue eyes, but sloppy around the middle from almost perpetual beer drinking. He had a tall can in his left hand right now, in a paper sack.

"We got time," Nella said. "Shit, Sheriff Duncan moves slow as molasses in January—in the Arctic." She grinned. Her teeth were yellow but they were straight. One was missing, on the left corner of her smile. She was a skinny white girl, freckled, but she kept her red-brown hair cornrowed—mostly so she wouldn't have to wash it much. She had a tattoo of a rose on her neck that said *Dickie* under it. The *Dickie* was partly crossed out, but he'd gotten back to her before she'd finished crossing it out and after a short beating Nella had decided she wanted to keep the Dickie tat. She'd even added another one, fancier, on her left tit.

He really needed to get another woman in the Sand Scouts.

"I'm pretty sure Buff was up all night," Nella added, one hand searching through her ski jacket pockets for a cigarette. "Buff went to sleep maybe two hours ago. That's what Twotty says." She found a crumpled pack, half a cigarette left, lipped it out.

"Twotty's always tweakin'," Dickie said. "Not reliable."

"Ha," Sten said. "Twotty tweakin'." He never actually laughed but sometimes his wolfish face drew back into a kind of snarl when he was amused and then he'd say, "Ha" out loud. Now, with a practiced, effortlessly dramatic movement, he zipped up his old-fashioned black leather jacket. Sten was skinny, got cold easy. His hair was receding, Dickie noticed. How old was Sten? Hard to tell, with him. He lived in some kind of cool-greaser Neverland where the inhabitants never seemed to age. Anyway, he was the oldest of the Sand Scouts.

"I'm already *on my fucking way* to see Buff," Dickie said wearily, pushing Liddy to one side so he could cross the road into Old Town Freedom. It had been Old Town Ferry Landing before the mayor got town council to change the name. Supposed to help the tourist thing. They'd aged the signs to make them look like the place had always been called Freedom.

Dickie strode across the highway, the others hurrying to follow, as a semi-truck pulling a trailer of logs boomed past, blaring its horn angrily, just missing them by maybe two seconds, its slipstream skirling the smell of wood, diesel, peeling bark.

They walked between the coffee-and-fish smells of the Rusty Pelican café, and the incense smells of Deanna's Gift Shoppe, where sometimes Sten bought rolling papers. Then they headed up the gravel alley to the thin, cracked concrete road that twisted its way up the hill rising over the highway. The hill shouldered most of the houses, old and new, in the central area of Freedom.

Near the top of the hill they trooped up a cracked concrete driveway to the little cracker box house where Buff lived with Twotty, when Twotty happened to be at home and not off on some speed run.

They found Buff snoring, alone, facedown, on a futon in the back bedroom. He was half-wrapped in a blue, unzipped sleeping bag on a foam-rubber futon, his fat, hairy ass exposed. His thick, pale bristly legs flopped off the futon, angled across the gray-painted wooden floor. Around him, open cardboard boxes overflowed with dirty clothes, junk food wrappers, dope paraphernalia, odds and ends of legal papers, leather pouches, dirty backpacks, empty bottles. There were no decorations in the room. One box contained brassieres, women's underwear, leggings—Twotty's shit, probably. Dickie didn't see any guns or ammunition, but he noticed that one of the nylon backpacks, unzipped close to Buff's disheveled head, was bulging just enough. He squatted by it, picked it up, felt the distinct weight of a handgun in it. He looked inside: yeah, a .45 Colt pistol. And next to it, a half-ounce of yellow-white crystals, probably bathtub meth. Didn't look like the stuff Dickie sold.

Dickie stood up, swinging the little backpack like a pendulum, as he looked around. Buff had been staying there more than a year and he was still living out of boxes. "See, I move into a place," Dickie said, as Sten and the others went to stand over the snoring man, "I like to spread myself over it, put my imprint on it, organize it." It was true: his own place, at what used to be Jenner's Jerky Ranch, was neatly organized, everything in its place, the walls covered with pictures of men he admired. Benito

Mussolini, General George Patton, Julius Caesar, Erwin Rommel, Al Capone, and the white supremacist metal-rapper, Skizmo. On his bedroom door was a poster for the 1960s Omar Sharif movie *Genghis Khan*. He'd watched *Genghis Khan* on VHS six times; *Patton* he'd seen seven times. "But this Buff, he's into living out of fucking cardboard boxes."

Buff groaned and snorted and changed position, at that, and went back to snoring.

"Ha," Sten said. "Sleeps like a baby just off the tit."

Nella laughed. "What a big smelly hairy fucker." She was from Winnipeg, way up north, had a slight Canadian accent. "He *used* to be buff, when he was takin' the steroids, that's why they call him Buff, but now look at him, all fat and flabby."

"Naw, they call him Buff because he used to sell buffalo meat," Randle said. He had a tendency to divert criticism from heavyset people. "He's got an uncle, dude had one of those buffalo ranches and he used to go around—" He broke off, seeing Dickie staring at him.

"Randle?" Dickie said. "Shut up."

Then Dickie kicked Buff hard in the ribs with a steel-toed boot; the boots still had sand on them from the beach. He felt a couple of Buff's ribs crunch. The snoring abruptly became a squealing, with Buff floundering about. The Grummon brothers laughed.

Dickie drew Buff's gun from the backpack, seeing at a glance that it was loaded, and made sure it was the first thing Buff saw when he tried to sit up, writhing around that busted rib.

"Ow! Fuck!"

Dickie pointed the gun at Buff's head. "Buff, you've been selling crystal in town here and you were told not to," Dickie said softly. "We had an understanding about who sells what, and where."

Sten had tugged out the little .32 he liked and Nella had her buck knife open. The Grummon brothers had their .45s showing.

"Whuh the fuck, what you doin' here, you bust my ribs, I never sold no fucking nothing in your—!"

"Stop lying," Dickie said, his tone all calm and advisory, "or I am going to shoot you in the nuts." He shifted the gun to point at Buff's testicles.

Buff went to whimpering, shaking his shaggy head. He scratched in his brown beard—the kind of raggedy beard a guy grows unintentionally, because he's forgotten about shaving. "I thought—you stopped dealing . . . "

"I did," Dickie said. "For a month—maybe two. Because the State Troopers came around. And we had to burn down our cookin' trailer too. But that doesn't mean somebody else can start up because I'm laying low, Buff. No. I was just waiting for the heat to die down. And it's only been a few weeks. Now—everything clear?"

Buff was clutching his side; there were tears trailing through the grease on his fat, hairy cheeks. His mouth twitched and pretty obviously Buff wanted to say something about his ribs. The pain. The injustice of it all, and such. But he didn't. He just bit his lower lip and stared at the floor. Finally he managed, "Clear. It's clear. I got to get to a doctor, get an X-ray and shit."

Dickie shook his head. "Oh—did I give you the wrong impression? That we were done with you just because you finally understood me? No, Buff. It's actually too late for that. Help him get dressed, Randle. You too, Nella."

"I got to touch the fat fuck?"

"Get it done."

It took them some time to get him dressed enough, red hoody sweatshirt and torn sailor pants—from before Buff was kicked out of the Navy—his big belly sagging over the buttons as he staggered out the door. They'd hidden their guns away again, except Dickie had the Colt out, down close to his side.

"You want me to get my *ve*-hicle?" Sten asked, as they went out front. For some reason he liked to say the word like that: *ve*-hicle.

"No need," Dickie said. "We got his. We gonna keep that one anyway."

They all climbed in Buff's big old rattletrap VW bus and drove him to the old salt quarry, about a quarter mile inland, a little ways off Seaward Road: a sandy depression in the ground where a broken earthmover rusted.

All the way there, Buff was saying things like, "I'll pay you whatever you say, you already punished me, Dickie, you busted my ribs, fuckin' hurts, and I didn't even do it!" with boring repetitiveness.

Buff was jabbering like that right up until they dragged him out of the van, shoved him up against the old earthmover. Then he got quiet. His gap-toothed mouth was open wide, one hand holding up his pants, as he looked at the guns ready in their hands; how they were standing around him in a circle. The realization was suddenly there on Buff's face. Like a man turning on the light to find he's stepped into a nest of rattlesnakes.

"That's right . . . " Dickie said. "Now you're getting it."

He noticed an abandoned bird's nest, a big one, in what was left of the tractor's seat, behind Buff. Maybe an omen. Dickie believed in omens big time.

That's when he felt the rumble under his feet again, coming from the direction of the sea. Whoa. He'd really made contact with the edge of the world!

The others felt it too, looking around, frowning. The ground shaking a little . . .

"That's right," Dickie went on, "you remember how we do it,

me and my people. All together, so we all take responsibility as a team."

"This'll be like bear hunting," Liddy Grummon said, his face twisted around a grin.

"Ha," Sten said. "Bear hunt. Cornered that ol' bear."

"No—listen—" Buff licked his lips. "I thought of something you want to know. It's about Shipman—he's—"

"Shut the fuck up," Dickie hissed, pointing his gun at Buff's leg. Good place to start.

"No!" Buff yelled, and tried to run, but Dickie shot the big man's right knee out from under him, and he went down, spurting leg kicking, and then the others were shooting down at Buff—the Grummons and Sten, firing with an ear-bruising racket of gunshots.

"Enough!" Dickie shouted, after a few seconds. They stopped, as the acrid blue smoke drifted around them.

What had Buff said? Shipman? He didn't like to think about Shipman so he'd told Buff to shut up, but now that he considered it, he wanted to know. "What'd he say about Shipman?" Dickie asked, waving smoke away.

Liddy Grummon squinted at him through the smoke. "Joe Shipman—from when we was in Sea Scouts. He came back to town. He's trying to sell his old house or something. Might still be in town . . . "

Joe Shipman. Within reach.

Buff gargled and sobbed and bubbled. All those shots, but Buff wasn't dead yet. He was dying, a pool of dark red already sinking into the sandy ground around him, but he was still wiggling around, and groaning. So Dickie gestured to Nella, telling her to get in close with the knife.

Everyone had to be part of it. They all had to commit. She got in close, knelt by Buff, and he thought he saw a sort of

Mother Teresa look on her face. Sometimes she pretended she was harder than she was.

Maybe it was more like when his mom had taken him to get the Rottweiler put down. The vet'd had a look like that, injecting the hotshot into the dog's neck. *Just getting it done.*

She cut Buff's throat. The ground rumbled in approval.

ONE

How LONG *had they been driving? Five hours?*

Russ's dad had picked him up at the San Francisco airport, and they'd started driving north in the old Volvo immediately, heading for a little town on the coast. The town was called Freedom. Russ had never been there. The road, clinging to the cliffs over the sea, was making him sick to his stomach, with all the curves. And Russ had to pee.

He didn't want to be a baby about it and complain. Probably his dad already thought he was kind of lame, about to turn twenty-one and still living at Mom's house, back in Akron. Then mom says she's kicking him out, gets dad to take him in. Even lamer. "Start over fresh in California," she says. What is this, Mom, 1850?

They had Karen for comparison. His sister, just two years older, was a sharp contrast: a star academic at Brown, a graduate research assistant. Russ had two years vaguely majoring in English with a concentration in American Literature at the University of Akron, and not much to show for it, except he'd read a lot of Steinbeck and Fitzgerald and . . . *some* Melville.

Why should he care what his old man thought? His father had moved away from Ohio, come out to California—and why? Dad kind of lost his right to judge him, when he moved out, didn't he?

Only, he was in his dad's pocket right now. He was broke and his dad had paid his way out here, claiming there was a landscaping job waiting in Freedom. Okay, he'd stay with his dad for a while. Didn't mean he was a loser.

Not that his dad had ever called him a loser. But "Your life has no direction" was more or less the same, wasn't it? Last time they'd had that talk, on the phone, it had been like:

RUSS: Dad, what direction have *you* had? Wandering around the country . . .

DAD: I wasn't wandering, I went where the work was. I have a degree. I have a job.

RUSS: Degrees are meaningless now. I need to find something that matters to me. I don't want to just *survive.*

DAD: You think nothing matters to me?

RUSS: I didn't say that. But you moved out of state. So . . .

DAD: You don't know all the facts, Russ—you don't know what *really* matters. That's where you're confused . . .

Russ had made an excuse and gotten off the phone. Then things got bad with him and Mom, and six weeks later, here he was.

And he still had to pee. "Dad? Is there a rest stop?"

"We're only about twenty minutes from Freedom."

Russ crossed his legs more tightly. "Twenty minutes from getting out of this car. That'll be freedom, all right."

He glanced at his dad to see if the remark had annoyed him. But Dad was smiling. He was a broad-bodied, tanned, solid man of medium height, stiff brown hair speckled with gray; a man who liked outdoors stuff, was reading a biography of Thoreau, wore thick plaid shirts that Russ associated with lumberjacks. His dad was a long way from being a lumberjack, but he was a contrast to his gangly, pale son, who had gotten his mom's jet-black hair and brown eyes. Dad liked Hank Williams, 1950s rockabilly, country swing, and folk; Russ liked ironic punk-styled bands—and the smarter hip-hop, like Immortal Technique and Aesop and Juji. Dad liked baseball; Russ hated sports. Dad didn't drink; Russ liked to get smashed with his friends. That was something he might have inherited from his mom too. Never an obvious alcoholic, she was irritable, in the evening, before getting a couple drinks inside her.

Russ missed his mom and he didn't miss her, at the same time.

"There's a wide spot up there," Dad said, suddenly. "You need me to pull over?"

"For sure."

Dad pulled over in a wide graveled place in the road and Russ gratefully got out of the musty car, into fresh air and room to move, the small muscles in his legs twitching with the stretch.

He walked a short ways into the fir trees, picked a spot behind a tree. The spot smelled, pleasantly and sharply, of the conifer needles dropped around its trunk. *Douglas fir?* he wondered, as he peed against the trunk, admiring the patterns of bright green lichen—and a small tree frog, like something carved from emerald, clinging just above the roots. "I'm being careful to miss you, little dude," he said. "But avoid this side of the tree for a while."

Halfway back toward the car Russ stopped, just standing there, feeling the ground ripple under him, hearing a distant rumble.

What *was* that? Big breakers in a sea cave under them? The car was just a hundred feet or so from the edge of a seaside cliff.

Russ hurried back to the car, feeling nervous, unsure why. But noticing the flocks of sea birds flying inward, from the sea, not far overhead, hearing their brassy collective noise. The birds looked like they were in a hurry, something frantic about their winging; their clamoring, piercing calls.

The wind picked up, ruffling his long black hair, making the tip of his prominent nose tingle. He sniffed, wondering, as he got back into the car, if he was getting a cold.

"Feel better?" Dad asked, looking in the side mirror at the road. Jerking the car back on the highway with the abruptness that so annoyed Mom, ten years before. Dad said it was "decisive" driving.

They'd fought about that, her and Dad; about lots of things, but especially, where to live. Dad had wanted to move away from Akron, find someplace rural in California or Oregon. "Somewhere a person can stretch out and breathe," he'd say.

Russ had been eleven when his parents had broken up: Dad insisting his mom quit drinking; Mom deflecting the drinking issue by claiming he was having an affair. After the divorce, one night, when she was in fact a little drunk, she admitted to Russ that "Dad's affair" had probably been in her imagination. That little revelation struck Russ hard, right in the pit of his stomach. He'd been sympathizing with Mom, had taken her side. Then it turned out her "imagination" had wrecked the marriage and damaged his relationship with Dad.

Life went on. Dad worked for two more years in Akron, then saw his chance to move to California. He'd taken a job teaching civics at a community college in Santa Clara. The teaching gig eventually ended—Russ had never been clear if Dad had lost the job or quit—and now he had some kind of county statistics job up here, in Deer Creek, and he was just getting by. He had to commute inland from Freedom for more than an hour to get to his office, but didn't have to make the drive five days a week; he did some of his work from home.

"You know, Freedom's got its peculiarities," Dad said, glancing out his window at another noisy flight of birds heading inland.

"You mean the town, right?" Russ smiled.

"Yeah, the town."

"How come it's named 'Freedom'?" Russ asked. "That's sort of a weird name."

"They changed the name of the town to Freedom about six years ago. It used to be called Ferry Landing. The town had a ferry, of sorts, long time ago, that went up and down the coast from there, like to Buried Cove and Molly's Harbor."

"How come they changed the name?" Russ asked.

"Oh, that's a long story. Basically—" Dad twisted about in his seat, trying to get more comfortable, audibly cracking his neck. "—basically, it was Lon Ferrara's idea."

"Ferrari, like the car?"

"No, *Ferrara*. Mayor of the town. He owns like four businesses in the area—maybe five or six, I lost count. Kind of guy who hates paying taxes and probably does just about anything to avoid them."

"Everybody complains about taxes."

"Yeah, but he says taxation is theft. Ferrara's extreme about it. He's a libertarian. Hard core. There's different kinds of libertarianism, but essentially the concept is to minimize government and maximize individual freedom. That's the main idea."

"Yeah, I've heard. Sounds good in theory."

"Doesn't work very well in real life. Plus Ferrara's tied in with that teabagger bunch. He's the local Tea Party chairman. Likes to quote that line of Ronald Reagan's—'Government doesn't solve the problem, it is the problem.' Ferrara's given his version a fancy monicker—the Decentralization Movement." He shook his head. "All I know is the schools are barely functioning now. We were supposed to have a privatized fire department here. Never materialized. Mayor sold the firetrucks we had to pay for the Old Town decorations. The privatization of garbage pickup never came through either, so we have to drive our stuff over to the dump ourselves. And he hassled people into voting the town a new name. That's how we got 'Freedom'!" Dad shook his head again in disgust. "I wrote a letter to the *Ferry Courier*, complaining we didn't have the *freedom* to say *no* to naming the town *Freedom*. They didn't print the letter, naturally—Ferrara owns the *Courier*. Which is now called the *Freedom Courier*."

Russ snorted. "They're not, like, skilled at picking up on irony."

Dad chuckled. "You got that right." He took another curve, and added, "You know, the libertarians pulled off a win on that Supreme Court case last year and the county's been going to hell in a handbasket since. Among other things, the Decentralizers have gotten rid of emergency services, dumped search and rescue in this area. Gotten rid of all the cops but two! One and a half, really—one sheriff and a kind of town patrolman up in Buried Cove. Punks running wild . . . "

"Hey, whoa, what's wrong with punks?"

His dad grinned. Russ had been in an Akron neo-punk band. "Not those kind of punks."

"I was just playin'. You mean the, uh . . . "

"Yeah, the drug dealing, thieving kind. Hey, check it out—up ahead, that's Seaward Road. It's a highway, really. We go east on Seaward and then turn right on Ferry Lane and we'll be home. My apartment. Not much, but it's warm. Just a block from the new apartment building I got you the landscaping work on, right down the street from us."

They passed a sign:

WELCOME TO
FREEDOM, CALIFORNIA
Pop. 2200

LON FERRARA was holding court in The Bobbing Buoy Bar and Barbecue when Jenkins first started yelling about the advisory. Ferrara stood at the end of the bar, one boot on the old-fashioned brass foot rail, facing half a dozen bar customers, five assorted men and one woman. He was hoisting a schooner of Doublehit from his own microbrewery up in Buried Cove, slopping some on the bar as he gestured in emphasis. "Privatization is efficiency!" he said, trying to ignore Old Jenkins. The haggard, white-bearded old man had worked for the government meteorological station for seventeen years, though he was no meteorologist himself— just a drunken retiree, really, at this point. Jenkins was stumping up and down the wooden sidewalk outside, pausing to wave his aluminum cane, bellowing about the warning he'd gotten on the Internet at the senior center, and how Monterey and Santa Cruz were on some kind of advisory or "seismo alert" or some fucking thing. Christ, Monterey and Santa Cruz were a long damn ways south, south of the Bay Area, even, what did that have to do with Freedom?

"Privatization is efficiency," Ferrara repeated, liking the phrase, looking around with satisfaction at the bar; sawdust on the sagging wooden floor, dark wood trimming around the high, patterned-tin ceiling. A hundred thirty years old, this place—a monument to the nineteenth century's way of doing things. *Make your own rules.* "Privatization changes everything," Ferrara went on. "No government waste. No inflated bureaucratic wages. And if we want firefighter services that's how we'll get them. We'll get our emergency services—they'll be privatized. I'm working on that one." Ferrara was a big-shouldered man with short legs and a long, heavy torso, dyed dark brown hair—the most difficult-to-spot hair plugs money could buy. He had dark, quizzical eyes, a tweedy blazer. "But to make it happen right you need competition for the service! Competition is practically synonymous with efficiency!"

"Synonymous," Hilly said, nodding, one hand combing his iron-gray beard, his rheumy eyes flicking questioningly at his whiskey glass. Like he was wondering how it had emptied itself.

Mario Ferrara, the bartender—an older, jowlier, aproned version of his brother Lon—came over with a bar towel and sopped up the ale without comment. Lon could slop all of the beer in the place, if he wanted. He owned the bar, and nearly owned his brother too, at this point.

"If competition makes for efficiency," Jill said, "then how come there's never any competition when private companies take over public services?" Jill Hushbeck was a willowy woman with gray streaks showing in her long, straight dark-blond hair; her hazel eyes were difficult to see behind her thick glasses. Why didn't she wear contacts, for crying out loud? She was almost legally blind without those heavy-duty specs. But Ferrara could feel her watching him attentively. Waiting to get the rhetorical jump on him. "There's just one company taking over—usually pre-arranged—and no one to compete with them once they've started."

"Well, Jill . . . I'll tell you . . . " He paused to look her over. Hard to read her face behind those Coke-bottle glasses.

They'd gotten in a lot of debates, him and this woman, last time he campaigned for mayor—to Ferrara she stood for the shrinking Old Guard liberal element around town. Which was why he'd eased her out of the editorial job at the newspaper. Now she worked full-time trying to sell real estate and she was barely hanging on in this market.

But despite the thick glasses, she was an attractive woman; a tall woman in her forties, she filled out the black turtleneck sweater and those designer jeans nicely. Her long, delicate fingers toyed with the stem of her glass, swirling her chardonnay. He'd never seen her drink two glasses of wine in one sitting.

Like to get in there, he thought. Get a piece of that.

But she'd never go for it. Maybe he could make some kind of real estate deal for her, maybe that'd make her more pliable. But he doubted it, even then. Anyway, his wife had moved out, gone to live in Monterey with her sister, was plotting a divorce, and he didn't want to give Wilamina any ammunition to use against him in court. He'd lose too much money if she got the divorce she wanted. He was already overextended.

"I'll tell you what, Jill," Ferrara said at last, "I don't know what sources of information you're trusting, but privatization has *got* to be more efficient. It's in the nature of things."

"Around here—who are we supposed to get to be the privatized fire control company, Mayor? *Your* company, that's what we'll get—no one else around to do it. Where's the free-market competition for that?"

"Heh, she got you there," Mario said, chuckling. "She—"

Ferrara shot his brother a glare and Mario, realizing he was risking his meal ticket, shut up quick—Mario owed his brother about sixty thousand dollars. Lon had bought out Mario's failed night club in North Beach. Sold it, and paid off his debts.

"You're just misinformed, Jill . . . " He paused, feeling the floor shivering under him. What the hell was that buzzing in the floor? Termites?

"Gotta stay informed, stay on the smart side," Hilly said loyally, vigorously nodding, toying significantly with his empty glass.

Ferrara ignored him, not in the mood to be nudged into buying Hilly's drinks. "The fact is . . . "

He broke off, frowning, as Old Jenkins stumped by the window again, then paused to bang on it with the rubber tip of his cane.

"You people listening in there?" Jenkins yelled, his voice muted by the window. "We got an advisory!"

"You break that window you'll pay for it, Jenkins!" Ferrara boomed back at him. "Senile old prick."

Some of the others laughed. Jill put her wine glass down, crossed to the front door, peered out, shading her eyes from the lowering sun.

"What's going on, Mr. Jenkins?" she asked.

He nattered something back at her, Ferrara caught the words *warning, evacuation, earthquake, global warming clustershake* . . .

"What horseshit," Ferrara said. "Back to this global warming nonsense."

Mario opened his mouth like he was going to argue—they'd lost some beachland to the sea rising right here, it was true, the beach was narrower than it used to be; the cliffs a little shorter. Then there was the crazy weather variance around the world. So what—global warming could be a natural cycle caused by sunspots—you get some variation.

"I heard those clustershakes around the oceans are a real thing," Mario said, shrugging. "Just saying."

"The whole idea that global warming could trigger earthquakes, tidal waves, and shit—" Ferrara laughed "—makes no goddamn sense! What's one got to do with the other?"

Jill came back into the bar, chewing a lip worriedly. "Mr. Jenkins is pretty certain there's an advisory for this part of the coast . . . "

Ferrara rolled his eyes. "Like we wouldn't have heard. Okay, Mario, put on the television."

Mario nodded, used a remote to switch on the television over the bar. It got its feed from a satellite and right now it was showing a rugby game. Mario had a thing about rugby.

"No emergency broadcast on there," Ferrara observed. "You see? Gimme another Doublehit, Mario . . . and what the hell, another drink for Hilly."

TWO

RUSS WAS LEANING on the redwood railing of the apartment's balcony, looking down at the town of Freedom and the sea beyond. The air did seem clean, bracing, aromatic here. Smelling of brine, and wood smoke, and the fallen leaves under the oaks flanking the apartment building.

There were binoculars on the railing—Dad was a "birder"—and Russ picked them up, thinking he'd look out to sea, but he held the binoculars against his chest, just looking around . . .

Two hills overlooked the sea, which was a bit more than a quarter mile away; the higher hill to the north, Russ's right, was ringed with old wooden houses, along a winding street—an almost ziggurat effect—set off by those seaside trees that seemed to lean back from the ocean, spruces shaped by years of exposure to the steady wind so they were sculpted like bonsai. A saddle dipped, where Seaward Road passed between the two hills. Ferry Lane circled south from Seaward, to the lower hill, with newer apartments and condos. Dad said a lot of them were owned by Lon Ferrara.

"Hi," said a girlish voice below. "So you got here."

Russ looked down to see a young woman about his age, maybe a little younger, with a tanned, heart-shaped face, sunglasses pushed back over her spiky honey-colored hair. She wore a dark green sweatshirt, Army fatigue pants, Doc Marten boots. Even at this distance he could see the sharp blue of her eyes.

"Whassup?" Russ said, casually, hoping that sounded cool

without trying to sound cool. "Got here—uh, yeah, we got here." That *didn't* sound cool. He wished he still smoked—better to have a cigarette in his hand right now, instead of binoculars.

"My grandma pointed you out, she knows your dad. If your dad is Drew Haver?"

"Yeah."

"'Kay, well, I'm supposed to invite you guys to have dinner, some kind of veggie stew. I think she really sent me so we could meet, which is, you know—lame." The girl shrugged. "But I don't know anyone around here. She worries about it. Wants me to make friends. My Gram's really nice, it's hard to tell her no. But she's a vegetarian. So it'll be, like, all tofu."

"Oh." Her grandmother had put her up to talking to him. He'd hoped she'd talked to him on her own initiative.

Another flock of birds passed raucously over, heading inland. "There go some more," she said. "Birds have been coming in, like there's a big storm out there. I felt the ground shaking too. There was something on the radio . . . " She frowned.

"What kind of something?"

"I don't know, it got fuzzy, something about Monterey and seismic advisories. Makes me nervous, I grew up in San Francisco."

"Yeah? Supposed to be a great place to live."

"It's not so great. Earthquakes. Two since the clusterquakes thing started. Not that big but—got kinda ugly. And it's expensive. And, you know—people get shot. I was living in Potrero Hill, though, that's pretty tight. But then my mom died, and my dad was already dead, so I came to stay with my Gram. What you looking at with those binoculars?"

"Um—nothing yet. Not even sure how to use 'em."

"You having the stew?"

"I'll ask my dad if he . . . I mean, you know, probably. Um—I'm Russ."

"Oh yeah. Pendra."

"Pendra?"

"Yeah. My mom was all about Celtic stuff. Something to do with that."

She looked at him and he could feel her evaluating him and he thought, *I look like a fucking worse dork than usual from this angle, for sure.*

He said, "I'll ask my dad about the dinner." He hesitated, then added, "I felt the ground shake too."

"Yeah?"

"Yeah—it was . . . a ways from here." Another ragged flight of shrieking birds overhead, and a rumbling from the ocean. He looked out to sea—and what he saw puzzled him.

The horizon had changed. It was white and frothy out there, now. A line of white, straight as a rule, erased the horizon's curve.

"Christ. I cannot believe I agreed to this," Brand muttered.

His full name was Brando Marlon Robinson. His mother had been a Brando fan. She'd also been more than a little crazy. But Mom was no longer in a mental hospital; at seventy-four, living in a San Diego condo, she was more cheerful than Brand, who was now forty-seven.

"You see?" Songbird said, leaning toward him, with her best look of compassion. "*You cannot believe!* And that is the problem." She shook her head sadly. "The way people talk is full of unintended messages about them."

Maybe he was sitting here with this woman because she talked like his half-cracked mom. Her real name was probably Susan or something, Brand supposed. She was thirteen years younger than he was, a pert woman with a mauve streak in her mane of curly red hair, a tattoo of a hummingbird on her right wrist, and she was presuming to coach him on his life. She was a "life coach."

They sat on his broad back porch on Highcrest Street, the covered porch people usually put out front on a big ramshackle wooden house like this one, but it had been built here for the view. Below the tiers of houses and highway, the beach was a swath of gray and tan at the foot of the larger hill that crowned the town of Freedom.

"Songbird" was wearing a canary-colored Patagonia hiking coat and Rain Bird pants; Brand was wearing a regular ski jacket, grimy orange, and jeans—it was cold out here, the wind always swiping at the house. They were drinking mugs of green tea, something he almost never drank. His daughter, who lived in Santa Cruz, had given him the tea, as well as this session. The tea tasted like wet hay, to Brand.

The life coach was gazing at him with a look of keen interest. Mixed interest, he suspected. She had no wedding ring and, inwardly wincing, he wondered if she was measuring him as a possible mate, a widower she could straighten out, remake into a healthy middle-aged, marriageable man.

He missed his wife; missed walking with Marilee, watching movies with her, having dinner with her, sleeping with her. He missed sailing with her. He'd sold their little sailboat when she'd died and had never gone sailing again. And another thing he missed—she'd insulated him from troublesome females.

Better give the conversation a chance. What else had he been doing? Sitting around, halfheartedly trying to illustrate his book. A book that would sell barely enough copies to keep his publisher interested in publishing him. But he wanted to please Annette. Talk to Songbird and get it over with.

His daughter Annette had paid the life coach to talk to

him—Songbird had a timeshare in Freedom, and supplemented her income, when in town, with "life coaching." Or tried. Brand doubted there were many takers. It was more of a Los Angeles thing. Most of the time she lived in Westwood. His daughter had found Songbird on the Internet.

There was no way he could bring himself to call her Songbird out loud.

" . . . you see," she was saying, "there's a secret that is so *obvious*, people overlook it. Believing is almost magic. You have to train yourself to *believe* . . . "

She went on in that vein. He tuned her out, nodding at the appropriate intervals, checking in now and then to be sure she was still on the therapy-lite refrain. He looked at the cacti he'd tried to grow in the Navajo pots along the wooden fence in his back yard. He was from Arizona, originally, and he'd thought they'd cheer him up. They were turning brown. It was really too cold and damp for them here. The vegetable garden he'd attempted was overgrown with weeds. A few onions had done all right. He really ought to dig down and see if any of the potatoes had made it . . . This time of year, though, they were probably ruined. Things grew—and died. Languishing and fading in dead soil . . .

" . . . there's a reason religions emphasize faith, because faith heals us and I don't mean like 'faith healers,' I mean . . . "

Brand knew he was being unkind, not following what she was saying—and by extension he was being unkind to Annette. He ought to play the game and let this woman "coach" him. Be mindful, listen to her nattering. That's what it was, nattering, but he could be nice about it. Why not?

" . . . belief is so subjective, but I know that when I believe in my own happiness, I'm happier. It seems like a paradox . . . "

"I don't lack belief," he said suddenly, surprising her. "I believe in various things. What I lack is denial."

"Uh . . . " She blinked. "Denial?"

"Denial. *I need denial*. I'm lacking in it. I need to be in denial that I suffer from a terminal disease, that we all do, from the time we're about twenty-five."

"What disease?"

"The long, slow terminal disease called aging. I'm missing all kinds of denial. Like—denial that we're using the rest of the world as our piss pot and denial about my own responsibility for that. Denial that my daughter will inevitably die—and most people, I believe, die unhappily. So—she will probably die unhappily too."

Songbird was slowly shaking her head, smiling sadly, but she'd never be able to 'coach' him if she didn't understand, at least a little, what he thought about life, so he went forcefully on: "Denial that millions of people are being enslaved—indentured servitude, sex slavery—and that hundreds of millions, *billions* of foolish, brutal people are going to have children and just make billions more foolish, brutal people who will have yet *more* children who will learn from their parents to be even *more* foolish, brutal, and cruel—and who will absolutely insist on believing in stupid superstitions, religions that spread ignorance and war. Denial about the hopeless wreckage we're making of the natural world. Denial about the ways that I myself have failed in this life—like the fact that I should have done a lot more to ease my wife's passing." His voice went hoarse, but he pressed on: "That maybe I could have saved her life if I'd worked harder so we had better health care. Denial about the isolation and suffering all around me. Denial about my failure to make a difference in the world in any consistent way. Denial! If only my denial was intact, I could look away from all those things. Insulate myself from them. I could look away from my own culpability and everyone else's. I could look away from the slow ruination of my brain and my health. But . . . I'm short on denial. Haven't got any at all, in fact."

She gave him a pitying look. "Brand—once you heal, you won't see things that way. Healthy people don't see it that way."

"No, healthy people have *denial*, that's all. Or they take Prozac. Which is pharmaceutical denial. But look—if it's spirituality you're talking about, I can grasp that. You've read the Diamond Sutra—or the Upanishads—or the Bhagavad Gita?"

"Um—I'm familiar," she said, blinking.

She hasn't read them, he thought. He shrugged and went on, "The Gita tells us to approach life head-on, accept your transience, identify with the eternal—now *that* has value. It also says accept death. But this approach *you* have—I mean, yeah, I know I'm a depressive but it seems so unbalanced to me to pretend that the dark side of existence is just a matter of having negative energy. No, it's part of living. And tragedy is part of living, and suffering."

"It's hard to see, from here," she went on. "But *things happen for a reason*. Everything happens for a reason."

"Oh Christ, not *that* one! Everything happens for a reason? You mean it all ultimately has a point? Really! Two weeks ago, in Sacramento, a man murdered a woman in front of her three children and then he murdered the kids one by one. And not quickly. What *reason* is there for that?"

She took a deep breath, sipped her tea, twisted her lips into a skewed cone. "Maybe we'll try another approach . . . Let's try a healing chant. This chant teaches that all things are possible."

She taught him the chant, took his left hand between hers— probably imagining she could transfer "good energy" to him that way—and she repeated the mantra softly, a faux Native- American incantation. Her hands felt clammy. He noticed that her nails were badly chewed.

Dutifully mumbling the chant, he lifted his gaze beyond the splintery gray line of his back fence, taking in the sea, an eighth-mile below: the blue and green waves tipped with horses of white; mottled, in the hollows, with the green and brown of kelp, and disturbed sand. The ocean seemed to be churning with more excitement than the wind would explain. And the horizon looked strange . . .

Hamish, his white-haired neighbor, popped his head up above the northern fence. He had a perpetual worried smile and big down-slanting dark eyes.

Brand knew Hamish was standing on a scuffed little boulder he routinely used to look over the fence. Hamish's thin white hair lifted in the breeze. "Brand, did you—oh . . . sorry."

"Sorry? About what? Oh." He took his hand back from Songbird's. "Not what it looked like." He was grateful for the interruption. "Did I what?"

"Did you feel that? Several times, the last couple hours . . . "

"Oh, hello there!" Songbird said chirpily, beaming at Hamish. "Did you feel something special, over there? Sometimes these mantras travel through the air and affect the neighbors! When the energy is lifting, it reaches out to everyone nearby . . . "

"I *did* feel something," Hamish said, adding puzzlement to his wide smile. "Like—the ground shaking."

"The ground shaking—wow! That's a powerful response."

"I didn't notice the ground shaking," Brand said, feeling sure that Hamish meant something physical, not metaphysical. "Anyway, the wind is always rattling the house so I tend to discount anything like that."

Hamish squinted at the sea. "The radio said something about an evacuation. For the whole county."

"Evacuation?" Brand was suddenly feeling more alert. Distantly aware that Songbird was rattling on about "having the courage to bring positive energy into a negative world." He glanced at Hamish. "Why an evacuation?"

"Because . . . Jeezus God, look at that!" Hamish pointed down at the sea.

Brand looked at the ocean, standing, shading his eyes with his hands. The horizon had lifted itself up, and now it was rolling toward them like an endless wheel, catching the light.

A sky-breaching wall of seawater was rising above the nearer sea, was rushing toward them. It came on thunderously, inexorably, toward the small town of Freedom, California.

Brand turned to speak to Songbird—and saw that she had gone. He heard the front door bang shut; heard her running feet on the walk.

Her footsteps were lost in the growing rumble, the rising, world-shaking roar from the infinitely populous waves of an invading army: the sea.

THERE WAS a long, deep, unprecedented rumble from the sea— and a sudden prolonged hysterical shriek from Old Jenkins . . .

They ran to the window, and saw the waves—and in a handful of seconds Ferrara had rushed from the front window to the back stairs.

The creaking staircase led to the second story of the tavern building and the splintery sun deck, which they hadn't used in years. Ferrara led the others by at least four steps, rushing to the top of the stairs; he unlocked the metal door from inside with a twist of the rusty lock-knob, shouldered through onto the sun roof, blinking in the sudden light.

Hearing—and feeling—the tympanic roll of the oncoming wall of water, Ferrara climbed up the steeply angled roof behind the sundeck, his feet slipping on mossy wooden shingles. Got to the top, straddling it, just in time, heart hammering, wheezing, to turn and see a mountain range of seawater, more than a hundred feet high, rising up, up . . .

It came booming toward him, stampeding across the beach below the town, the churning at its base like countless running white feet . . .

Some beachcomber in its path screamed hoarsely, the scream cut off as the wave swept the man up, sucked him tumblingly in, and swallowed him, the onrushing wall of water—a hundred feet high—not slowing as it hit the beach, seeming to lean eagerly toward the town as it smashed onward, across the highway, coming at the buildings facing the sea, including the Bobbing Buoy Bar and Barbecue . . .

Then it was looming over Lon Ferrara, pushing a cold wind ahead of it that made Ferrara's clothing flap. The great wave was dark brown at the base, then tan, then transparent green, brilliant white, flecked with flotsam, veined with seaweed . . .

The wave. A dirty but translucent mountain. Throwing a shifting mix of reflected light and gloom.

Monumentally towering, beyond time, throwing a chill, fulsome shadow across Freedom, California . . .

THREE

RUSS WAS WATCHING from the balcony; his dad hurried out, and Pendra was watching from the ground under the balcony, and they all three stared down the hillside at the wall of water, its bigness on an apocalyptic scale, its crest seeming to hang over the highway, and the streets spread out below them—to hanging there like a cobra poised to strike . . . for a single long second. It took him a moment to fully comprehend. *A tsunami . . .*

And then the wave came crashing into the town with a growl within a rumble within thunder, all bursting into one master roar. The ground shook with it; a wind was forced up the hill toward them, smelling of sea and petroleum.

"Oh God, oh no," Dad muttered. Staring.

Seeing the vast wave slam the town Russ thought of a really big, muscular man standing in front of a miniature model of a village on a table, the man suddenly sweeping his arm into the little buildings, bashing them to flinders with one sideways massive swipe, crushing one little house into the next . . . A giant, smashing the town . . .

Instinctively, he raised the binoculars to his eyes . . .

It was more than Russ could take in. The Pacific Ocean had *displaced* the town, below the hill: every building along the beachside highway was submerged, or sucked from its foundation like plants torn up by the roots. And the wave—the word seemed inadequate, it was more like *the muscular shoulders of the ocean*, lifting up—this immense surge from the deeps was changing its color as it scooped up dirt and debris, so the trough behind the wave became the color of an old bruise.

Russ became aware of another sound, through the ongoing roar: a thin, many-sourced warbling. Then he realized he was hearing *screams.* They were attenuated from here, icicle-thin: hard to hear, yet icily penetrating the malicious bellowing of the mountainous wave.

And the bodies . . .

As the wave splintered and tossed the line of boxy wooden buildings, moving on to the next row of houses, Russ saw bodies—tiny figures at this distance—flipped up as if the wave were throwing them over its shoulder, like a big vicious dog killing its way through trapped rodents. It was impossible to tell if any were still living, or if their apparent flailing was driven by the churning, gray-brown element. They were just more debris mixed in with the shattered timbers, drifting doors, whole sections of wall, furniture, cars upside down, unrecognizable objects rising and subsiding—as the wave moved on, plowing over the next street and the next, redefining shapes as it went, human artifacts liquefying into the chaos of the dirty living sea. The water went from dark brown to black with debris; the odd shapes of broken walls, panels of wood, debris that had lost all identify merged into one grinding irregular mass, bullying its way forward. The tsunami heaved against the hills like a football player trying to tackle a bigger man, the tackler flying asunder in dirty foam. And *another* great wave, not quite as big but as forceful, followed quickly, picking up new flotsam: a minivan spinning like an overturned turtle, a man trying to climb onto it, slipping back, vanishing in a whirlpool; logs that had been at sea for years were hurled like javelins, crunching into the houses on the hill. Houses collapsed down into the hysterical sea with a squealing and wrenching Russ could hear even at this remove, the shattered faces of buildings disgorging furniture and people. And the wave moved onward, upward . . .

"Dad—" Russ asked suddenly. "—should we run?"

"If we do, we . . . we'd be on lower ground. This is the highest ground around here. Don't think we'll need the roof . . . "

And then the entire town, below their vantage, was engulfed by the sea—except for a narrow, peaked building, close to the submerged highway, where a group of people clung to the roof. The structure was on a rocky spur of land, significantly higher than the rest of the buildings. The tidal wave swept over it—and a few people remained, afterwards.

Scores of bodies were being whipped about in the white and brown water, entwined with crackling power lines and kelp and carpets . . . The tsunami, grinding everything before it with bladelike pieces of what it had destroyed before, seemed to erase life as it pushed ahead. Russ felt a small blossom of hope when he made out several people climbing from the swamping debris, climbing onto a free-floating wooden two-car garage. Most down there, clearly, would be drowned, crushed, blenderized. But some lived; some struggled free of the vector of chaos . . .

A mist rose from the crashing of the wave like smoke over a forest fire. Everywhere, dogs barked, birds shrieked, and the hillsides thumped and echoed with sound.

And piercing through all was the persistent keening of screams.

THE SOUND of weeping reached Russ through the vastly amplified, *basso profundo* of the tsunami. He looked down and saw it was Pendra, turned to look at the wave crashing below them, hugging herself and shaking her head.

"Up here, Pendra!" he yelled. "Better come up here!"

The tidal wave was rushing up the hill toward them, another great wave close behind it—like great gelatinous creatures charging, crashing into trees and houses, breaking up into competing waves that thrashed back and forth, pitching pieces of buildings. A couple of small boats, a badly broken yacht, one dead horse and an overturned pickup truck, were all tumbled together with the floating roof of a house—and it was all coming up the hill at them, rising, mounting up to make them part of it, an expression of nature, as if the tsunami was a commonplace natural process that was *supposed* to crush the town into boiling liquefaction.

Russ watched, hypnotized, helpless, as it came up for them. As the tsunami came on, rearing colossally . . .

. . . and finally broke, just before it reached the apartment building. Just as Pendra came onto the balcony beside him, shouting but almost inaudible in the massive noise of the displaced sea, the sounds of cars flung to crash through rooftops just about eighty feet below them. Two flowerpots fell off the corners of the balcony, with the reverberation of the tsunami's slam; a window cracked and dust sifted from the edge of the roof overhead.

The rapacious wave was collapsing. Still it refused to back away completely. Gray and sickly green and filthy, the ocean raged almost within reach of them. At last it began to suck back, back toward the open sea.

People were drawn with it—they were some distance away but he saw them clearly, living people thrashing in terror as the wave recoiled. The ocean was swallowing its victims. For a time it roiled restlessly in place, seemed reluctant to pull back.

SEVEN BLOCKS from the beach, CHIEF TOMMY'S MOTEL was a squat building clinging like a barnacle on the side of the hill.

Nella was in room 22, second floor, thumbing her cell phone, trying Ronnie again, when the thundering and screaming and crashing started.

She had been trying to get a certain someone out of her head and a certain someone back in. Buff—him she wanted out. She kept seeing Buff dying, something terrible about a big guy like that becoming such a scared little thing and then dying miserably, like a fat puppy getting chased around and killed by a speedfreak with a golf club, something she'd seen a few years before: something else she wanted out of her head. And she wanted Ronnie Burke *in*, she wanted Ronnie to fill up her whole mind and fill her body and just sweep her out of where she was, because he was the last guy who'd been able to do that for her. He'd been so sweet, like he really did care about her, but later he'd heard someone call her a skank and the day after that he didn't show up and that was almost a month ago and she'd sent him some text messages but cell phones worked for shit out here—well sometimes they worked, depending on where in town you were, but not reliably like around Sacramento—and every time she thought she'd got him almost agreeing to meet her, then the call got dropped.

Nella had rented the motel room to stay in, partly to be away from Dickie Rockwell's bunch and partly to shack up with Ronnie if she could get him to really commit to just coming here and giving her a chance (something was booming and crashing outside) if he would just give her even a few minutes, she might—

The picture window at the front of the motel room heaved itself inward and sprayed broken glass over her as if the battering ram of muddy water had been deliberately fletched with shards, but she couldn't scream because her mouth was full of brown water and she was being shoved up against the wall, pressed into a corner, the water quickly filling the room, pouring through the window like a dam's spillway, turning the motel room into a whirlpool, the water crashing around and rising, rising to her neck, making the TV crackle and the dresser lift up and dance around. The mattress whipped around to suck against the window—and the mattress blocked the window, for a moment, so that the pushing waters subsided to an angry back-and-forthing. Trying to wake up from this nightmare, Nella saw a dead cat swirling, all tangled with kelp and the clothes from her suitcase, her best clothes almost indistinguishable from muddy sand, and then—

The walls started to crack, and lean bulgingly inward, then outward, then inward, like cheeks inside a panting mouth—and the door just *exploded* outward, and she found herself flying headlong, her whole body drawn in by an unrelenting suction, her left shoulder cracking hard against the splintered frame as she bounced through. She was swept out, whirled under water into dirty brown darkness . . . then she popped up like a cork into the air, coughing, just another part of the sodden, blended, filthy medium the world had become, ocean everywhere, ocean and debris and a school bus that seemed to be swimming like an orange whale, dragged along in the flood . . .

The flood.

The phrase "Biblical Flood" came into her mind, the two words almost shouted in her head, and she remembered Bible lessons with her folks in Winnipeg and how withdrawn and angry they'd been when she'd asked "But how could *that* happen, if . . . ?" and how they hadn't let her eat for two days, not anything, to punish her for lack of faith. When she tried to slip down to the kitchen her father caught her, dragged her by the neck back to her room. And now Nella was being hustled by another unstoppable force, as if Papa was dragging her through the filthy roiling water thirty feet deep where the parking lot had been. She felt her bare right foot slapped by what was probably a car antenna jutting from beneath, other cars and vans all crookedly surfacing before sinking again. A blue-haired old lady in a torn nightgown was scrabbling at a floating mattress with long red fingernails, trying to climb onto it—the mattress tipped her back into the water and she sank gurgling and didn't come back up; the Mexican woman who cleaned the rooms drifted by, face down, the back of her head bashed in, hair matted and wet; the old Indian guy who ran the motel office went by, clinging to a big piece of Styrofoam, staring at her with dull shock but, she realized, almost triumph too, and she looked away from him at the sky to see if God was looking down. She saw nothing but the quite ordinary gray sky, and when she looked back the old Indian guy was gone and she was suddenly aware that the water was cold. She'd been too stunned to notice the temperature before, but she felt as if the uncontrollable chattering of her teeth announced it, and she was sure, now, that this wasn't a dream, remembering the passage from Genesis about the flood sent by the angry Jehovah that her parents had read to her many times: *The Lord said, "I will blot out man whom I have created from the face of the ground, man and beast and creeping things and birds of the air, for I am sorry that I have made them."*

Nella couldn't think about anything else, after that—there was no room for it. Because a steep wave had knocked her under, tumbling her, and she was choking. She opened her eyes and saw the world had gone brown-black, she was under a layer of obscene chocolate, looking up at a ceiling made of the rippling murk; she was afloat in a lower level of translucent green water, lit by light shafting through breaks in the murk overhead; bits of wood drifted up, and down, and a refrigerator was slowly sinking, its door open, and a ray of light coming through a hole in the surface-scum spotlit a child floating upside down about thirty feet away: a pale-haired girl who must surely be dead, her limp arms splayed; and a little lower, several overturned sedans, seeming colorless, were finding their own level. Blankets swept from the motel had become aquatic creatures billowing like jellyfish. Nella felt she should let go and die but she couldn't. She kicked and clawed at the water, trying to climb a ladder that wasn't there.

Kicking, kicking. It seemed to take forever to ascend into the brown layer, into opacity; pushing splintery debris out of the way, getting tangled with rubber-coated wire, fighting free . . .

Then she was thrusting her head out of the dirty water, gasping, clasping a floating crate and spitting foulness. The crate was pretty buoyant and she pulled it down between her legs so she could ride it like a horse, keeping her head and shoulders above briny water stinking of sewage and oil. She saw another body floating by, face down—a man, vanishing under waves that twitched every which way. Her teeth clacked like castanets in the cold water, she kicked her feet, instinctively trying to get to the place where the water slapped against the hill above the sunken motel.

But the sea was still surging, sucking her the other way. Towards crackling, sparking debris . . . she saw an electrical cable hanging down from a leaning pole, the cable wriggling and snapping like an angry snake. She didn't want to be electrocuted and if she got close enough the water would transmit the electricity and she'd be fried in shit-water.

She wriggled the crate up, clinging as if it were a beach toy in her bruised arms, and she kicked crazy-hard, rasping out "No no no no no no not gonna no!"—the words almost stuck in her caked throat. Little by little she was making her way through the churning; thrashing along toward a tree to one side of the motel near the hillside, a pushed-over oak tree, some of its roots sticking up at the sky like the tentacles of a giant wooden squid. She was heading for it, trying to keep to the left of a big morass of random floating items: a small car on its side, a couple of spare tires, overturned plastic coolers, and a great deal of jagged timber—

There was a man in there, a naked man with a spike of wood, a giant splinter, right through his body under his right nipple, and he was feebly trying to pull himself up on a higher chunk of floating wood. He vomited blood and fell back and tried to thrash up again but the turbulent water slapped him down and he vanished in the churning swell—

Spitting blood herself from a split lip, she looked away, focused on the roots of the oak tree, and kept kicking toward it, past the motel—glanced to one side to see that the top of the motel was covered in brown sucking water but someone was clinging to the 1960s-style sign above the roof: a crying heavyset middle-aged woman with her red hair pasted down; she was wearing only a brassiere, her white ass looking doughy.

Someone else was screaming, behind Nella, near that sparking cable—and suddenly the scream cut off.

Then Nella had almost reached those roots, twisting toward the sky, the gray, kelp-twined tree trunk revolving slowly in the water; a naked man clinging, farther up . . . why was everyone naked?

She saw people watching, up on the hill above her, standing on dry ground up there, on some house's back deck, about thirty yards over the dirty, invasive new breakers. And she recognized them.

It was Dickie Rockwell and Mark Sten and the Grummon brothers. They were passing a bottle and laughing at her.

FOUR

Only a single building was left standing—partly standing—along Highway One in Freedom, California. It was the tallest building in town, three stories, once housing Ferrara's Bobbing Buoy Bar and Barbecue. Several walls and a large piece of the roof remained.

Lon Ferrara, soaking wet, shivering, crusted in salt, was straddling the spine of the peaked roof, his brother and a woman clinging nearby. Ferrara was asking himself if he was dreaming. He was feeling like he was at a significant remove from *real*. The cold wind, the spray, was cutting at him, but he didn't feel it much; his hands, clamping the wooden shingles, were just dead things at the end of his arms. The wave had passed over him and had pressed him crushingly onto the roof and then tried to pull him free. Tremendous pressure, but he'd wedged between a drain pipe and a deck post and the roof had been slightly turned aside and a lot of the pressure had been turned from him too and then the water had receded, to just below his perch . . .

He did feel one thing: the sensation of smallness, of inconsequentiality, was like a big burning hole in his middle.

The bar was destroyed; the guts of the building had been literally sucked out from under him. He fully expected this roof to collapse too. It was almost all that remained, except the upright teak beams that supported its frame—hard timber extracted from an old ship, the beams had withstood the tsunami, holding

55

the peaked roof over the sun deck. The walls were gone, but the beams, the frame of the building, were still there. The deck itself had washed away in the thunderous surge—the massive wave had been weakened in this area by the rising slope of the sand, the tidal break of boulders lining the beach, the highway, the spur that the bar stood on—and an empty semi-truck that had been passing at just the right moment, right for Ferrara but fatal for the truck, which had been kicked over on its side and spun, slammed into the building housing the Surf Shop and the Gift Shoppe and Amir's Frozen Yogurt, all of them stoved-in and reduced to floating debris. Amir himself had gone floating by, face down, limp in the agitated surf. A dead sea lion, cloven almost in half, rippled bloodily by, a few yards from Ferrara's feet.

The tsunami had boiled past them, Ferrara and Mario and the woman, rising, rising, rising over them as it was forced up the hill by pressure from behind—but after it had crashed over their roof they were still there. And the three of them were still clinging, shivering but holding on when it receded part-way, leaving a great deal of foul water to toss furiously around this little wooden island. The tsunami was reluctant to leave the land, like a swarming army that had captured new ground and was not going to give it up.

Ferrara heard the cries of people in a building that had stood behind his bar—a two-story apartment building on First Street, made of concrete and redwood, standing pretty stoutly for a while. He pictured the currents, sluicing water invading the house, instantaneous flooding, rip-currents like poltergeists tearing through the rooms. He could hear the faint yells of people smacked against walls, against one another, against tubs and tables—saw someone bashed out through an exploding window. The sea drowning those it didn't simply pulp first. He heard the creaking crunch of the building collapsing.

Then there was just the sound of water from back there. Sea noises replacing human noises.

He glanced over at the woman, clinging not far from him. His dazed mind wouldn't find her name.

His brother was there—his stupid brother Mario. He saw Hilly's body, just below his little wooden island: stuck on a twisted piece of drainpipe, head half torn off, flaccid arms waving in the waves like he was doing a hula.

Jill was telling Mario—even as enormous waves danced crazily around them, trying to pull down the roof that was the only thing keeping them alive—that they should try to pull others up here with them. That they should help that man who was clinging to a tree trunk, over there, his gasping mouth wide open. But the more people who came up here, the more weight, the more strain on the roof, so the Ferrara brothers ignored her and soon the man disappeared under the waves.

It would most likely be death to slip under those waves. There was no swimming in there—it was like a blender, that churning sea, slashed by blades of splintered wooden edges and jagged glass on broken window frames and pieces of cars. There were oil slicks that would choke you and pull you down . . .

No, he wasn't going into that mess for anyone. And *no one else* was going to be allowed up on this roof. The more people up here, the more chance it might collapse. They might even crowd him off. No, if anyone tried to climb on, he was going to kick them in the face.

Ferrara simply held on, feeling almost numb with cold; feeling just that one certainty: he wasn't going to let anyone take anything else that was his . . .

———

THEY SAT on the balcony for a long time, in white plastic chairs, Russ and Pendra and Dad, staring down the hill as if someone had slapped them all repeatedly until they could no longer think or speak or move. Sat there, awash in the raw, overwhelming smell of the flooding; watching the waters slowly, slowly recede; looking at a town turned inside out, its interior broken up and scattered below them. Hearing the hissing, the crackling . . .

Russ realizing that, somehow, fires had broken out, just above the waterline, in many places. Fire seemed a strange offspring of a tidal wave. The smell of smoke mingled with the reek of displaced sewage and decaying fish.

But finally, Pendra said, "My Gram . . . my Gram went to the store. She didn't have any sodas for guests and she went to the store right before . . . " She put a hand over her mouth and her eyes teared up again and Russ put his hand on her shoulder.

"We'll check on her," he said. "See if she came back before the wave . . . "

"No, she—left right before the . . . "

But they went and looked through the apartment, the three of them. Dad leading the way.

The apartment, in the same untouched building, in a downstairs corner, was empty but for two cats—a tabby and a fat, grumpy old Siamese. Pendra picked them both up, the cats mewing complaints, and hugged them to her, as Russ and his dad made a show of searching through the neat, cluttered old two-bedroom flat, with its 1960s artifacts. Framed posters of Summer of Love shows, their art as enigmatic as the stoniest tag graffiti.

Russ felt foolish; he knew the woman wasn't there. Knew she was probably dead.

Russ and his dad returned to Gram's living room just as the Siamese got disgusted with the enforced hugging and scratched

Pendra. She dropped both cats and burst into tears, covering her eyes with her hands.

"We've got to see if we can help people out, down the hill," Russ's dad said. "Pendra—you should stay here, take it easy." He flicked a light switch. "There's no power here either, I see. No surprise. No gas in this building. Nothing to turn off. Wait here for your grandma and we'll have a look down the, uh . . . "

Pendra exhaled windily, shaking her head behind her splayed hands, then dropped them, wiping her eyes with the motion, and said, "Let's look for her. See what we can do. We better bring Gram's first aid stuff . . . "

Pendra found the first aid kit and they went outside, struck instantly by a smell of exposed oceanic muck. Leaving the orderly little apartment and walking down the hill was like leaving the mortal world and descending into Hell.

The tsunami was visibly receding, slowly draining back into the Pacific. They saw a few intact roofs below, like wooden islands in the lapping water, with people clinging to them. It was impossible not to see the water as a person, somehow—it had seemed so self-directed, so malicious—and now, even as it slowly withdrew, the churning, nervous, silty waters seemed to Russ like a mass murderer after a rampage, still shaking as his fury subsided.

Many of the killer's victims were floating around the rooftops, so discolored by mud and slime it was difficult to make them out from the flotsam and mucky water. There was a car, maybe a Corolla, jammed through the middle of a house, tail up, like a giant automotive tombstone leaning toward the sea. Fires licked just above the waterline; smoke gathered over the little town and the still-restless brown water.

A barefoot woman ran by, a block down, shouting a name, over and over again, and Russ knew, somehow, she was calling a lost child. The terror in her voice was deeply maternal.

Debris choked the street below as the waters drew back; high, ungainly lumps of wood and plaster humped up: the remains of houses. About a block down, the street below them was obstructed by a great unruly dam of timber and assorted objects, including one precariously tilted Volkswagen bug, and two twelve-foot boats, crammed into the giant deposit of rubble at odd angles. The accidental dam was at least thirty feet high, muddy water still streaming from its every crevice. Even from here, almost a block away, Russ could see a body, bent all wrong, worked into the splintery mass. Several men were dragging a limp woman, muddy from the water, from the barrier. One of the men was sobbing, his shoulders shaking.

Russ thought it was like pictures he'd seen of a war zone.

Birds wheeled frantically overhead; dogs barked. Cats screamed with agonized shrillness, trapped somewhere. A fierce-eyed, heavyset black man with salt-and-pepper hair, naked from the waist up, was stalking back and forth, shouting at people. "If your house ain't been hit, get your water from the pipes, fast. Get it into buckets, whatever you got!"

Good advice, Russ reckoned, but most everyone remained standing about on the street, gawking. About ten yards down, a crying teenage girl was staggering up the street, yelling hoarsely, "Does anyone have a cell phone that works?" Her blond hair was matted, a broken left arm turned sickeningly sideways, one small breast exposed in her torn blouse, her eyes blacked by bruises, "Did anyone call for help? Hey! Does anyone have a . . . "

Russ and Pendra waited while his dad went to talk to the girl, gently putting his coat over her shoulders, telling her to sit down and wait for help. Pendra shouted for her grandmother a few times, but the street echoed with shouts for other missing people, and she gave up, staring around, one hand over her mouth, now and then shaking her head.

Russ wanted to put his arm around Pendra, but thought better of it. "She drove, right?" he asked.

She nodded. Staring at the wrecked houses. At sodden furniture, flipped over in the street. At a middle-aged woman, her face twisted with emotion, dragging a man's body out from under a soaked mattress. "She . . . the store is down the hill, past all . . . " Pendra waved vaguely, as Russ's dad came back. "Oh God," Pendra said, her voice breaking. "Russ . . . I think she's probably dead! She would have been in her car! She's old! She . . . " She wiped her nose on a sleeve. "I don't have anybody else, just no fucking body at all . . . "

Dad didn't think twice, he put his arm around Pendra. "We don't know what happened to her. What sort of car was it?"

"Um—a Honda Accord. Kind of like . . . metallic blue."

"Let's see what we can find a little farther down . . . "

A naked boy, perhaps four, his face streaked with blood, was wandering wobblingly across the street, crying, waving his arms. Russ thought he ought to take the child in hand till they could find his parents. But a skinny Hispanic woman in a water-stained housekeeper's dress scooped the boy up—the woman was clearly not the child's mother, and he resisted with shrieking, white-faced hysteria. She clasped him even closer, hugging him as he thrashed, and said, over and over, "We find her, we find her, *niño* . . . "

People were emerging from Dad's apartment building, and from other houses above the waterline; some were openly weeping, most were gaping around in shock.

A lean, thin-bearded older man, an aging hippie, shuffled up to Russ's dad. He had long gray hair worked into dreadlocks, leathery tanned skin, a marijuana leaf in gold outlined on his green T-shirt. He gestured vaguely at the panorama of wreckage and said, "This is like the shit that was supposed to happen in 2012. They only missed it by seven years. Probably this is, y'know, *the beginning*, and it'll end with everything going all fucking sideways at once, man . . . "

"Tsunamis have happened before, Lars," Dad said. "That's all it was."

The phrase *that's all it was* struck Russ as inadequate. But it was impossible to know how much "it" was. He had been wondering if the tidal wave had hit San Francisco. The scope of it even here in Freedom was difficult to grasp. The smell alone—of briny sea-bottoms and oil and smoke and sewage—was overpowering. And that would only get worse. When the bodies started to rot.

"Just an earthquake under water, Lars," Dad went on, patting him on the arm before moving on. "They happen."

They walked on down the hill—till Dad stopped, staring at a chunky, balding man, in a polo shirt and loafers and khakis, in the driveway of a two-story house built over the hillside. The man throwing Samsonite bags into the trunk of a gold BMW. Dad shook his head. "Dr. Spuris? What are you *thinking?*"

Spuris jumped at the sound of his name, his eyes wild, his mouth open. "I . . . oh . . . it's you . . . " he said vaguely. But his eyes stayed wild. "Drew, I'm just . . . "

Dad walked calmly over to him, "Dr. Spuris . . . "

"For God's sake," Spuris said, holding up both hands in warning. "Keep your voice down! If people know that I'm . . . "

"It's noisy out here," said Russ's dad. "But there's a noise missing. You notice? Sirens. You know why—Ferrara and his cronies ended that service. The Decentralizers got rid of it. We have no ambulance or EMTS, no firefighters; we have no cops in this town to speak of—the closest cop might well be dead, he went up and down the highway a lot. No hospital in the area, anymore. So that leaves . . . you. And the other doctor—only he lived across from the highway. Chances are he's dead. You can't go anywhere, Dr. Spuris . . . "

But as Dad spoke, Spuris's eyes got wider. He only seemed more panicky. "Oh my God. No sirens. I can't stay! FEMA will send help. These people will keep me working till I have a heart attack! I'm not a well man! I can't deal with all these people. I'm retired, for God's sake!"

"You were a GP for years. You're only semi-retired. You can help. Did you see that little boy down the street? He needs treatment, Spuris."

"There'll be hundreds, *hundreds!* All at once!"

"People will help you. We'll find a way. You can do this. And anyway—we're on a hilltop. The wave went up the hill, and around it. It had to have gone up Seaward Road a ways—the only eastward road out of here. It could be blocked with debris. The coast highway is totally unusable. Probably for miles. There are a lot of rocky hills—and no other roads. So where are you going to drive *to?*"

"Oh my God. Do you really think we're stuck here?"

"Doctor!" The shirtless black man ran up, breathing hard. He was wearing jeans, and mud-caked sneakers. "You're a doctor? We got a dozen people need you right down here—"

"No!" Spuris made a dart for the car door.

But Russ stepped in, his face grim, blocking his way, a hand raised. "Uh-uh."

Dad reached behind him with his other hand—and Russ was amazed to see him open the car door, lock it, slam it shut.

"Oh Jesus, I think you just locked my keys in!" Spuris blurted.

"I'm telling you again, the only road out is almost certainly *blocked*, Spuris. You're not going anywhere anyhow."

"And I'm telling you I can't deal with this!"

But four more men were striding up, and one of them was carrying a 12-gauge single-barrel shotgun: a man covered in mud and blood. So was the shotgun. Maybe it would fire, maybe it wouldn't.

Hard to say what the man's race was; but blue eyes looked out of the cracking mask of yellow mud. "You're coming with me, Spuris. I've got a little girl down here. She's hurt. You're coming."

Dr. Spuris gawped at them. They surrounded him. Four large men, including the shirtless black man.

He stared around at them, panting, and then turned slowly to his bags. His voice dull: "Let me get my . . . " They parted for him, but watched him closely as he went to the open trunk of the car, unlatched the largest suitcase—and inside, crammed in with the wadded clothing, was a doctor's bag.

Russ's dad nodded, and he and Pendra and Russ went on down the street. Looking for Pendra's Gram.

A strange feeling was growing in Russ. He was trying to hold the feeling down, push it away. But keeping it down meant he had to stop thinking about people who must be trapped, alive, in the fallen houses, around them; about the people who must be trapped in overturned cars, lying in there, broken and dying: Women, children, every sort of person, trapped and suffering and facing death. How many were there? *Don't think about it,* he told himself. *Get through this, one thing at a time.*

But it wouldn't keep back: his own inner tsunami, rising up and up, threatening to crest and crush him. Rising up, up.

And then there were two adolescents, a boy and girl, caked in mud, half naked, dragging a groaning man who was missing most of his lower half . . . leaving a wet red trail on the street as they dragged him up it, away from the debris.

Russ groaned, and turned aside from Pendra and his father, and vomited against the side of a slime-coated parked car.

Everything Is Broken

JILL CAME TO HERSELF climbing up a hill.

She couldn't remember, exactly, how she'd come here. She'd been clinging to the roof of the bar with Mario and Lon. People had died, nearby—they were almost within reach, but she could do nothing for them. The cold, hungry wave had washed over them and she'd clung stubbornly thinking *No no no*. Then it had receded somewhat, but its gray waves jumped around them like angry wolves. She had tried to shout something to Mario Ferrara—not sure what—then lost her hold and slipped into the water. No one had tried to pull her out. She'd swallowed water, flailed to the surface, spitting up burning salt water. She had dog-paddled—then clung to something slippery and wooden. A post? Her glasses were gone, but she'd seen bodies floating face down. Glad for once not to see clearly. She'd lost her grasp on the post and forced herself to keep paddling. She'd thought, *I can swim, dammit*, and made herself stretch out into the long strokes that she used at the Y to do laps. Eventually she'd found herself climbing up out of the water, onto a street . . .

Someone was screaming in a building nearby her, now. Water was pouring out its broken windows as if from a dam's spillway. Jill just kept climbing . . .

She was barefoot, covered in slime, shaking with cold, her hair plastered to her head, as she struggled up the hill. She was not so far above the thrashing water that still sucked at the lower, beachside part of town. What had become of her shoes? She didn't know. Her feet hurt but somehow it didn't seem to matter.

She stepped delicately over debris. A twisted car fender; a bent mailbox; a broken window pane, the whole frame lying in the street; mounds of shattered glass; beach toys—something ironic in the beach toys, lying here, amongst the seaweed and trash in the street, and so close to that dead child. The child was just more debris. She knew the boy was dead because his head was turned around backwards on his neck and his eyes were staring into emptiness and a crab was walking across his forehead. She reached down and flicked the crab away, though it seemed pointless to bother.

A filthy, beach towel reading *FREEDOM CALIFORNIA— FIND THE FREEDOM!* had been plastered by the wave to the windshield of a small car. Water bubbled out the edges of the Honda's partly closed windows—still filled with water, the little two-door sedan had become a dirty aquarium on wheels, with the pale dead driver inside it, brown hair floating like Sargasso weed over his head; the dead man staring through the water, out the windshield, as if amazed that the traffic light had never changed.

Find the Freedom! Irony—and it struck Jill that she had written an article warning about all this, several years earlier, when the clusterquakes started. She'd written an article—but she hadn't moved away from the coast. Mocking irony . . .

"Around the end of the last Ice Age, there was a great increase in seismicity along the margins of the ice sheets," Professor Garland said. *"We've got a clear-cut geological record of that sudden rise in seismicity. That tectonic change in pressure, in turn, triggered these huge submarine landsides—which generated enormous tsunamis. So yes, global warming can lead to volcanoes, earthquakes, and massive tsunamis . . . "*

She'd blithely typed those words, published the article in the paper—that was before Ferrara had taken it over—and everyone had ignored it. She'd ignored it herself, her own warning—she'd stayed right here.

And here she was . . . stepping over a drowned dead woman as she climbed the hill in her bare feet . . .

Everything Is Broken

Suddenly fatigue washed over Jill, and she was shaking too much to keep walking. She stumbled toward a small passage between two buildings on the left. She stepped over some driftwood and when her foot came down, her ankle seemed to give out, her leg wouldn't hold her up, and she pitched forward onto the wet pavement . . .

FIVE

NELLA FOUND that some of the dead lady's clothes fit her. Anyway, they fit her good enough.

The dead woman's house was built on two levels, the foundations of the lower a little down the hill, and that lower section had collapsed, rammed by debris carried on the crest of the big wave. Some of the upper floor and the interior stairs were exposed, the stairs descending down to the lower level suddenly cut off, the last tread left hanging over a mound of steaming ruins. The outer walls of the lower section were gone; some of the woman's family pictures were still hanging on an exposed inner wall. There was something naked about that. Especially when Nella looked down, through a shattered doorway, into the pit of the fallen section, to see the woman's purpled arm sticking out, endlessly reaching upward, from under heaped furniture, pictures, appliances, and broken timbers—as if reaching toward the pictures.

But just now Nella was putting on the woman's New Balance walking shoes. They were only a half-size too big. There'd been enough water left in the upstairs pipes to wash with, and Nella felt a little better, cleaner and wearing clothes. She'd scavenged a pair of designer jeans, a blue sweater, A little loose on her but close enough.

She stood up, wincing at the pain in her shoulder and right knee, looked around the upstairs living room. It was almost undisturbed, like a furnished dollhouse, except for some broken glass from a picture window resembling crusts of ice on the carpet. A driftwood sculpture was attached to the wall over the fireplace.

Nella felt the house creak in the wind and wondered if it would collapse. The other Sand Scouts had already looted the intact parts for anything that looked valuable. Jewelry, an iPod, a flatscreen TV. They'd gone to check next door. She could hear them over there—whooping and hollering as her mom would say. They'd found a lot of liquor in their house-to-house searches. So far all the houses had been occupied only by the dead. People had gone up the hills as far as possible, scared of a follow-up wave.

She saw the crucifix, then. A large one, made of brass, alone on the wall over the sofa, as if to guard a television viewer from evil. She crossed to it. Jesus seemed to writhe, for a moment, on his cross, looking down at her; brass eyes narrowing as he focused on Nella.

I'm just seeing shit, she thought.

But she shuddered and looked quickly away.

I will blot out man, whom I have created, from the face of the earth . . .

That's when she heard the screaming from across the street.

Nella stepped to the door—and saw that the Grummon brothers were chasing a young woman out the front door of one of those flat-top houses covered with shingles all over—even the outer walls, covered in those yellow shingles. The young black-haired woman was dressed only in a sweatshirt, no pants, no shoes, naked from the waist down. She had plump thighs, was running across the gravel drive, her round face twisted into a fright mask, and Randle and Liddy were right on her tail, Randle puffing and Liddy giggling, and then she slipped, with a squealing cry, fell in the gravel, and Randle grabbed her by the ankles and dragged her backwards.

The woman clawed at the gravel, convulsively shaking her head, then looked up at Nella and mouthed, *Help me!*

But Nella just shrugged. Like, *sorry*. She couldn't do anything about it.

Then Dickie was there, breathing on Nella, like he suddenly appeared, blocking out the scene. He was grinning like a panting wolf, smelling of booze as he pushed her backward, closing the door. "We found the keys for the pickup truck next door," he said conversationally, as he pressed her back on the sofa under Jesus. "And . . . " He tugged at her pants. She knew, from the tight hunch in his shoulders, the quickness of his movements, there was no putting him off, he'd just hit her if she tried, so she unzipped the jeans and peeled them off as he undid his fly, still talking. "We can't get out to the ranch, road's blocked with all kinda shit, but we found a house at the top of the hill with a good view for defense, we're gonna bunk in there. No one to argue anymore. No one to say shit. Freedom in Freedom. We're gonna go see Joe Shipman. He's still in town. I know right where that motherfucker is." He was rubbing his hand around her vagina, trying to get her wet. Wasn't working, so he put a lot of spit on his hard red thing. "Got a lot of stuff Sten's puttin' in the truck, to take up there . . . "

The girl was screaming, from across the street. Distant. But Nella could hear it.

"Spread your fucking legs . . . you're gonna need us, girl . . . "

Her bruised shoulder hurt as he heaved himself onto her. She cut off a yelp of pain, hissing to herself as he jammed into her. But the girl across the street did Nella's screaming.

Nella thought about Ronnie. Wondering if he were alive. Glad he couldn't see her now.

But someone was watching: Nella glanced up, past Dickie's

head, seeing Jesus Christ gazing back at her: Jesus upside-down. Jesus looking down at her as she surrendered to Dickie.

TWILIGHT WAS easing over them. The stench was increasing as the seawater drained away.

Russ worked at clearing debris from a man who was probably dead. Pendra had been helping, but she'd gone to sit down for a while.

They'd found work gloves somewhere. Electric lanterns, flashlights, and there was a nurse who kept a supply of bandages in her basement, and topical antiseptics, things like that, boxes of them. They'd already used up most of supplies—Dr. Spuris and Lucia Greia, a retired Filipina nurse, and several elderly ladies had gone through the medical stuff—and there was nothing much for people in pain, just some scavenged prescription painkillers, like codeine. There were no rescue helicopters in the sky, there were no ambulances, no working phones, cell or otherwise, no working Internet, all cable lines broken. Nothing.

Nothing. They were alone.

They'd sent two young volunteers to ask for help. Two college buddies who said they could take their dirt bikes, get over the hills past the giant mound of debris that blocked Seaward Road, head inland to find help. How long would it take for them to get help to Freedom, with all the other towns, up and down the coast, that must be devastated by the tsunami?

So they coped, one step at a time. Russ's dad had found some disposable paper masks to filter out the worst of the dust that rose around them as they pulled at splinter-ended timbers and sections of drywall. But some of it got through and Russ coughed, from time to time. He was working stolidly, alongside about six others, in this shell of a house, but he felt like a zombie.

They'd been at this for hours, one house after another. It was just going to go on and on.

Russ was hungry, and some sandwiches had gone around at one point, but he was afraid to eat. He wasn't sure why. Something about the smell of the dead.

Up the street, toward the top of the hill, there were a couple of big empty houses where people were laid out on blankets, on the floor, groaning, some of them dying. Being treated with almost haphazard selections of prescription painkillers, along with ibuprofen and, sometimes, hard liquor, if the pain was too much.

Dad had only mentioned cholera to Russ just once. But the notion had stuck in his head. *Cholera.* When would it start? Doctor Spuris had recited the symptoms: watery diarrhea, vomiting, muscle cramps. To start. Then cold skin, incessant thirst, sunken eyes, thread pulse, weakness. Death.

Some radios had picked up news. The little radio station in Buried Cove had been right on Highway One, and it was gone, along with almost all of Buried Cove, which was on lower ground than much of Freedom—but more distant stations were heard in a static-choked way, and they weren't encouraging. It was said to be the biggest tsunami in recorded history. Parts of San Francisco had been hit, and hit hard. And Monterey and Santa Cruz and Long Beach and other towns between, and Santa Monica. It was said to be part of the clusterquakes phenomena, which was, in turn, linked to global warming in some way. Ships at sea had capsized, the Coast Guard was trying to rescue hundreds of people from a sinking cruise ship that had been headed for Mexico, along with more than two thousand other boaters; an oil tanker caught in the tsunami had dumped an *Exxon Valdez*-sized oil spill over Half Moon Bay; hundreds of thousands, maybe more than a million people up and down the coast were dead or dying; a million more displaced.

Freedom, California, was the last town on the government's mind—especially since Lon Ferrara had worked so hard to make it that way.

"There's a car, like the one you were looking for, the other side of that big logjam, Russ," said Carter, coming in. Dale Carter was the big African-American, who'd tried to get people organized, early on. He'd put on a San Francisco Giants baseball jacket. "Some of us were climbing over it, trying to get past."

"I'll go look," Russ said, his heart sinking.

His dad, looking pale and bone-weary, shook his head. "I knew her. I'll go. Don't say anything to Pendra yet."

Dad left with Dale. Russ went back to work, he and Lars pulling the last timber off the dead man. The man's chest was crushed, part of his esophagus had been forced out of his mouth. Russ tried to jar the image from lodging in his mind and turned away.

"I'm gonna smoke a doob," Lars said. "You want some?"

Russ shook his head, wondering how Lars could combine marijuana with anything this grim. But Russ had always had a low tolerance for marijuana. If he took a hit of pot everything became hyper-real, vibrating with painful meaning. Not good timing just now. He was already feeling that way. He wanted a drink.

He wandered into a back room of the house they'd been working on. He raised a Coleman lantern and saw that the room was intact—there was white debris dust, wafted from the wreckage in the others rooms; it coated the little bed, the stuffed animals, but everything was in place. He glanced out a broken window, and saw a leafless tree he hadn't noticed before, behind the house; rubbish hung in the tree by the high water, dangling like trashy Christmas decorations. A movement caught his eye. After a moment he made out a human silhouette near the very top. He approached the window, peering up—saw the silhouette move. The face turned, caught the waning light. A child was stuck in the tree, washed there by the wave, wedged in a crotch of two branches. A naked boy. The boy's eyes were closed but he moved one arm twitchily. Maybe it was the child who'd slept in this bedroom, torn from taking shelter on the roof. What, maybe seven years old? Deposited there by the wave like the flotsam hanging around: ropes and kelp and a sodden blanket and a small dead dog and unidentifiable swatches of trash.

Aching with fatigue and fear for the child, Russ went to get help, and a ladder.

Outside it was dusk, and darkening. Streetlights would normally come on, in most places, this time of day. But there hadn't been many working streetlights in Freedom, before the wave, and none worked now: the electricity was gone. No lights on in the houses. Just pools of light around Coleman lanterns, beams flashing from flashlights. People moaning—that sound was part of the very air. The sounds of people moaning, weeping. Perhaps a bit less now. He could hear the sea, in the distance, its hiss rising and falling, the sound of waves breaking as they did any other day, as if nothing had happened.

It took four of them to get the child down. The little boy was naked, bruised. His face swollen. They couldn't tell if he was badly hurt inside. The rusty-haired boy was delirious with fatigue and fear and disorientation as they gave him water from their meager supply of the bottled stuff, carried him to an improvised stretcher—they'd made it out of a long piece of carpet and a stepladder—and toted him up the hill to the houses being used to shelter the injured.

As Russ came back down, he paused to watch a mud-coated figure toiling up hill like a drowned man risen from the sea. He was perhaps forty or older—it was hard to tell—clothed in slime, mud, underwear, and socks, his face a mask of dried muck. The man was staggering along in the twilight from one person to the next, begging every one he met to help him get his wife back, she'd been sucked out to sea, when the wave receded, but he was sure, absolutely sure, she was still alive. He explained this calmly, speaking in a mush-mouthed way. Tear streaks marked the mask of mud like erosion lines. She was a strong swimmer, he told them, repeated it over and over, she was a strong swimmer and they'd only just gotten married a few months before, he'd waited all his life to meet her, and they'd been on the deck of her uncle's guest house and the wave had come and it had separated them and he'd found himself deposited on a chimney, and she'd been sucked out to sea and he'd tried to go after her but he was tangled in some old clothesline, and he'd lost sight of her, and it had taken him a long time to get out of the wire, and get down from the roof, and come up higher on the hill for help, but he was sure she was alive, somewhere out at sea, drifting.

Several people, one after another, explained to him that they had no working boats, that she was surely dead by now, but he wouldn't listen, he would wave them impatiently away, and go to the next person and the next. When he passed, Russ saw that all his teeth had been knocked out; were reduced to bleeding stumps on his gums. Soon he wandered off, and Russ never saw him again.

Up to his knees and elbows in stinking dried muck himself, Russ went back to clearing debris away—and sometimes bodies. His movements became mechanical and weary.

They'd laid out hundreds of corpses in four houses on a side street a block up; one body right beside the next, on the floors. The dead that could be identified by those who knew them included a retired cop, two ministers, a pharmacist, another nurse, a part-time paramedic, a doctor in town to remodel his vacation home, a retired fireman, a former Army medic just a month back from the Middle East. They'd all had nice houses close to the beach.

All people they needed. As if the tsunami had selected them out, to make sure they wouldn't be of help.

Russ needed a break. The men around him worked either silently, or cursed to themselves. Some despairing quality in their perseverance depressed him. He dropped his crowbar and muttered about finding some water, drifted outside and, carrying a small flashlight, trudged along a side street, just at the high water mark, looking for a place to be alone. He chose a house he knew they'd already searched. It was intact except for the front room, which was mostly occupied by a fourteen-foot aluminum boat, complete with a big Yamaha outboard motor. The empty gray-metal boat had slammed into the house prow on, smashed through the picture windows. There had been a body in the house, an elderly widower Russ's dad had known; they'd carried the body up the hill. The widower had kept a store of Irish whiskey, and Russ helped himself to some, pouring a half tumbler in the bedroom, drinking it off. He was slightly ashamed to be looting the dead man's whiskey, but he felt a little better afterward.

He poured another shot, drank that off too. *Don't get plastered. You need to be there, helping Dad.*

He stared at the bottle—Jameson—and then screwed it shut, stuck it in a shoebox, hid that under the bed. Went a little unsteadily to find his dad.

Dad was about two blocks up the hill, sitting by Pendra, on the curb, his arm around her. She was crying. Russ figured the car Dad had checked out belonged to her grandmother.

"I want to go see, make sure it's her," Pendra said. "My mom and dad died. I never got to see my dad's body. People just told me he was dead. I need to . . . " She broke off, squeezed her eyes shut. Took a sighing breath, getting control. When she opened her eyes again tears slipped from their corners. "Lots of people have lost people, in this. But I need to really know she . . . that it was her."

"I've seen her many, many times," Dad said. "I knew your grandma pretty darn well. It was her. I saw her face clearly. She's really and truly gone. I'm sorry. She died quickly."

Pendra sobbed, one hand over her eyes. "How do you know she died quick?"

"I just . . . it's obvious." Dad winced. "The car was upside down. Believe me, she was killed right away. She didn't suffer. Just—boom, like that. I promise."

"I don't know what to do."

"You stick close to me and Russ here, we'll all look out for each other. Eventually the rest of the world will get around to us. Okay?"

She nodded. She wept. And then . . .

It got darker.

SIX

THE WAVE towered over Russ, cresting, about to crash down. Then stopped. Just froze up there.

Russ walked toward it. It was like a wall of green glass. Just frozen in place, unmoving and unmovable. He reached out and touched the smooth surface of the wave towering over him—it was actually made of some kind of transparent green synthetic. It squeaked like a balloon when he touched it. Silhouettes of people were suspended inside it. He stared, and their shapes became clearer . . .

Stuck in the wave were bodies, corpses in various positions, upside down, angled, fixed like fruit in Jell-O. And closer, inside the wave, looking out at him: was someone who was alive.

It was his mother. Gaping at him. Saying his name, without words.

He reached for her. *"Mom? Mama?"*

Russ sat up, head pounding, the nightmare receding like dirty seawater drawing back after the tsunami. He had a septic taste in his mouth. And he was terribly thirsty.

What time was it? Russ wondered, looking through the window at the light outside, the overcast sky. Maybe about ten?

He had laid down on the sofa "for just a few minutes" about five a.m., after working all night, and he must have fallen deeply asleep.

He made a croaking laugh, looking at his hands. He still had the work gloves on.

"Russ?"

Dad was standing in the doorway, looking like he'd just woken up himself. "How you holding up? Get some rest?"

"Kind of. Where's Pendra?"

"Sleeping at her grandma's place. How come you slept here, son?"

Russ sat up, pulling off his gloves. "I didn't mean to, just did. You sleep?"

"A couple hours." Dad rubbed at his eyes. "We've had a lot to do. The danger of cholera around here—" He shook his head. "We're going to try to relocate everyone to the high school. The gym, the classrooms. Use that as our base till some help gets here."

"You see any helicopters?"

"One did fly over. Circled once. We tried to signal. It kept going. We figure someone'll come from Deer Creek first. We haven't seen any Coast Guard."

"Where's Deer Creek?"

His father sat wearily on the arm of the sofa. "Deer Creek's about sixty-four miles east. They've got a fire department, a small hospital, all kinds of stuff we don't have." He paused, added bitterly, "In the Ferrara regime."

"Ferrara? Oh right. The mayor. If he's alive he's probably hiding."

"Him? I don't know. He'd never blame himself. The absence of emergency response would somehow be Big Government's fault." He wiped his mouth. "Anyway, people in Deer Creek'll get the word from the guys with the dirt bikes. If they don't get through, for some reason, right away, hell, there are merchants from Deer Creek who supply us here—they'll realize the road's blocked off. Send someone to check on us. We'll get some help from that quarter . . . when they get here."

"How badly blocked is it? Maybe we can clear it."

"Maybe, but it could take days. It's a huge pile of logs and every kind of debris. There's even a pretty good size cabin cruiser stuck up there. But we can expect help to come, son. Two volunteers went already on dirt bikes, remember—taking the trails up through the hills."

"What about all the injured?" Russ's mouth was so dry it was hard to talk. He tried to work some saliva into it. "People dying. They can't just *wait*, dad. We've got to get them out! Get them down that road. We could take some in the cars that still work, if we got the road open. It might be days before those two guys get people organized to come. If they don't get lost on the way . . . "

"We can't move the injured over these hills. Trying to do that might kill them. Gotta get the road cleared to get them out. No boats we can count on so . . . " He made a sound that was almost a groan. "I mean, that blockage is *high*. Dangerous. There's hundreds of tons of the stuff ready to fall on anyone who tries to break it down . . . "

"How about dynamite?"

"You got any? Me either. The hardware store was on the highway. It's under three feet of sand and debris. Flattened." He sighed. "So was the pharmacy, by the way."

A man appeared at the door behind his dad, a man maybe in his late forties, looking as dirty and worn down as everyone else, his tired face marked by sardonic affability. He glanced at Russ. "This your son, Drew?"

"That's him," Dad said. "Really pulled his weight last night."

Russ felt a trickle of inward pleasure. *Pulling your weight* was a big deal to his father.

"Russ—this is Brand Robinson," Dad said. "Friend of mine. His place was damaged and looted. He'll be staying with us."

"Looted?" Russ was startled. "I wouldn't think this'd be the kind of place where people would be looting."

"Oh yeah," Dad sighed. "We got all kinds here. Some of those fires were *set*—and there are people in this area . . . " Dad shook his head. "Lot of meth heads, biker types, couple of gangs . . . we have our share of thugs out here."

"You got anything to drink, Dad? Water, or even a warm soda?"

Brand reached into his coat, pulled out a half-quart plastic bottle of water, a third full. "Here." He tossed it to Russ. "Knock yourself out. There's quite a bit of bottled water around. People here stocked up on it. The water from the reservoir was kind of chancy even before this."

"It's okay for me to drink this off? I'm hella thirsty."

"Go for it."

Russ drank the water, all at once. It wasn't enough, but he felt a little better. Strange how good plain water tasted. He'd never noticed the taste of water much, before. "Thanks. I got so sweaty and dehydrated. So there's no fresh water coming into town?"

Dad passed a shaky hand over his forehead, leaving a trail of grime. "Water was piped along the coast to the town water tank. The wave smashed that pipe to scrap and the water tank too. So . . . it's gone. We sent someone to check. Water in the taps and hot water tanks is all but gone." He shrugged. "We'll work it out till help comes."

Russ rubbed his head. He really wanted a shower. Wasn't in the cards. "We were here, like, just a few minutes and bang—it hit." He shook his head in amazement. "It's like we had an appointment with the tsunami."

Brand gave a dry chuckle. "Well. I understand you guys came up the coast. So maybe you *missed* your appointment with the tsunami. You missed being drowned by just a few minutes." He snorted. "I can't believe it. I sound like that damn life coach woman. Wonder if she made it."

"Who's that?" Dad asked.

"Oh—someone my daughter put up to bugging me this morning. Funny little woman. Hope she's all right."

A little breeze came through the open door from behind Dad and Brand, bringing with it a charnel smell from the sea. A thought came to Russ. He was slow to voice it, afraid his dad would say, yes, we should . . .

"The bodies on the beach," Russ said at last. "So many bodies down there. Shouldn't we go down and . . . *do* something with them? Move them up for identification, or bury them or, I don't know . . . "

Dad shook his head sadly. "Too late. I'm afraid. We didn't get to them in time. The tide came in. Most of those bodies were swept out to sea. They're just gone."

Russ felt a flash of relief—and then a flush of shame.

Dad stood and stretched, grimacing. "Muscles are killing me. Come on, Russ—we've got a little food left at our place. Let's get something to eat before it spoils. I've got to empty out the damn toilet tank."

"Do what?"

"We're reclaiming the water from the toilet tanks. We'll need it."

On the way out, Brand muttered, "I wonder if Ferrara is dead. There were people on the roof of his bar."

"I don't think I've ever said this about anyone," Dad said. "But I do hope to God the son of a bitch is dead."

And despite all that had happened to make Russ feel the capacity for shock was wrung out of him, he was shocked when he heard his dad say that.

NELLA WOKE on the sofa, first thing she saw was that brass, cold-eyed face of Jesus Christ staring down at her. She closed her eyes again—but someone hammered on the door, one of the Grummons yelling that they had taken over a house at the top of the hill, and Dickie said to get her ass up there.

She made herself get up, tried to clean up a little, and went up the hill through the biting wind, the watery morning light. She found the new place pretty easily, a split-level house, brown trimmed with rusty red, at the very top of the hill; part of a strip of identical houses, a small development. She was walking up to the house—knew it was the right one because there was Sten coming out, yawning—when she heard the shots, two distinctive thudding noises. The sounds coming from the house.

Who was shooting who? It could be they were just taking pot shots at pictures on the wall. But maybe they were shooting that girl the Grummon boys had raped. If she was still whining, like as not she'd get on their nerves, and they'd have shot her. But they'd probably done her earlier, if they hadn't let her go, or tied her up and gagged her.

Nella felt like she was going numb, thinking about it. And so tired. She had slept badly and her crotch hurt from Dickie forcing himself on her. She wanted to go back to sleep, go into the house and find a place to lay down. She figured they were all done fucking for a while. But she was afraid to go in, what with the gunshots.

Sten had a pistol in his hand, held down by his side. He saw her looking at it and stuck it in his coat pocket.

"Hey, Sten?" Nella asked, as she walked up. "You seen Ronnie? You know, Ronnie Burke?"

"I know, the one you were hot for. Nope haven't seen him. Probably dead. Seems like half the town is dead at least."

"What's the shooting?" Nella asked numbly, as he went to the back of the pickup, grabbed the last thing in it, a case of beer waiting on the tailgate.

He stopped, holding the case of beer, and nodded toward the open garage. "You see those little motorbikes in the garage there?"

Nella peered that way. It was dark in there. Might be dirt bikes. "I guess."

"Couple of weedy frat boy types. Their dad owns the place. Came up here to get those dirt bikes yesterday, they were, gonna ride 'em over the hills, get the National Guard out here or something. One of them had a .22 target pistol. We took it away and tied them up. Dickie just decided this morning what to do with them."

She squinted at the dark shape of the motorcycles, silhouettes at the back of the unlit garage, like they were ghost bikes. She nodded. "Both of 'em?"

"Sure, yeah, kid pointed that gun at Dickie, pissed him off. And he don't want nobody getting the fucking National Guard out here. If it happened that they got away . . . " He shrugged.

"The National Guard?" She shook her head. "This thing hit more than just us. They're too busy to mess with us here."

"For a while. Meanwhile—this is sweet. While it lasts, we got to milk it. Dickie's got a whole vision of what he wants to do. Just a whole . . . big . . . vision. Come on."

Nella followed Sten as he carried the case to the garage, put it down in a greasy corner—and Dickie came through the inside door to the garage, right then, the Grummons with him.

Dickie glanced at her. "You're coming with us, Nella." He turned to Sten. "Let's get another car, make sure we don't run outta gas. There's a Buick down the street. We're gonna get going right fucking now."

He was like a general, giving orders. She always liked that side of him; made her feel safe.

He had a Glock stuck in his waistband, she saw.

She hoped he wouldn't make her kill anyone, this trip. She really didn't feel up to killing anyone today.

———

DICKIE HUMMED an old Pantera song to himself as he rode shotgun in the boxy metallic blue Buick they'd found in the driveway of a house down the street. If there was anyone in the house, they were hiding. No one tried to stop them taking the car, though they made a lot of noise.

Sten was driving; the Grummon brothers and Nella were crowded in the back. Dickie had his pick of most any car in town now—and after Sten had gotten this one started up, they'd headed on down the hill, toward Corning Street, where Shipman was. Maybe he was there, still, like he'd heard from Buff and some others, and maybe not. But the current from the horizon was carrying everything to Dickie. This town belonged to him and now Shipman did too.

"We gonna get some shit, Dickie?" Liddy Grummon asked, trying not to sound scared as he said it. He was nervous about asking, which was a good thing, from Dickie's point of view. "Sure like to get high. I mean, now, with all that's happened, we don't have to worry about keeping, what, under the radar and shit. We can go ahead and—"

"You going to cook some up?" Dickie asked. "You expect other people to do the work?"

"If you want me to, shit, I'll cook it up. We could get the makings from the drugstore. They might have some dexies and shit too."

Sten shook his head. "Wave swept the drugstore away. First thing I checked."

"We got that shit of Buff's but it looks pretty rank," Nella said.

"We'll do up some shit when I say," Dickie said.

The smell of the Grummon brothers was too heavy in the car, making him feel stifled, so Dickie rolled down his window, but only got a worse smell—the breeze was coming in off the beach, carrying the reek of all the death the tsunami had dumped there. Maybe some of it was the smell of nearer dead people too, from the houses collapsed close to the water. The wave came; the wave cleansed. The smell of rot was also the smell of cleansing. So Paps had said.

Dickie remembered hunting, when he was a boy, just turned fourteen, one misty morning with his old man. His dad was raised up back in Kentucky, in the hills, and he knew how to shoot. Dickie watched as Paps shot a deer right through the heart at fifty yards with a 30.06 that cold morning; it took a few steps and then said fuck it, blew out a final steamy breath, and flopped right over. Paps sawed away some parts of the doe with that big serrated hunting knife, left most of the animal to rot. "Just gonna leave it there, Paps?" Paps' half-brother, Gunny, was a full-on poacher, back then, taking wild pig, deer, bear, even eagles, most anytime he wanted, and Gunny said it was better to cover over the carcass. "Gonna stink bad," Dickie went on. "People'll find it, know someone was shootin' deer out of season." Dickie was showing off, a bit, to his dad, with this wisdom cadged from Gunny.

"Won't stink long. Lots of goddamn animals die out here," Paps had said, dumping the deer's sliced off rump and thigh meat on a tarp in the back of his truck. He had red-brown deer blood on his gnarled hands and arms, halfway up to his elbows. "Nobody pays it no mind. The stink, that's just the cleansing."

"I start to stink no one's gonna say it means I'm clean," Dickie had pointed out.

"You're giving me smart mouth shit," Paps'd said, smacking Dickie on the side of the head with the palm of his hand. He did it almost casually. It had stung some, but Dickie was used to it, and hardly felt it. Mom's belt buckle treatment, now that one you felt.

Paps had taken a flask from his coat, pulled thoughtfully on it, and then, staring at the mass of red flesh in the back of the truck, he'd said, "The stink means the germs are getting to it. That's the start of the cleansing. Then maybe along comes a coyote or a bear, take some meat from the carcass. Then comes the bugs. Yellow jackets, maggots, and such. They clean it right up. You see that deer next year, nothing but white bones. Nature's fucking way, Dickie. Get in the goddamn truck and shut up, for Christ's sake. I promised your mom you were going to Sea Scouts today. She's got it in her pea brain it's going to straighten your ass up."

Paps was dead a year later: he'd taken a handful of black beauties, and driven his car off a cliff—down into that cleansing sea. Mom said it was an accident, crazy-driving on drugs, and not suicide. Maybe. Dickie hadn't known him that much anyway. When Paps wasn't in prison, he was just plain not around. Uncle Gunny, he was in prison for poaching, by and by. After Dickie started getting in trouble pretty much 24/7 and went to juvie, not quite seventeen years old, he lost touch with his mom. She moved back east to be with her sister. He never heard from her again. No one was there to pick him up at juvie, when they let him out, once he turned eighteen. Then he met Sten. Shipman had left town already . . .

Shipman. Funny name, Shipman, for a Sea Scouts skipper. Shipman skipper of the ship. Real funny.

"Here's the street," Sten said, turning the Buick.

"It's that kinda brown-colored house, there," Dickie said, after a moment, pointing left.

"More tan colored," Sten said. He was capable of being picky like that.

"Okay, tan, fuck, whatever, just pull up there, double park to hold that van there."

Sten chuckled as he pulled up to block the van. "You shoulda been a cop, Dickie."

There was an old U-Haul cargo van in the driveway. The back was open, crammed with furniture, boxes, random things from the house. Looked like they'd got here just in time. But then, with the town hemmed in like it was, where would Shipman go in that van?

"That him?" Sten asked, as Shipman came out of the house, carrying a metal briefcase. He had gotten chunky. He wore khaki pants, loafers, and a blue windbreaker. He had that stupid fake-looking little beard and that stubby nose. His gray comb-over didn't do much to hide his balding head, especially with it flapping around in the wind.

"Yeah," Dickie said, hearing his own voice grating. "It's him. Get out, everyone, right fucking now, and make sure he doesn't run."

Another man stood with Shipman, and the guy looked familiar to Dickie. He had close-cropped dyed-blond hair, a tan that looked almost orange, teeth that had been blindingly whitened, and a sheepskin jacket. Waters, that was his name, Ron Waters. Had a hair cutting shop—called it a *salon*. Dude always looked gay, to Dickie.

"Hey, there, 'skipper,' " Dickie said, calling to Shipman, as he approached the men at the back of the cargo van.

They both turned to stare at the group coming toward them. Waters took a step back, bumping into the rear of the vehicle. "Uh—that's *Dickie*, isn't it?"

"Yeah." Sten said. "It's Dickie."

Shipman's mouth dropped open. He licked his lips, turned, closed one of the van doors. "Okay, well, you folks'll have to move that vehicle, there, I'm about to leave . . . " His voice was high-pitched with fear.

Sten nodded toward Waters. "You want this fag to stay here, Dickie? He cuts my hair—we'll need somebody to do that."

"Waters, go back in your house, and keep your gay ass in there," Dickie said. "You want to save some trouble, get anything valuable you have, put it on the porch. If it looks good, we might not even search the house. Today, anyhow."

Waters did something with his mouth that made Dickie think of a goldfish he'd seen gasping for air on the surface of a dirty aquarium. Then the haircutter turned to go, looking ready to just boogie out of there fast—but Shipman, staring at the gun in Dickie's waistband, grabbed Waters' elbow. "Wait . . . wait. They're . . . Ron, don't leave me here with . . . "

"With who?" Nella said, pretending to be shocked. "Kind of rude, put it that way!"

Randle laughed at that. "Rude, dude."

Waters jerked his arm free. "I gotta get home, I . . . " He rushed off toward the house next door.

Shipman was fishing in his pants pocket for something—probably a cell phone. "Look, what do you people want?" He tugged the cell phone out. "You've really got to stop blocking my van—"

"You got to know by now, skipper, that cell phone's not going to work, anymore," Dickie said. "Not around here. Towers are down." He pulled the Glock from his waistband, held it loosely in his hand. "You go ahead and try to use it."

Shipman stared—and put the cell phone back in his pocket. "Okay, well, I heard what you said to Ron about . . . valuables. All mine are right here in this van. I'll just . . . leave it here. And go."

He started to push past Randle Grummon who propelled him back with a single stiff-armed motion. Shipman staggered back, almost fell, staying on his feet only because the closed van door was there. "Now look—!"

"Look at what?" Nella asked, as if genuinely puzzled.

Sten said, "Ha. She got you there. Ha."

"The sheriff—"

"Word is," Dickie said, interrupting sharply, "the sheriff is dead. No law enforcement anywhere around here. Disaster all over the damn country, everybody busy, nobody got time for this town. So that leaves you and us, Shipman."

"I'm curious, where'd he think he was *going?*" Sten wondered. "Got to know the roads are blocked off. Moving to another house in town?"

"What?" Shipman looked startled. "No, I—I'm selling this house."

"After all this shit—" He pointed toward the ocean. "—you think you're selling the house?" Sten asked, grinning wolfishly. "Man, the whole town'll go for ten dollars when this is over. There's more tidal waves coming."

Shipman looked desperately from one face to the next as he chattered. "No, no, we'll be able to put things together, and they, we—well, like I said you can have the van—there's some stereo equipment—not much of real value. I live in Bakersfield, I just came back to town to clear out the house and then the tidal wave came and, you know . . . I'll find a boat, if I have to. There are trails out of town—I thought I could find some place to store the van and—"

"And boat out of here, or hike out?" Dickie said, nodding thoughtfully. "Man, I got good timing. But that's no surprise. The world's giving it all to me." He pointed the pistol at Shipman's middle, tempted to shoot him in his fat gut right here. "We've got the trails covered. No one leaves. And you couldn't boat out. So much debris out there, no draft for boats to get out. We're watching. Anyone finds a way, why, we'll see and we'll shoot 'em. So you got no place to go. You're coming with us, now, skipper. We're gonna go all together in the Buick."

"What? No! I don't have to go anywhere with you! There are people watching, across the street . . . "

"If there are, they won't do shit for you. I doubt if they even *like* you. Don't remember anyone really liking you. Now, skipper, you want to get gut shot, right here and now? Okay—" He made a show of aiming the gun at Shipman's middle.

"No!" Shipman sidestepped, turned, hustled toward the Buick, with his hands up. The Grummons parted to let him go by.

Dickie could tell he was thinking of running for it, dodging across the street. "You run, I shoot you down, bullet through the spine, Shipman."

Shipman's shoulders slumped. He walked woodenly up to the car.

"How about that van of his? We could use that to move stuff," Sten pointed out.

"We'll come back later, go through it, check the other houses around here," Dickie said.

"Where's he going to fit in the car?" Nella asked, walking over close to Shipman, looking him up and down.

"In the trunk," Dickie said.

The Grummons laughed—and Shipman shouted "No!" and started to run. But Nella saved Shipman from being shot by tripping him. He went down on his face, crunching his nose, and the Grummons dragged him to the Buick.

Sten popped the trunk and they popped Shipman into it.

Not even half an hour later, they'd come to the top of the boat launching ramp at the north end of the beach. The beach itself was partly awash, all studded with debris, including cars and parts of buildings. He saw some people way down the beach, poking through the debris. Too far away to worry about. The stench was heavy here but a hissing wind off the ocean carried away some of it.

Everything Is Broken

Aground on the old, cracked boat launching slipway was what remained of a white, wooden sailing vessel, about thirty-two feet long. The tsunami had tossed it onto the ramp almost upright. The vessel's masts were snapped off, and there were big ragged holes in the hull. It looked like it had drained out through the holes. It would be just dry enough. "That'll work good. Take him outta the trunk, Randle, you and your brother, drag him up in there, tie him down in the hold."

"What do we tie him with?"

"Dumbshit, there'll be all kind of rope on that boat there."

Dickie turned to Nella and Sten. "I need you to get me some gasoline . . . wait, the Buick's got half a tank, we can use most of it. Looks like a long piece of garden hose over there, on the beach."

It took another forty minutes to get it all set up to Dickie's satisfaction, partly because Shipman fought being taken into the beached sailboat—kicking and screaming the whole way—and they had to work that gasoline up into the hose, but once they got the gas started it was pretty easy to get it flowing since the hose was going down the ramp—downhill, after all—and into the sailboat. They ran the other end of the green hose through the uppermost of the holes in the sailboat's hull. Shipman was in there yelling the whole time. Nella was starting to look sickly and pale, by the time it was all set up, Dickie noticed. She was a chick. But she'd looked sickly all day.

"All set up," Randle said, coming up the ramp with his brother, wiping his hands on his pants.

"Okay. You guys stay here, keep watch. I don't think anybody'll fuck with us but just keep a weather eye out, mateys, while I talk to the skipper."

Sten said, "Ha!" at that one.

Dickie handed Sten his gun and went down the ramp, climbed up the rope ladder at the stern, into the boat. It shuddered a bit as he climbed inboard, but didn't seem in danger of toppling over.

He went up the slanted deck to the hatch and then scrambled down the ladder to the cabin, shouting over Shipman's angry sobbing, "Hey skipper! Yo yo yo! All hands on deck! Ship the starboard main! Batten the fucking asses and shit!" He coughed, once, from the gasoline fumes.

Shipman was tied to a broken wooden folding chair, in a pile of debris—old rope, a narrow mattress from the cabin, galley trash. The stuff was pretty wet from seawater. Shipman was wriggling around, hands tied behind him, trying to get out of the rope.

Dickie grinned. "Hey skipper—you remember your Sea Scout knots? I should've told the boys to use a fisherman's bend, or a Bowline on the Bight—remember those? I was going to take that first knot test, so you said you'd tutor me on knots, remember?"

"Dickie . . . I don't know what you think you remember but . . . Some other skipper, maybe . . . "

"Oh no, it was you, Mr. Shipman. You're the Skipper and I'm Gilligan, right? 'Come on, Gilligan, it'll be a three hour cruise.' You took me out to your boat—not too different from this one!—and you took it out to sea a little ways and you put out the sea anchor and . . . let's see, what'd you say—you said I'd *remember* the knot if it was used on my wrists, said it was an old sailor's trick, right? And after you tied me to that frame you tugged down my pants and said something about you read my signals and you knew I wanted this and you pushed my face down in the pillow and you raped my ass, for quite a long goddamn time."

"Dickie, I might've misunderstood, I might've thought . . . "

"That I wanted it? That what you going to say next? That I *wanted* you to tie me to the bunk frame, down below—You knew from my screaming and begging you to stop, and my crying and stuff? Was that your clue?"

"I really thought it was—"

He broke off when Dickie stepped close and kicked him in the mouth. Shipman sobbed and spat bloody teeth.

"No, skipper, you never thought that and after that other kid in our crew started acting weird, because you raped him too, you left town, right? Believe me, you'd have been dead a long time ago, skipper, if you hadn't left town. I meant to go look for you, but no one seemed to know where you were. Bakersfield! Never thought of that. Who lives in Bakersfield on purpose? You do! But—here we are! Wait—what's that smell?" Dickie coughed. "Some fumes in here . . . "

Shipman was wheezing now, looking around desperately. Dickie couldn't stay here much longer. The fumes were getting to him. "I'm gonna miss talking to you, old times and shit, skipper, but . . . I gotta go . . . where's that cigarette lighter?"

Shipman gasped and stared at him, mouth hanging open. "Dickie, I'm sorry, take me to the State Police, I'll confess everything!"

"Yeah? You tell 'em about how you got a kid to trust you, a kid who really fucking needed somebody to trust, kid who lost his old man, mom was a drunk—kid never had no parents he could count on, but here's someone gonna show he *cares* about me, gonna teach me something . . . You *did*, man, you taught me something. About trusting people. You taught me about knots, skipper. You really did."

Dickie tossed the lighter up once, caught it. Then he turned and climbed up the ladder.

"Dickie! Bring the police here! I'll confess here if you want! Find someone, anyone, a citizen's committee or something, bring them here! I'll tell them everything! *Dickie!*"

Dickie could hear Shipman wrenching around, trying to get loose. He hoped those idiots tied him good. Should've taught them some Sea Scouts knots.

Dickie got awkwardly up on deck—the slant of the deck made it hard. He was glad to be out in the cleaner air. Coughing, he found an old piece of triangular blue-plastic boat pennant lying on the deck, snapped the lighter flame on, held the point of the pennant in the fire. It curled up, started burning, dripping molten plastic.

He got it going good, then tossed it down the ladder, into the hold. Into the gasoline. Shipman yelled, "There's still time to—DICKIE, you can still—!"

Dickie went quickly to the railing, was climbing over, wondering if the pennant had gone out without setting off the gasoline—he dropped to the ramp right when the fat *WHOOMPH* sound shook the boat. The little vessel rocked on its keel. Shipman squealed loud and long—reminded him of the sound a wild pig had made, when Uncle Gunny's hunting dogs dragged it down by the neck.

Dickie backed hastily away from the boat. He felt light, unreal, quietly happy, grinning without being able to help it, as the flames licked up from the hold, and the screams bubbled out, and smoke roiled up into the sky . . .

He watched it burn for a long time, long after Shipman stopped squealing, till there wasn't much left but the charred ribs of the boat, and a blackened, greasy mass in the sizzling ashes . . .

SEVEN

DALE WAS SITTING on the sofa next to Russ's dad, turning the crank on the emergency hand-powered radio he'd set on the coffee table. "Early twentieth century tech coming to our rescue in the twenty-first century," Dale said, chuckling, as he cranked. Russ looked out the picture window of Dale's front room at the gray afternoon; the sea, far below, still flecked with floating debris, in the distance. *Like the sea's trophies*, Russ thought. He noticed smoke curling up from the north end of the beach, near the old boat ramp. Maybe someone was burning debris.

"Okay," Dale said, twiddling the dial. "Let's see if we can get some news . . . I got this baby hooked to an old roof antenna, we should get something . . . "

"What about everybody else hearing this?" Russ asked. "They should know."

"We'll tell them," Dad said.

Antsy with apprehension, Russ remained standing, arms crossed over his chest, looking at the radio, as if that would somehow help him hear the news. The world seemed to be collapsing around him and just the fact that big media was still rolling, the talking heads still babbling, the tickers still ticking— it felt good to him. "I hope we get local reports," he said. "Rescue efforts for—"

His dad shushed him—which Russ found irritating—as the voice of a female radio announcer said, " . . . the death toll for the West Coast is expected to approach one million, and some estimates put it at three million . . . "

"Oh God in heaven," Dale breathed. *"No."*

"For those who do survive, flooding due to storm surge is still ongoing. Most of the West Coast is without power and with extensive damage to highways just getting repair crews into the area is very, very difficult. Emergency medical aid is similarly limited. Clean water is a serious problem up and down the coast. Evacuations around damaged nuclear power plants are ongoing. We have had reports the Diablo Canyon plant is close to meltdown but this has not been confirmed. Estimates of the overall cost of the disaster are incalculable at this time . . . "

"I don't think this little town's gonna get any kind of high priority from these people . . . " Dale muttered. "Can't blame 'em."

The radio voice went on, "FEMA undersecretary Leonard Coolidge made this statement about half an hour ago: 'We're asking everyone to try and cope with the supplies they have for now. If you are near the sea, move inland in an orderly fashion . . . '"

Dad snorted. "We'll do that right away, Coolidge. Christ."

DRIVING HIS extended-cab pickup through the twilight, Mario beside him, Ferrara almost felt like he was still clinging to that wooden island, the roof of his bar, with the waves sawing frantically around him. Chaos was still crowding him, now, as he drove up the hill—a kind of still-motion chaos—a whole block of burned houses. Just a few blocks back down the hill, the houses were damaged by undermining, half collapsed; a block below that it was all flattened debris, still wet from the tidal wave.

After the water had gone down, Ferrara and his brother had made their way to Ferrara's house, just above the great wave's high water line. Found the four-bedroom house partly burned. Looted. His golf clubs, some cash, guns, jewelry gone. Worse, his vintage T-Bird was missing. Some clothes remained, a few other things.

He and Mario cleaned up, got bandaged, spent the night in sleeping bags on air mattresses in the empty garage.

"Who you think is going to help you with this plan?" Mario asked.

"Cholo and Steve are kind of equipped for that kind of . . . heavy lifting." Cholo and Steve were a couple of beefy types who worked at Ferrara's brewery.

Mario looked at the burned houses, shook his head. "How'd that fire get going like that? We're lucky it didn't spread. "

"Somebody set it, is what. Some gangbangers maybe. All the more reason we need our own muscle."

Ferrara found Cholo and Steve about six blocks north, lolling on the roof of Steve's house, drinking beer—halfway through a case of Ferrara's Doublehit Ale, which they claimed they hadn't stolen from the brewery. They sat there on the roof, looking down at the devastation like a couple of guys watching a football game in the park. Steve was a blond bohunk with a crooked nose, broke from his time as a ham-fisted boxer; Cholo was Indian-Mexican, an ex-Marine getting fat around the middle but with bulky shoulders. Dark blue tattoos on his neck and forearm of a winking, grinning vulture and the Marine Corps symbol. Ferrara pulled over, staring.

"What the hell you doing up there?" Ferrara asked, as he and Mario got out of the big glossy-black Ford pickup. "You guys work for me! There's shit to be done! The real work's starting right fucking now!"

"We're off at the brewery today," Cholo said. His voice sounded thin coming from the roof. "Don't work today, boss."

Ferrara wasn't sure if he was serious. With that wide, inscrutable American Indian face, like something on an old-time nickel, you couldn't much tell. "Work schedules washed away with that fucking wave. You got any guns in that house? We're gonna need guns, water, anything you got. "

"Yeah, sure, I got some stuff," Steve said. "Guns and ammo, and a subscription to *Guns and Ammo.*"

Ferrara shook his head. Fucking smart asses. "How long you had that case of beer?"

"Bought it employee discount on Friday," Steve said. "Why?"

"After the wave, somebody stole two fucking trailer-truckloads of beer from my fucking brewery *and* they took the fucking safe, and *then* the cocksuckers set a fire to cover shit up. So I lost the vats and all the grain too."

The factory was about a quarter mile up the coast and a short ways inland, nestled in the shadow of rocky bluffs that cut off access north, if you weren't a rock climber. The highway north was mostly knocked down, and blocked where it was intact—so someone from Freedom had looted his factory. And maybe they'd had help from an insider. Some brewery employee.

"You think we got two truckloads of beer back here?" Cholo had asked. "Where we be keeping that?"

"I'm not saying you did it," Ferrara allowed. "Fucking VVs probably got it." *Valle Vatos*, a Mexican gang. "My fucking brewery gone, my *bar*, my T-Bird—it's too goddamn much."

"Brewery's insured, ain't it?" Steve asked, looking out to sea. He sipped some beer.

"No, goddammit, I don't do insurance. It's a way the IRS keeps tabs. I stopped insuring about— Never mind, that's none of your goddamn business . . . just get the guns! There's somebody squatting in Mario's house and we gotta get 'em out!"

"How you know somebody's taken over Mario's house?"

"Because he went up there and they took a shot at him and said to keep the fuck away!"

Cholo and Steve conferred in low tones, then Cholo shrugged. "Let's do it."

They got the guns, climbed into the back of the Ford four-by-four and drove a circuitous route to get past debris, up the hill to Mario's place. It was at the crown of the hill, just west of a small woods of tall, wind-shaped firs between the house and the rugged, boulder strewn chaparral.

Ferrara pulled up, they got out of the truck—and someone fired from the side of the house, two shots that clanged into the pickup. Big caliber bullets were punching holes right through the passenger side door.

"Mother*fucker!*" Ferrara hissed, ducking down on the other side of the truck. In moments the other three scrambled around beside him, hunched for cover, peering past the hood and cab of the truck.

"Hey!" Ferrara yelled. "You in the house! Get the fuck out or we open fire!"

The only response was a hoarse bellowing: *"Fuck off, we're staying here till we don't need to no more! Stay back!"*

Another shot, whining off the pavement in front of the truck, this time from a window. Ferrara raised his .45 semi-auto pistol, and fired back twice. The window shattered. No other response. The gunshots echoed across the quiet town.

"Shit, Lon, that's my house!" Mario muttered.

"And that's my fucking truck they just shot."

He and Mario were hunched behind the hood of the big black pickup, on the driver's side—the truck was turned parallel to the front of Mario's house

"You can go out the back!" Ferrara shouted. "Go through the woods, get the fuck out! But that's my brother's house! Get the hell out of it!"

Another two shots, overhead this time, and whooping laughter from the house. Ferrara raised his gun to return fire—and his brother put a restraining hand on his wrist.

"Lon—Antony could be in there. I don't know where the hell he went. Maybe he didn't get out of town. They could have him prisoner."

Ferrara growled to himself, but Mario had a point. His nephew Antony, Mario's son, could be in there. So they waited. Minutes passed.

And here they were. Seemed like a half hour watching the house. Cholo with the 30.06 rifle, Ferrara and Steve with the semi-auto pistols, Mario with a shotgun and revolvers and ammo they'd taken from what was left of Ferrara's place, his house on the northern side of the hill, overlooking the ruins of the brewery. Lon Ferrara's house was above the high water mark of the big wave, but somehow in all the chaos it caught fire—maybe one of the local gangs again, fucking around—and most of the house had burned. His gun cabinet had been locked up in his garage though, hidden behind a false wall because he knew, sooner or later, the liberal government was going to come and take his guns away if he didn't hide them. So no one had seen the guns when they'd taken his classic T-Bird out of his locked garage.

"Stand-offs are bullshit," Steve said, now, as they peered over the truck. No sign of life from the house. But no way they could just decide the squatters had left. "I mean—they could use the time to flank us."

Ferrara nodded, wondering if Antony Ferrara was in the house. Maybe the same gang that had reamed out his brewery was in there. Maybe the same fuckers who had started a fire at his house, and stolen his T-Bird. For all he knew the T-Bird was parked out back. Could be the fuckers who stole it were in his brother's house, here, right now.

Everything Is Broken

"I can see my son's dirt bike in the garage there," Mario said, his voice hoarse with worry. He was pretty het up about his kid. The boy had been visiting from college, hanging out with a friend his age, a dirt-bike buddy. Mario hadn't seen him since the big wave.

There was another possibility that hadn't been spoken about out loud. That these pricks in Mario's house had killed the boy.

"Well," Steve said. "There's no cops to call . . . So . . . I guess it's on us . . . "

Ferrara looked sharply at Steve. "What are you saying, with that 'no cops' remark?"

Steve looked quizzically at him, eyebrows raised. "Just that it means we're stuck with doing something about this ourselves."

Ferrara stared. Maybe Steve hadn't meant it that way, but he figured some people were going to blame him if there were looters, gangs out of control, after the wave. He'd stopped the bond measures that paid for cops in Freedom; for the fire department, for emergency services.

He'd had a plan and it hadn't worked out. Well, now he had a new plan. And that plan was going to hit the town like the tsunami, only this wave was going to be a good purging, a good way to cleanse and start over. He was going to change the town from the bottom up. Because he'd lost everything. The bar, the brewery, his other businesses—all wrecked.

He had to recoup. He was going to take it all back. This was his chance to remake Freedom, get rid of the last ties to the welfare state.

"I gotta get in, see if they've got my son in there," Mario said. But he made no move. They could feel someone watching them. Someone who'd shot at them already.

But Ferrara was sick of this. His back hurt from hunching down. Maybe they could come at the place from the side . . .

"Someone coming out," Cholo observed.

"Hey!" the guy yelled, from the front door. Just his head poking out a bit. Skinny guy, hair slicked back. "Coming out to parlay, talk shit over! Don't shoot! There's a lot more of us with guns in here! Don't fucking shoot or they'll open up on you!"

"That's Mike Sten," Steve said. "Runs with that crazy fuck Dickie."

"I don't know him," Ferrara said. "Not personally. Seen him around." He lifted his head up a bit, and shouted, "Come on out, keep your hands where we can see them!"

Sten came out, hands raised. No gun visible. But he probably had one in his waistband, behind.

He walked slowly toward them, squinting in the light. Smirking a little, it seemed to Ferrara. He stopped about five paces from the truck.

"Okay I put my hands down?"

Ferrara nodded, keeping his pistol trained on Sten. "But you reach behind you, I shoot. Now—you know who I am?"

"Sure." Sten's mouth twisted with some unspoken irony. "You're the mayor."

Ferrara sometimes rejected the title, though he'd campaigned for it; other times he wore it proudly, if it served his purposes. This time, he needed all the authority he could muster. "You bet your skinny ass I am, Sten. You know whose property you low-lifes are squatting in? *Mine*. Mine and my brother's—I own it, he lives there. Not you."

"Sorry. Emergency situation. Got to do what we can to survive in this, you know, emergency shit. We ain't giving up anything we don't have to."

"Yeah? Like my Thunderbird?"

"Your what? There a Thunderbird on this property? You sure hid it good."

"Not here. Someone stole it from . . . okay, that wasn't you. You guys break into my brewery?"

"Naw, that was Jorge. Him and his brothers, they split off from the VVs. Just three or four of them, holed up on the north edge of town. Don't come out much. We saw the fire, saw 'em go by after."

Ferrara nodded to himself. Looking around after discovering the burned out brewery, Ferrara had found a neighbor, an old man, said he'd seen some Mexicans drive a truck up the road not long after the big wave hit.

"Those Crystal Mexes around?" Cholo asked, glancing nervously around. "I mean—there must be a hundred of those guys."

"Not around here there aren't," Sten said. "Just Jorge's little crowd. Four of 'em. Like I said, he's on the outs with the VVs. Most of the Mexes are way east. Stuck on the other side of the hills, with the road blocked. You want your shit, talk to Jorge. But they'll probably blow your head off you come close. We were nice to you guys, see—we fired warning shots." He grinned. "We're like, civilized."

"You civilized enough to get the hell out of my brother's house now?" Ferrara asked.

"Naw, man. Emergency. And you guys are being covered right fucking now, you know. Don't be shooting at me."

"You got any hostages in there?" Ferrara asked. "Couple of young men?"

Sten shook his head. "No hostages. No prisoners."

"Hey—you seen 'em, at all?" Mario put in, looking at the garage, then back at Sten. "Couple of college kids. My son Antony was staying here, in the house you're in, right there—he went out yesterday morning, camping, had another guy with him, kid about the same age. College sweatshirts?"

Sten looked at him a long, blank moment. Something too flat and steady in that look, Ferrara decided. Finally Sten said. "Nope. Ain't seen 'em. No Antonys, no college kids."

"I get that we got an emergency situation here," Lon Ferrara said. "But what makes you think you can just take over the house and shoot at people come to claim it?"

"Like you say—emergency," Sten said. "But I'm not here to apologize, Mr. Mayor. I came here with an offer."

"What kind of offer?"

"Dickie, he's had another vision."

"A what?"

"That's sort of how he figures out what to do. He has visions. And he says you and him should partner up. He knows you've got your peeps. And he knows you've got plans. Says he's been watching and thinking on you for a while. Says your peeps aren't enough. You're going to need some . . . militia. To help you out. Act as your point men, out there, till this thing blows over, right? Lot of property available, all of a sudden, with people swept out to sea. Valuable stuff's being dug out of the mud. There's cars that won't be claimed. All kinds of stuff. Jewelry. We can make a deal . . . "

Ferrara was surprised. He'd expected a trade, like they'd leave peacefully if he'd let them go with no trouble, something like that. But a partnership?

If the VVs had looted his brewery, and gotten his T-Bird, that made them the primary enemy. And Dickie might be the ally he'd need. Not only for the VVs. There was another reason.

To put the fear of God into people who were likely to stand up against him, when he carried out his plan.

"Okay," Ferrara said. "Tell Dickie we'll talk about that. We might work something out—short term."

EIGHT

THE SUN was a blazing red-orange oval on the sea, melting into sunset, replicating in the windows, and Russ, searching through the damaged houses at the water line for survivors, was feeling tired and hungry.

They'd been at it all day, digging people out. Putting the bodies in the corpse houses. Treating the survivors. Giving the badly injured ones the Vicodin, other prescription painkillers they'd scrounged from medicine cabinets in abandoned homes. Making up lists of the dead, for later. The list included the sheriff. They'd found him in his inverted car, half buried in the sand on the beach. Hanging in there upside down.

Russ was trying not to think about some things he'd seen. The memories were like bruised muscles—if you tried them, they punished you with their aching.

He'd been drawn to a ranch-style house mostly covered with slimy mud, drawn there—drawn to it and wanting to run from it, at the same time—by a yipping, an intermittent high pitched whimpering. His dad arriving at the same time, wearing the green rubber wading boots he'd scavenged from the house of a dead crab fisherman: the man's forty-foot ketch, with a pile of smashed crab pots, dropped by the tsunami through the roof of his garage to crush him at his workbench.

Dad had found the large collie, toward the back of the house, its lower half badly crushed, blood bubbling from its jaws, under a collapsed wall. Dad had patted the dog's head with one hand, the other hand cutting its throat with a box cutter.

They'd had to dispatch a lot of wounded pets. Others, rescued, were in a series of abandoned back yards near Dad's apartment building.

But this one—the collie . . .

Russ turned away, dropped his tools, and just walked away from it all for a good hour.

A little later: A gasping, semiconscious young woman trapped in her slime-swamped Audi, mud up to her neck. People digging her out. Finding that her belly was sheared open by a big shard of metal from the car door, mud crammed up inside her, she hadn't lived long after they'd dug her out. Russ had made the mistake of letting her get a grip on his hand as she lay dying. Just couldn't bring himself to break the grip. Had to watch her die.

Later still. Two children, a small boy and girl, in an attic. Dead beside their father—their dad had shot them and then himself as the muddy water began to fill the attic. And it had receded before they'd have been drowned. But by then . . .

Russ made the mistake of looking into the little boy's dead, staring eyes . . .

Brand had asked him to help move the bodies but he'd gone floundering out of there, and found the whisky bottle he'd hidden . . . and made himself sick drinking it too fast.

Dad finally had to crash for a while; Brand was taking his place, him and Dale Carter, the older black guy who'd helped make Dr. Spuris stay. Spuris, though, had all but collapsed, and was snoring away in his house. Lucia Greia, the retired nurse, tirelessly making splints, setting bones, comforting. She was a small woman, but seemed indefatigable. Spuris had done everything under duress and it seemed to Russ that Lucia did a better job than the doctor anyway. But there were some people you couldn't really help. Some . . .

. . . her belly was sheared open, mud crammed up inside her . . .

"Hey Russ . . . " Brand, coming over a pile of rubble, smiling.

"You see Pendra around?" Russ asked.

"She's okay. She was helping Lucia but it seemed like she was going to collapse so we sent her to take a nap. I found some juice, hasn't gone bad. Not too bad. Some kind of tropical punch, you want some?"

"Sure." Russ took the bottle gratefully. Wished he could mix in some of the whiskey he'd hidden in that shoebox.

Russ glanced over at Lars. The aging hippie was across the street, peeing against the partly-standing wall of a stucco house. Still wearing that same marijuana-leaf tee shirt. Which maybe he didn't change much even before the tsunami.

"Got to figure out about sewage," Brand said, visibly shivering. A cold breeze had picked up with the sunset. They all had on at least two layers of clothing. "There's that compost toilet concept."

"Lot of people are just digging holes in back yards. I was thinking—the pipes out to sewage treatment—are they broken?"

"Some of them. Lots of them don't seem to be. But there's no water for flushing."

"Well—what if we filled up some containers with seawater? We could run it through screens to get out the worst of the mud or whatever, and then keep buckets of seawater around in the houses, use it in the toilet tanks for flushing?"

Brand stared at him. "What a great idea! We're gonna organize that for sure!"

Russ shrugged as if it were no big deal but, aware he was milking Brand's approval, he went on, "It'd make the cholera Dad worries about less likely. For a while."

"Yeah! Come on, let's go up, tell people about that. And we can help out pulling down the blockage." He grinned. "Or maybe help even more by staying out of the way."

Brand turned and went back up the hill, Russ started after him. "That blockage on Seaward Road? They find some dynamite?"

"No, Dale's got it figured we can—" He broke off, and they both turned and looked out to sea, drawn by the drone of an aircraft. Russ saw it first: a military seaplane, dipping out of the clouds, about a quarter-mile out, heading south.

"Hey!" Russ yelled, waving. Realizing it was pointless to yell, no way the guy could hear him.

He shielded his eyes against the glare of the setting sun, watched the plane head south. And vanish in mist.

Brand growled, shaking his head. "You'd think they could come and look at us up a bit closer anyway. But nothing. Not even a flyover. One chopper this morning, didn't even circle. I mean Jesus fucking Christ. There are people dying up in the gym." They'd moved the worst-injured to the school gym, up by the Seaward Road blockade, to get them closer to the rescuers they kept expecting from Deer Creek.

They continued up the rubble-edged street. Russ suddenly feeling much tireder, much colder. A feeling of hopelessness making him feel like he was shrinking inside his skin.

Brand glanced at him, seeming to sense his mood.

"Listen, I'm bitching, sure, but we've got to remember all the other people who're hurting, up and down the coast. The radio said there was a fault-line they didn't even know about out in the Pacific, east of Hawaii. Who knows what was caught in the wave, between here and Hawaii. Islands, ships. Then it hits the coast for hundreds and hundreds of miles. The whole Richmond District in San Francisco was pretty much wiped out. *Eventually* they'll be here, I guess, but meanwhile . . . "

"Meanwhile we fend for ourselves. But what about those people at Deer Creek?"

"They'll come. They have to know we need help. Deer Creek'll be organizing a caravan of volunteers to take our injured out. But they can't just dynamite that barricade."

"Why?"

"Because—they need to have engineers make sure no one gets hurt on our side first. Even if we stay way back—it's downhill from there, you could have all that stuff roll down on people."

"Yeah, but meantime people die from neglect!" Russ thought about the two hours he'd spent that morning helping out in the gym. He'd had to leave, finally, look for something else helpful to do. He couldn't deal with the misery, the suffering, the feeling of helplessness in that room. People begging for relief from pain. For help he couldn't give. He'd felt guilty, leaving. But he hadn't been much use to anyone.

"Anyway we're gonna take the ball and run with it—try to pull down the barricade with chains and trucks."

"Pull it down? We can do that?"

"Dale is an engineer, turns out. He's out of work, came up here to sell his summer place, got caught out by the tsunami. He's got it figured that if we can pull out some of those big logs at the bottom, the thing should partly collapse, enough to get some vehicles through. There's some risk, the trucks we use to pull it down could get crushed. We've scrounged enough big chains to try it, but . . . the damn chains aren't very long."

"What happened to those two guys who were gonna go for help on their dirt bikes?"

"No one's heard from them. Could have been caught by the VVs."

"Who?"

"Valle Vatos. Local people call them Crystal Mexes. Most of them are out east of here but there might be a few in town. There's a guy named Jorge, gets into arson for the fun of it.

They're the reason a lot of people are carrying their shotguns around. Them and Dickie's Sand Scouts."

"*Sand Scouts.* You going to tell me who that is?"

"Just another gang. Smaller. Maybe ten or twelve of them all told. There's a hardcore group you see around town, five or six of that bunch. This guy Dickie's their leader. Was in the Sea Scouts growing up so he named his gang the Sand Scouts. Thinks the name's real funny. If we'd had enough real cops here, Dickie'd be in jail by now. And now we haven't got any at all . . . "

"So—maybe we should all be carrying weapons."

"I don't know. I'd hate to get too paranoid. But maybe. Just don't think we're really as forgotten here as it seems like. People are probably working on it."

"Yeah, but . . . All those people, dead. Nothing anyone can do about *that*. I mean—I don't know what my point is. It just makes me feel so . . . " He hesitated. Wondering why he felt so comfortable, opening up to Brand. In a way he couldn't with his dad.

"Feel so . . . ?" Brand prompted, gently.

"Like we're nothing. Less than gnats under a sledgehammer."

Brand smiled crookedly. "Not less than that. Human beings manage to do more damage to the world than gnats. But I know what you mean. I feel the same way a helluva lot. Insignificant. Times like this—" He half-turned, gestured vaguely at the wreckage down below them. They could smell the dead animals, pets caught in the wave, fish dumped by it. Half-a-dozen human bodies washed up on the beach. "You look around and think: so much for denial. Now we can see our real situation. Insignificant, temporary, and . . . it can feel meaningless."

"It *is* meaningless." Russ remembered a little boy dying in the gym that morning. Ten years old, kept asking for his mother. Russ had gone to get some water for the boy and when he'd come back, the kid was dead. Internal injuries, Spuris said. The feeling of meaninglessness, the perception of randomness as a tyrannical king over existence, had swept over Russ then. "Those bodies on the beach. You know what I was thinking—they're seafood for seafood. I mean, that's what we are, right? We're worm food on the land, seafood for sea creatures out at sea."

Brand's smile was cynical but somehow sympathetic. "I know what you mean. I kind of think we have to make our own meaning. Until we find some kind of . . . of metaphysical meaning. When we put a broken town back together, we're making things a little more meaningful and . . . well . . . that kind of meaning is all we can be sure we have. But it can be enough, I guess." He grimaced. "I'm not much use at looking on the bright side. If you only knew. I'm sorry I'm not more . . . I mean, I should be talking more positively."

Russ chuckled. "If you were, I wouldn't trust you, man. But one thing I . . . *what?*"

Brand was staring open-mouthed into a space between two houses. Russ turned to look, saw a woman sitting there, leaning back, motionless, against the house closer to the sea. Was she dead? But then she moved her right leg, just slightly. She was a tall slender woman in a dirty, tattered jogging suit, She wore mismatched sandals, her long flaxen hair awkwardly bunched on top of her head.

"Jill?" Brand called. "Jill!"

They went to crouch beside her, and she opened her eyes, squinting at them. "Who's that?" she rasped.

"It's Brand—oh! You haven't got your glasses!"

"No, I . . . I was in the wave, lost 'em . . . " Her voice was a husky whisper. "I was . . . on Ferrara's roof. Up there with him and Mario. Been making my way up here for some time. I was sick . . . yesterday I guess. Still kind of feverish. Had to find some clothes to wear. I just hid out till I felt better but I'm . . . "

"Oh Jesus, you've been on your own? Didn't that prick take care of you?"

She chuckled raspily. "I slipped off the roof. Into the water. Neither one of them—Lon nor his brother—lifted a finger to help me back on. Haven't seen 'em since . . . But I can't see much. I was kind of reluctant to move around . . . all alone. Half blind like this."

"Is your place intact? It was up the hill a ways."

"I'm not sure. I couldn't get over there. There's all kinds of debris . . . "

"Jesus, Jill—come on, let's take you where you can stretch out, get some food." He helped her stand. "Oh shit I should've asked—you got any broken bones?"

"No, don't think so. Bruises, and I lost a tooth. And I'm half blind. But . . . so many other people . . . I swallowed a bunch of . . . I don't know, mud and . . . Can't hardly talk . . . "

"This is Russ, Jill, Drew's boy. Let him take your other arm. Come on. Just come on with us."

NINE

MIDMORNING—and Nella's flash of hope went out like a fizzled fuse.

She was on a windy, mostly barren hilltop with the others, under aluminum-gray cloud cover. Dickie and the Grummons and Sten and Lon Ferrara and his boys. The men wore long black and orange fire fighter's coats, taken from a storage shed on the brewery property. They wore the coats against the weather and to cover up their weapons. Kind of gave them an almost official look too.

Ferrara had said it was lucky the VVs hadn't gotten into the storage shed—and lucky none of the townspeople knew about it. Ferrara had hoarded a few old boxes of town supplies in there— stuff other people would have appropriated, if they'd known. Nella wondered, though, what the other people in town were going to do when they found out the mayor had been keeping town stuff on his private property, and not handing it out to people.

Nella was huddled in a ski jacket she'd found in Mario's closet, her hair whipping in the intermittent wind, her nose stinging. Wondering how she'd gotten here. She felt like she'd been just swept along to this hillside, like the refuse carried by the wave.

The shrubby, boulder-strewn hill was on the east side of the barricade deposited by the tsunami. The "barricade" was a three-story-high blockage of debris left there when the Big Wave had pushed a flood up Seaward Road, the highway east.

The wave had crested on the hills to either side of the road, but crashed between them as if through a break in a dike, carrying everything that would float, and it had blocked up the only intact road out of town with enormous logs, pieces of boats, the occasional small car, the wreckage from houses, furniture, mattresses, tires. Fish and flotsam, kelp and corpses. The roads to the north and south along the coast were just *gone* for long stretches, slapped down off the cliff by the wave. The beaches ended in cliffs. The only way out of Freedom was cliff-climbing or overland on faint animal trails wending between outcroppings of granite and sandstone—or along Seaward Road, if you could get past the tsunami's barricade.

Nella had traipsed mechanically over the hills behind Freedom, straggling after the others. The hike had been mostly uphill, a couple or three miles, and they were footsore. But Ferrara had insisted they had to know what was happening with Deer Creek. His timing had been good. When she first got to that low hilltop, Nella felt a flash of hope, seeing that caravan of trucks and vans and ambulances and fire trucks coming from the east, arriving at the blockage in the pass to the coast.

But now, tired and cold, she felt drained of ambition; felt pretty sure these men wouldn't let her go down to the people on that road, five hundred yards away.

She was trying not to look at Lon Ferrara. Ferrara had said, earlier, "What's she doing with us? She won't be much use."

"Hell she's some use to me, now and then!" Dickie had said and everyone had laughed except, of course, Nella.

But Nella hadn't felt anything, hearing Dickie say that.

She thought: *That should bother me, shouldn't it?*

But what he said didn't bother her. What bothered her was Ferrara's glowering appraisal, whenever they'd stopped for a rest on the trail to get here. Ferrara looking at her with that mix of want-you and hate-the-sight-of-you. Made her feel more scared, more vulnerable. Like in a dream of being naked in public.

But in the sight of the eye watching from above, she was always naked. The eye looked right through her skin. She could almost, *almost* see the eye when she looked up at the clouds. The watching eye was beyond the clouds but she could *feel* it looking through them—it could look through anything. She could feel it and she could almost see it. And when she thought about it she realized there were *two* eyes, two of them made of brass, looking at her upside down . . .

And then another flicker of hope—mingled with a shudder of startlement—as, *boom, crash, thump*, the barricade started to fall in on itself. It was being pulled down, undermined, it looked like, from the other side, the town side.

Nella caught herself thinking that maybe she could go with those people in the emergency vehicles; maybe she could ride with them back to Deer Creek.

"Yeah, see, it's the chains on those trucks," Steve said, adding, "Over in Freedom." He'd gone earlier to see what the town rescue groups were doing. "Maybe we oughta . . . " He broke off, seeing Ferrara glaring at him.

"We're going to do our own organizing for this community," Ferrara said, squinting at the dust cloud rising from the falling barricade. And frowning when they heard a thin chorus of cheers from the road.

"Looks like the authorities is in town," Cholo said glumly, staring down at the emergency vehicles from Deer Creek. Including three cop cars.

"You know what, I can deal with that," Ferrara said. "They're here to take the injured out—let 'em do it. That's more we don't have to deal with. I'm gonna go have a talk with those boys. Chief Fetzer is down there for sure, from Deer Creek fire department.

He's mayor of that town too. He's the real power in Deer Creek—runs the place as much as anybody. I'll work it with him—we'll make sure Freedom is good and bottled up."

Dickie's eyes crinkled and he chuckled to himself. Then he put on a fake look of puzzlement. "But, mayor—if you bottle it up, doesn't that fuck with the 'freedom' concept? You know, full-on liberty, do what you want, and all? If you keep the people in the town, isn't that . . . not so damn free?"

Ferrara stared at him, face going red. The wind blew his hair around as if its motion were part of his anger. "What the fuck are you saying?" Ferrara demanded. "Whose side you on? We got a deal or not?"

Dickie winked at the Grummons and they burst into laughter. Sten just gave that wolfish grin. "Hey, I'm just fucking with you, man. Like I give a flying fuck about their freedom. Sure we got a deal. But right now I'm gonna get off this cold-ass hill. My balls are clinking together like ice cubes in a fucking cocktail."

With that, Dickie turned to go, still chortling, jerking his head at Nella like, *Come on.*

She hung back. But she thought: *They'll never let me go with those people, to Deer Creek . . .*

"Hold it, Dickie," Ferrara said, gesturing to his men. Mario and Steve and Cholo stepped up close beside Ferrara.

Dickie paused, looked back at him. Quiet and serious now. "There's cops down there on that road. I'm not staying up here." He looked steadily at Ferrara. Finally adding, "Lon."

"Don't expect you to stay here. But if we got a deal, then you take directions from me. What I need you to do now is get back over those hills, and wait for my signal. You got that walkie-talkie?"

Dickie looked at Ferrara like he was thinking of telling him to fuck himself.

Nella knew Dickie was just biding his time. She knew he

wouldn't put up with Ferrara forever. Probably Dickie figured he needed some kind of semi-legal cover for his vision to come true. And that's what Ferrara would give him for a while. Camouflage. Backup. Till the time came . . .

Nella knew Dickie and she could see all this going through his mind.

Finally, he said, "Yeah, I got the walkie-talkie . . . " He patted his coat pocket. "So?"

The walkie-talkies, not much bigger than cell phones, had belonged to Mario—he'd used them to talk to hunters he went out with, on hunting trips. They weren't good for a long distance, but within the confines of Freedom, or close by, they'd pick you up. Lon had one, and Dickie, and Mario, and Sten.

"So—you turn it on, Dickie, when you get over there by that high school gymnasium. Keep an eye on what's going on there. But keep out of sight. And I'll get in touch when I've worked up a plan."

"Sure. Long as we understand everything we take in, we split. Like we talked about."

"That's the deal," Ferrara said, turning to squint down at the road again.

There was a big creaking sound from the pass, followed by a clack and crunch and series of thumps—and a twenty-foot boat went tumbling down from the barricade, rolling sideways, falling to the gravel shoulder of Seaward Road and splitting open—six or seven yards from the nearest ambulance waiting on the highway below with its lights flashing.

"They're gonna get through pretty soon," Sten observed. "Big mess, but they can start moving people out of Freedom."

Ferrara nodded. "Cholo and Steve and Mario—you fellas wait up here. Watch my back. You others go on with Dickie. I'm going down to talk to the chief—"

"Lon?" Mario said suddenly. "Uh-uh. I'm coming with you."

Ferrara looked startled, Nella thought, to hear his brother contradict him. "Mario—just do what I tell you, we got an emergency here—"

Mario shook his head. "My son's missing. And his friend Roger."

He glanced at Dickie. Who was following the exchange closely, eyes narrowed.

Mario suspects, Nella thought.

"I'm going down there to see if they've got my son," Mario went on, looking down at the caravan of cars and trucks and emergency vehicles pulled up on the road below. "Maybe he's with them—helping out. That'd be like him." His voice broke. "Just like him. Or he could be on one of those stretchers. He could be . . . they could know where he is . . . "

Lon stared at him. Finally he nodded, quickly. "Come on, then. Let's do it."

Nella cleared her throat. "Can I . . . can I go down too—and see if I can help, or . . . " She licked her lips, dried out by the wind. Then she said it all in a rush: "Can I go down there with you, Lon? Please?"

Say yes. If she didn't go down to the road with Ferrara, Dickie would stop her from going.

Ferrara glanced at her, surprised, shook his head. "No, no, I need to control how all this looks."

Meaning, she knew, Ferrara thought she was too much of a skank to go down there with him.

She turned, saw Dickie scowling at her. "Come on, Nella. I told you. You're coming with us."

She could run, maybe. Down that hill. They wouldn't shoot her in front of all those cops.

But then what?

She'd be on her own. No one to protect her. It wasn't like she could trust cops. And probably Dickie'd find her in Deer Creek, in time. He'd be afraid she'd talk about what she'd seen. He'd track her and kill her. And Ronnie, if he was alive, was probably somewhere in Freedom.

So finally she just nodded and turned away from the road—feeling the last little spark of hope burn out as she did it.

I'm making a mistake, Nella thought, *walking with Dickie and Sten, back down the other side of the hill*. But it was the side away from the people on Seaward Road and it was too late to run now.

"You sure about that, Lon?" Fetzer asked, looking at Ferrara with lifted eyebrows.

The two of them were standing on the asphalt edge of Seaward Road, in the cluster of emergency vehicles. Cops in slickers and firemen and paramedics bustled near the volunteers from Freedom already moving the injured into the vehicles. A stench of briny decay blew from the half-fallen barricade of mud-caked debris.

Chief Fetzer was a tall, slope-shouldered man with a big head and a chin to match it, a red face—he liked his bourbon—and an immaculate blue fire chief's uniform. The uniform kept changing color because the lights on the ambulance nearby were flashing red, blue, red, blue, so it'd go kind of purple and then blue and then purple again.

"Sure I'm sure," Ferrara said, buttoning his coat up against the keening wind. He was glad he'd left the shotguns and rifles back at the house. The only weapons on him and his men were pistols, hidden under their coats.

"I was thinking we'd take these people into Deer Creek," Fetzer went on, sounding like he was thinking aloud. "We've got just enough room, with the volunteer vehicles, for most of your injured, maybe all of them. And then we can come back and evacuate everybody else."

"It's the come back part we don't need, Chief. The road's open now. We still have a lot of working vehicles on our side of the hill. We'll take people out, ones who want to go, when the time comes. But we have to check them out first. Sort out who's who . . . what's what."

Ferrara winced inwardly, aware that he wasn't making too much sense.

Fetzer stuck his hands in his jacket pockets. "Sure getting cold. Damp cold too." He looked at the sky. "Might rain." He looked sharply at Ferrara. "Your people don't have power for heat or lights over there, I wouldn't think, Lon. No clean water. And FEMA's busy as hell, down the coast—going to take them a long time to get to you."

"We got it covered. You know us, we like to be self-sufficient in Freedom. We're grateful you're taking the injured people. We find any more, we'll send someone through to let you know. But we don't want anyone running out of town right now—there's law enforcement considerations. We got looters who're trying to get out of town with their stolen goods, Chief. You can tell the sheriff for me—we're not gonna let 'em do it. We need to check everybody out before they leave town. All except the injured."

"Didn't get them out any too soon. Must've been rough as hell over there for you, pulling people out of the rubble and mud, the last couple days."

"Sure it was," Ferrara said, glancing away. "Busted my ass doing it. But we've got it covered now. Just keep your vehicles back, let us do our own policing. We've got police officers over there."

"Do you? Didn't see any. Just a lot of volunteers carrying people through. Going back for more. Working hard, those people. We could go in there and help out, when we get your injured to the hospital."

Fetzer glanced over at Mario who was talking to paramedics, checking the injured coming from Freedom. Ferrara knew Mario was looking for his son.

"Not necessary," Ferrara said. "Look, Chief—am I the mayor of Freedom or not?"

"Last I heard."

"Then probably the mayor'd know what the town needs, right?

"Um—yeah."

Fetzer didn't seem convinced. They'd argued, once before, about politics—about necessary infrastructure. Ferrara didn't want that can of worms opened.

"Okay, so, Chief—let me handle it. Like I say, I'll send somebody through to get you folks if we need more help. You don't want to be overwhelmed by refugees, right?"

"Well—it's not just up to me. But I know Sheriff Williams is concerned about protecting Deer Creek from . . . what would you call it, from looters, problem refugees from the coast. Like they had in New Orleans after Katrina. The VVs worry us. And those Sand Scouts." He raked a hand thoughtfully through his graying, wind-tousled hair. "Yeah. I expect the sheriff'll be glad to let it go at that. For now anyway . . . " Fetzer shrugged and turned away. "I've got to see how we're doing. These people are hurting, over here." He started toward the men pushing gurneys, toting the injured to the emergency vehicles. Calling out to a man at the back of an ambulance:

"Reuben! You got the morphine going?"

"About run out!" the paramedic responded.

"Well, let's go, let's get some more out!"

"I'm opening up a fresh box right now, Chief!"

"Chief!" Ferrara called. "One more thing."

Already ten paces away, Chief Fetzer stopped, turned to look wearily back at Ferrara. "Yeah?"

Ferrara strode up to him, leaned close to speak in a confidential tone. "Do me a favor, there, Chief—and don't make any announcements on what we talked about. I've got to think about crowd control. This is an emergency. You know how it is. People don't like to be told where to go but in an emergency . . . Got to do it."

"So—what you want me to tell FEMA? I mean—you people haven't been in touch with 'em, I take it. I need to tell them something."

"Tell them we're all right. Don't need their help. Now that you've taken the injured out. We'll take care of this our way. Those people—it's all a shuck to set up a dictatorship, Chief."

"What is?"

"FEMA. All they do is come in and tell you what to do and can't do. You can't get in your own house. And they keep local people from volunteering, going in. They got this whole plan, see—"

"Oh sure, all that, I remember you believed that stuff. I don't have time for it, Lon. You don't want FEMA, well—I'll tell 'em that. But look—you have a town hall meeting and decide you want them there, why, send someone through to Deer Creek, we'll tell 'em. Get the National Guard out here for you, the whole shebang."

"Not going to need them, Chief. That simple. We're keeping the peace. We're in better shape over there than you'd think. And I'd sure appreciate, like I said, if you didn't make any announcements about all this. Let me do that."

Chief Fetzer stared at Ferrara for a long, doubtful moment. Then he shrugged. "Sure thing. Anyway—I'll give it some time. But I'll check back, in, I dunno, three or four days." And he turned back to the crews moving the stretchers.

Three or four days. They'd have their hands full with these injured. There'd be time to do what needed to be done. He could send word in a couple of days that all was well too.

Mario came back, and Ferrara could see by the slump of his shoulders that he hadn't found his son.

And Lon Ferrara, his brother trailing after him, went back to the hills, taking the long way back to what was left of Freedom. Not ready to confront the men on the other side of the pass yet.

Ferrara wondering, as he went, if he could trust Dickie and his Sand Scouts.

Maybe, maybe not. But he wouldn't need them forever. Still—if it was true that "Jorge," whoever the fuck that was, and some of those Crystal Mexes had his Thunderbird, maybe his beer too, he could use Dickie to help him get them back. And if that worked . . .

"YOU'RE GOING to walk right up to that door, Nella girl," Dickie reminded her, standing on the sidewalk close by her, in the twilight. The Grummons had gone to Dickie's "ranch" at the eastern edge of town, in a hollow of the steep hills, where Chuckles and a couple of the other guys might be holed up. Supposed to recruit them.

Dickie was here with Sten and the Ferraras and his men, standing near the black pickup. "You're gonna knock and you're gonna ask if Jorge's there . . . ."

"Do I have to do anything with them?" she asked. Shivering as the wind shook a little cold, thin rain from the lowering clouds.

"Do anything?" Dickie looked up the street to the Mex's place as he spoke, slapping the big .45 into the palm of his left hand, over and over, as if slowly clapping with it. "Like sex, you mean?"

"Not unless you want to have sex with dead bodies," Sten said. "Ha."

"You just get out of the way, when someone opens up," Dickie said.

The big black Ford pickup was parked at the corner, almost a block down from Jorge's place. He and three of his buddies, split off from the VVs, Dickie said, were staying in the fading white one-story bungalow, trimmed in green shutters and half hidden behind squat fir trees. To one side of the bungalow, not touching it, was a wooden, paint-peeling, slightly-leaning garage that looked older than the house. There were only a few other houses on the tree-lined, potholed street. It was in a run-down outer corner of Freedom, almost in the shadow of the crumbling sandstone bluffs that hemmed in the town's northern side.

Ferrara was standing with Steven and Cholo and Mario, at the back of the truck. His mouth clamped shut, lower lip stuck out as he looked down the street the other way, Ferrara glared toward the gravel road that led to his brewery, or what was left of it. They could just see the charred tops of the buildings on the other side of a stand of pines and nearly leafless poplars.

"I think I got it figured, Mayor," Dickie said, just loud enough for Ferrara to hear.

Ferrara came over and Dickie whispered out his plan and Ferrara shrugged. "Like I said, this is you showing us you can handle shit, Dickie. Go for it. We'll back you up. Try not to hit my car, it's probably in that old garage."

Dickie nodded. "Be a shame to nail that old Thunderbird. Come on, Mike, Nella."

They walked slowly, quietly up the street, watching the house as they approached it. Nella could see a glimmer of light between two half-open green shutters. As they got closer she heard Mexican music playing, with accordions and guitars and people saying

"*Haii!*" She could hear the sound of a generator running behind the house. They knew it was there. It was part of Dickie's plan. He loved to plan things out, and make them happen, like an army general.

They got close and Dickie nodded to Nella, then signaled the others to wait by some fat decaying oak trees that made the sidewalk buckle up with their roots.

Her mouth was dry, but apart from that Nella didn't feel any real fear as she walked up to the house alone. She had wanted to live, when she was in the wave, dragged out of the motel. Now she didn't seem to care much anymore. It might be good to live—and then again, it would be okay to be shot down. Just as long as she went quick. Lately she went back and forth between those two feelings like the waves that had swept her to and fro in front of the motel . . .

She went up the steps. Seeing Sten, out of the corner of her eyes, sneaking around, hunched down as he went, to the left side of the house. Going to the back, where the generator was. Music thumped from inside. *Haii-yi!* She waited . . .

The music switched off suddenly—and the light too. So Sten had turned off the generator out back. Voices speaking Spanish, inside. Hushed, urgent voices. She heard a faint sound that might be the back door of the bungalow opening, men talking back there. They were blundering out to see what was wrong with the generator. Just like Dickie figured.

She knocked on the door, hard. A little paint came off it when she knocked. She waited. No response. She knocked again, harder.

Footsteps. Whispered voices. "*Quién es?*" someone called, through the door.

"Is Jorge there?" she called through the door. "My girlfriend said he might want a date. I don't have any food, my motel was all swamped in that wave, I got no place to stay, she said I could trade with you guys, you know?"

"What girl sent you?"

"Consuela!" There was always a Consuela, wasn't there?

Soft Spanish argument on the other side of the door.

Then it started to open. She backed away, as if she was scared. Saying, "Maybe this wasn't such a good idea . . . " *Why am I being such a good actor?* she wondered. *Why do I care if this works?* But it was best to please Dickie. Who was now easing up into the yard to her left, moving low up to the wall beside the door, under the front window.

A good-looking young man peered out at her. He wore a long blue-plaid shirt, buttoned up to his neck, hanging down untucked to half cover his jeans. He had shoulder-length wavy black hair, a *VV* tattooed on the side of his neck with a skull that looked like it was from *El Día de los Muertos*. He held a 9 mm pistol down at his right side and tattoos twined his slim arms. "I don' know you, *puta*," he said. He looked her up and down. "I don' think we want any of your—"

Gunshots from out back of the house. Yells of pain.

She ducked to the right and Jorge—she knew it was him—was raising his gun, starting to close the door, but Dickie stepped onto the front walk, was already firing his .45 through the open door as he came, three shots fast, *pop pop pop*, and Jorge shouted agonized dismay in Spanish. As Nella backed up she saw him staggering backwards into the shadowy house, falling . . .

Dickie rushed in, firing at someone else. Muzzle flashes at the windows. Nella saw a man limping toward the street from the side of the house, his teeth bared white in the twilight, a pistol in his hand, his right leg streaming blood. Sten pursuing, firing his pistol. The man turned, as he went, stumbling, firing toward Sten, missing. Cholo and Steve fired handguns at him from the oaks, the guns cracking, flashing in the dimness, the man's body dancing around with the impacts. The gangster sobbed and fell, tried to crawl. Sten ran up behind him and shot him through the middle of his back. He writhed and Sten shot him again.

"Took that Mexican a fuck of a long time to die," Sten said as Cholo and Steve came up.

The gangster was motionless, now, face down.

Nella almost fell backwards, tripping against the edge of the cracked sidewalk. She steadied and saw Dickie come out of the house, grinning at Ferrara, giving a thumb's up. Ferrara was walking slowly up, the shotgun in his hands, looking a little awestruck. Trying not to seem too impressed.

Mario trotted over to the garage, opened it up. The Thunderbird was there. And cases of Doublehit Ale.

"Ah," Ferrara said, brightening. "Good job."

Steve looked around at the other houses. Not a movement, not a peep. Not a sound from anywhere. "Jeezus. No one even looking out a fucking window."

The men gathered in front of the house, their eyes bright, flashing their teeth in grins. Ignoring the dead. Ferrara telling Mario to move the Thunderbird into some kind of town storage shed. Everyone talking excitedly.

Nella waited over by the sidewalk. She didn't want to be near them when they were excited by killing. She didn't want to have sex with anyone.

"Caught two of 'em out back at the generator," Sten was saying. "Dumb fucks."

Steve was looking down the street. Seemed to be listening, shaking his head in wonder. "No sirens. Nothing!"

"That's right," Dickie said, looking over at Nella. Winking. Pleased with himself. "And there won't be any sirens. Ain't it glorious? Sheriff's dead. No other police. None going to come at all. This is freedom, dude. Welcome to freedom."

TEN

"MAN, I'M TIRED," Russ said, settling onto a couple of wrestling mats, impromptu mattresses piled in the corner of the echoing gymnasium.

Dad and Brand hunkered down near Russ. Pendra was stretched out on her back, one arm thrown over her eyes, seeming to nap. Russ sat with his legs drawn up, back against the wall, looking around at all the people in the gym, most of them sitting or stretched out on wrestling mats, sleeping bags, futons cadged from deserted homes, a few talking in groups near the door. Hundreds of people. He was feeling more hopeful and the others seemed more cheerful too, now that they'd made contact with Deer Creek, and gotten the injured out. Laughter was heard, now and then—for the first time in days.

The fire chief from Deer Creek had decided that the injured would be carried on stretchers through the gap in the road blockage. There was still a big shaky pile of debris to one side—they couldn't force large vehicles through. But people could walk through and be picked up by the next caravan from Deer Creek.

A few of the uninjured had gone along to the hospital with their children, their spouses. But most every survivor not badly hurt was still waiting here in the Freedom High School Gymnasium, or in the more intact houses. That seemed to be what Deer Creek wanted—they didn't want to be overwhelmed with refugees, all at once. At least they had power and running water in Deer Creek.

But there were more Coleman lanterns, brought by Deer Creek's caravan of trucks; stacked boxes of canned food, bottled water, first aid kits, carried by DCFD to the gap in the tsunami's blockade. Not quite enough room to safely get trucks through, yet. The goods had been passed through, then trucked in to the gym.

It was getting toward evening and the light, from the row of windows near the gym's ceiling, was dimming. Getting hard to see the painting on the gym's wall, opposite the row of high windows: A cartoon sea lion grinning rakishly and balancing a basketball on its nose. The Freedom High Sea Lions had been the school's basketball team, once upon a time.

Russ leaned forward, rubbed at a persistent ache in his lower back. They'd spent the morning helping out at the debris barrier, setting chains, clearing part of the debris after some of it was pulled down. The afternoon they'd spent moving the injured through: a long, slow, arduous, emotionally stressful process— the injured crying out with pain every time they were jarred.

Everyone in the gym had helped move the injured, and they were all dead tired. Russ just wanted to get to Deer Creek, find somewhere more comfortable to rest. "So how long we got to wait here?" he asked.

Dad looked at Brand and shrugged. "Any thoughts on that one, Brand?"

"I don't know—Chief Fetzer and the sheriff were kind of fuzzy on that."

"They're fuzzy?" Pendra said, face still under her arm. Not asleep it seemed. "What color is their fuzz?" She sat up, groaning. "My shoulders hurt."

"They ought to hurt," Russ said, grinning. "You and Lucia carrying that huge woman on that stretcher. She must've weighed three hundred pounds, at least. I don't know how injured that woman really was, either. She probably could've walked to the ambulance." They all suspected the big lady had been malingering to get out of Freedom. "Here comes Dr. Spuris. He was really pissed off when they told him they didn't have room for him on that trip."

Dr. Spuris didn't look angry any more. He looked afraid. His mouth was slackly open and his eyes seemed sunken as he stalked up to Russ's dad and Brand. "You two—I want to talk to you. You're a couple of organizers for this . . ." He gestured flutteringly around at the people in the gymnasium. " . . . this thing!"

Russ's dad looked genuinely surprised. "We are?"

"Just tell me what the hell is going on! I walked up to the gap, to see if the people from Deer Creek were coming back for us—and there were armed men out there, with barbed wire across the road, telling me no one else is leaving town!"

AT FIRST, the razor wire was hard to see in the failing light. But then, as Russ walked up Seaward Road, with the unofficial deputation from the gym, the bonfire roared up big and bright and teeming with red sparks when one of the armed men tossed a match on the gasoline-soaked pile of debris. Broken wooden chairs, driftwood, and a large, intact wooden doghouse were all heaped seven feet high in the gap they'd made in the tsunami's barricade. The flame leaped up, towering over them all, a single enormous blue-yellow flame that rippled with a rumbling and crackling sound; it hissed and sucked at the sky, delineating the antipersonnel wire across the gap.

"Theatrical," Brand muttered, as the group stopped a few strides from the armed men at the bonfire. Russ's father, Brand, Russ, Jill, Dale Carter. Russ felt the heat of the fire on his face as they got near; his eyes watered when the smoke shifted, whuffed past him. About fifteen others from the town gathered behind Brand and Russ's father, including Pendra, close behind, and Dr. Spuris.

Jill squinted at Ferrara and his men and shook her head in disgust as if they were unruly drunks in front of a bar. She was still wan but more or less cleaned up, wearing scavenged clothes: jeans that were too short for her, a designer leather jacket someone had salvaged from their house. Rudimentarily washed in seawater, her hair was tied back in a long stiff ponytail.

"Christ, Ferrara, what now?" she asked, only half aloud. "What's all this about?"

The razor wire, behind the bonfire, was stretched across the gap in the great barricade of debris: an X-ing of taut, crisscrossed antipersonnel razor wire. The wire, the shotguns, rifles, pistols in the hands of the men back-lit by the bonfire—Russ thought it was a pretty clear message.

He counted eleven men, all of them wearing long black firefighter coats, trimmed in traffic-cone orange; each of them sporting a gun. One of the men stepped forward to meet Brand and Russ's dad, who were carrying flashlights—Dad gesturing for Russ to stay back. But he couldn't do that. Pendra was watching. He stepped up beside his father.

The people behind the deputation eyed the guns and stayed several paces back.

The wind had dropped some—but now it returned, carrying the charnel reek from the beach and the smell of brine from the sea, whipping up the bonfire so that it roared and exhaled gassy fumes. Barely feeling the warmth of the fire, Russ zipped up his coat, buried his fists in his pockets.

"Well, Ferrara," Brand said, stopping just a pace from the mayor. "I'm sure you've got an explanation for blocking up the pass. I mean, for Christ's sake—razor wire? Your idea of a safety measure?"

Everything Is Broken

So that's Ferrara, Russ thought. His hair looked dyed, Russ decided. Even his eyebrows. He had two days growth of beard that showed gray. He had short legs and a long body and a way of holding his head tilted to one side. He held a pump shotgun cradled in his arms.

"What I've got," Ferrara said, "is a declaration of emergency and a plan for this town, all in one. There are people looting, for one thing. They've got to be stopped. For another, all you people are getting set to just abandon the town—that's what I've been hearing."

"From whom?" Russ's father asked. "You haven't been around to hear anything."

"Doesn't matter if I've been right here with you or doing my own thing. We're just not going to let this town fall apart."

"*We*, huh," Brand said. "Isn't that Dickie Rockwell back there? I seem to remember the highway patrol was looking for him."

"That was awhile back," said one of the men, stepping up behind Ferrara, grinning at them. A pistol in his hand pointed casually at the ground. A lean, sardonic young man with long hair snapping in the wind like the flames from the bonfire. "All that false accusation blew over. I am . . . an innocent man."

"Blew over from lack of evidence?" Brand asked mildly.

"Naw, just a big misunderstanding. We're here to help, dude. We're the emergency militia."

"Ha!" said a wolfish looking man, taller and skinnier, behind Dickie. "Militia!"

"And that's Mike Sten," Brand muttered musingly. "Some of these others I don't know. Except Cholo, him I've met. The Grummon brothers I know by sight."

"Those other boys, those are Lucas and Remo and Chuckles," Dickie said proudly. "Just got 'em with us about an hour ago. They were out at the ranch waitin' for me and—"

"Dickie," Ferrara told him, abruptly. "Just let me deal with this."

Dickie's grin only widened—he exchanged a wink with Sten.

Not good, Russ thought. It was clear that Dickie didn't take Ferrara seriously. Which meant Ferrara couldn't control Dickie's bunch all that well. They were playing Ferrara, in some way.

Somehow, Russ knew these were men you either controlled—or you ran from. There was no real neutrality with them. He just knew that, looking at them. They were like some gangbangers Russ had known back home. Just a different variety.

Russ looked up at the still imposing wall of interlocked debris, to one side of the passage they'd cleared. The wave had mortared it together with seaweed, mud, and arbitrary swatches of trash. Russ could see the detached side of a house, up there, bizarrely angled, with part of a window still in it.

One day you're sitting in your house, the next day it's taken apart, the wall decorated with your kid's pictures jammed into a pile of debris a quarter mile up the hill. Where were the people belonging to that house? Dead probably. Broken and drowned.

Russ looked back at Ferrara—and Dickie, whose face was lit from below in the indirect glow of flashlight beams. This Dickie guy seemed to Russ another kind of force of nature. Just another point man for death.

"What's this plan you allude to, Ferrara?" Jill asked.

"In the present circumstances I feel it's important you call me Mayor, or, if you want, Mayor Ferrara."

"And I don't feel like it," Jill said, instantly. "Because you're not acting like a mayor, you're blocking the way out of a bad situation with guns and razor wire. You're part of the problem."

Man, Russ thought. *These people are armed and dangerous. That woman's nervy.*

Ferrara looked steadily at her. "Lost your glasses, I see, Jill."

"Yeah. I did. But I still have my sense of smell."

Russ smiled. Ferrara pretended not to understand her. He stepped to one side, raised his voice to be heard over the crackling of the bonfire. "First, we simply can't let people just walk away from town till we know for sure if any of those people have been looting! We need to make sure no one is getting away with what you folks have left! Second—we can't let Freedom become a ghost town! Third—we can't accept help from Big Government because their help isn't really help. So we need our own plan—and my plan is to get everybody working in a new company. I call it the Freedom Corporation! What we'll do is, we'll privatize the restoration of the town. That means we *pool our resources*. I mean to rebuild this town! I lost everything in that wave. Either in it—or because of it!" He seemed to lose control of himself, in that moment. Something feral flickered in his eyes. "I lost every . . . fucking . . . *thing!*"

He was breathing hard—and Russ stared at him. Russ's father, Brand, Pendra, Jill, Dale. They all started, realizing that something had happened to him in the tsunami. If it wasn't madness, it was close.

"Your insurance didn't cover tidal waves, I expect," Jill said, after a moment. "You're not alone in that." Sounding like she was trying to calm him down. "But there's FEMA help coming, there's—"

"No!" He stabbed a finger at her. "See, I don't have any insurance *at all* because that's really just one arm of Big Government. Insurance commissioners, it's all smokescreen! The insurance companies pretend to be independent but they're not. Look at the AIG bailout!"

"So, since *you* chose not to insure—you're going to make the town cover your losses?" Jill said, the words mixed with sad laughter. "How about cash assets, in banks? Stocks, that kind of thing? You must be able to . . . "

He grimaced, shook his head. "I don't want to talk about that. That's a personal matter."

"I heard you overextended yourself, building the brewery and that little casino in Deer Creek that you invested in—they wouldn't license it and you lost all that money . . . "

"Jill—that is personal business—we're here to talk public business! Now, I've got a plan for the corporation written out—I'm going to post copies of it. We've got a generator going up at Mario's place and I've got a copy machine there. But—now don't interrupt, let me get this out, let me say it plainly to everyone—I said it before and I mean it! *This town is not taking any help from FEMA!* I have made that clear to the authorities at Deer Creek. Told them to pass the word on to FEMA that we're okay. We are flat-out not taking *any* help from the US government or state government. These people from FEMA are planning to put anti-socialist Americans into detention camps! We are not going to trust them and we don't need them! We are independent! *We are Freedom!*"

"Oh God, Lon!" Jill stared at him in shock—then covered her open mouth with her hand. "You told FEMA *not to come?*"

"They'll come anyway," Dad said.

"Actually, not for a while," Brand pointed out. "They are sure to be way overextended right now. Stretched to the limits. Some town mayor says we don't need help, they'll check on them last. Maybe not for weeks. I mean—millions of people are displaced down the coast . . . "

"We don't need them ever!" Ferrara insisted. "Letting Big Government overrun us is not what this town is about! This is an opportunity to increase our decentralization from the power centers! Eventually we might even partner up with some other communities in the area and secede from the country—"

"Secede!" Dad burst out. "Jesus, Mary, and Joseph, Lon!" He shook his head, laughing bitterly. "You are *out of your fucking mind!*" He groaned. "I mean—seriously—you are having a nervous breakdown of some kind. You don't need our help—you need a doctor's help, Lon!"

Dad was probably right. Ferrara probably was. But it made Russ nervous when Dad spoke that way to Ferrara. Dismissively, angrily. Because Ferrara had a shotgun in his hands and he was backed up by other armed men. Including that Dickie guy.

Ferrara glared at Russ's father. Seemed to be controlling his temper. Then he said, "We'll just see. Government might be pretty weakened by this whole thing, they might just shrug us off. There's precedent for that. But we're getting ahead of ourselves. First off, we *create a company*. We're all going to be employees of it, see! We invest whatever we have in goods, right here, and in a special account at a bank over in Deer Creek—it'll be invested by the Freedom Corporation. We'll have a completely privatized town!"

Jill spoke up sharply. "That bank—you mean Deer Creek Savings and Loan? And who's going to oversee that account? You?"

"Someone has to. That's just practical. You're getting hung up on petty—"

"Where did you get the razor wire?" Brand interrupted harshly, looking past Ferrara at the crisscrossing wire glimmering in the bonfire light. Something in his voice suggested it was a more important question than it seemed.

"The wire?" Ferrara shrugged. "It's your standard antipersonnel stuff. For emergencies. I had some town goods, leftover stuff, stored in a shed out by the brewery. We got these coats, some emergency supplies, there was some wire . . . "

"Wait—emergency supplies?" Russ burst out. Hardly aware he'd spoken aloud. But immediately aware that Ferrara and Dickie were now looking curiously at him.

"Who's this?" Ferrara asked.

"That's my son," Russ's dad said distractedly, frowning at the bonfire.

"Hey," said another man, stepping up, catching Dad's eye. A Remington hunting rifle cradled in his arms. "We met before. I'm Mario, Lon's brother. You're Drew, right?"

Mario Ferrara. Russ could see the resemblance now. But this Ferrara didn't dye his hair, he let it go gray. And his eyes looked sadder, his face heavier, as if the sadness had collected like fat to sag in his cheeks.

"Yes," Russ's dad said, looking at the hunting rifle. "Mario. I remember. You worked at your brother's bar."

"Yeah—I'm looking for my own kid, about the same age as yours. Boy named Antony. With his friend. They're just a couple of college kids."

"Sure," Dale said, stepping up. "Antony. He and his friend went for help. Said they were going to take some motorcycles— dirt bikes. Take the trails past the blockage."

"Did they? They—" Mario broke off, blinking. "Dirt bikes? Did you *see* 'em on the dirt bikes?"

"No, no, they were going up to your place and getting those bikes. Not that long after the wave hit. We haven't seen 'em since, so we thought they'd gotten through . . . "

Mario shook his head, frowning at his rifle. "People from Deer Creek say they haven't seen them. Found out on their own the road was blocked, so they started up the rescue. Nobody had to tell 'em."

"Could be the bikes didn't have any gas in them," Dale said. "They might've gone by foot. Or they went somewhere else. Lot of places they could be. But I tell you one thing for sure, they didn't die in that wave. We saw them after."

Mario nodded slowly, brow furrowed. "I just don't see why they wouldn't be in touch with me by now."

"*Fuck* this noise!" Dickie said suddenly. "Mayor—you going to give them the plan, or what? I'm hungry, and I want to set up a fucking watch on this pass and go back to headquarters."

Dad snorted. "Headquarters!"

"Wait—" Brand interrupted. "Ferrara—'Mayor'—let's go back to these emergency supplies. Does that mean *medical supplies*?"

Ferrara shrugged. "Some. Just some old stuff from . . . when we closed the fire station."

There was a collective gasp from the crowd behind Russ; he heard Pendra mutter, "Jesus fucking Christ."

Brand and Russ's dad looked at one another—then both turned to stare at Ferrara. "When did you come into medical supplies? When exactly were you going to make it available to people in town?"

"Doesn't matter when."

"Sure as hell does!" Brand shouted. "*People died!* People died in my arms and that stuff might've *saved* some of them!"

Ferrara sniffed. "I had to think ahead. We're going to be here for a while. Now listen—we're getting off-track here."

"No, we're not getting off track!" Russ's father said, his voice taut.

Russ was still trying to get himself to believe that Ferrara could have sat on medical supplies during the emergency. With people dying.

"What supplies were they?" Dad demanded.

"Not going to discuss that." Ferrara's face twitched. "That's . . . that's off-track. What we want to talk about—"

"What we're going to talk about with the State Attorney General's office," Dad grated, "is prosecuting you for holding out on medical supplies in an emergency! We're going to talk to the families of people we lost about *suing* you, Ferrara! You think we're going to partner with you? We had no emergency services in this town because *you got rid of them!*"

"That tsunami was bad timing—I didn't make the tidal wave!" His eyes had that feral flicker again. "I don't make earthquakes!"

"No, you make us helpless when we have one! Now you tell me this—I've got a wire cutter right here in my coat. I've been using it to get people out of tangles for days—while you were AWOL. Now if I step around this fire and cut that razor wire there, what are you going to do? You telling me you're going to shoot me for cutting that wire and walking through this pass? I don't think so. You have no authority to do this."

Dickie stepped closer—and suddenly there was a pistol in his hand, pointed at Russ's father. Inches away from his head. "We could make an example right now, Mayor Ferrara. This is an emergency. What you call a crisis. We got, like, martial law. We can—"

"Put that damn gun down now!" Dale barked, seeming to swell with rage.

"Easy, Dale," Brand said. Raising a hand for caution.

Russ's dad just stood there, the muscles working at the corner of his jaws, glaring at Dickie. But when he spoke it wasn't to the man pointing the gun at him. "Ferrara? You in charge or not?"

Jill said, calmly, collectedly: *"Lon."*

Dickie grinned. He steadied his gun-hand with his other hand. The firelight gleamed on the blocky chrome plating of the pistol, still pointing at Drew Haver's forehead. They could hear waves rising and falling, behind them, just a susurration at this distance; they heard the bonfire hissing with damp wood.

Russ's father had arms rigid at his side, hands fisted. He was staring at Dickie. Seemed to be trying to figure out which way to jump. Russ thought he looked more angry than scared.

But staring at the gun, Russ felt hollow, like he might crumble in on himself. *I have to stop this.* But if he tried to rush Dickie he might prompt him to pull the trigger.

"Oh God," Pendra said. "Russ?" She moved closer to him, taking his right arm in her hands. He could feel the fear in her touch.

I've got to do something, Russ thought. *But what?*

Lon Ferrara reached out—and slowly pushed Dickie's gun-hand down. "Just—hold your fire, Dickie. Christ. We're disagreeing here, we're not fighting." After a moment, he added. "Not yet."

Dickie was looking at Ferrara now. His mouth was pressed into a line; his eyes shiny. He looked like he wanted to raise that gun—at Ferrara this time. But finally he stuck it in his waistband, and smiled. "Time and place for everything. I'm going back to headquarters." He turned and stepped to one side, spoke in a low voice to several of the gunmen.

Ferrara glanced at Dickie—a quick, cold look. Then he turned back to Russ's dad. "One thing's for sure here—we're serious. We're not going to let you go through that wire. That's right—that answers your question. We've got emergency rules here. We stay in town for now till *we figure things out!*" The last four words were shouted—seemed to escape of their own. He seemed startled by the sound himself, and spoke more quietly. "And—and we're going to take a vote on the corporation."

"A vote?" Jill said. "Really. And who counts the votes? You?"

Ferrara made a dismissive wave of his hand. "I'll pick a committee to do it. I'm the mayor."

"Ferrara," Brand said. "You want, you can ask these people here if they want to sign up for your company. Hell, why not." He turned to the small crowd. "How about it? Anybody want to sign on with him?

Dr. Spuris opened his mouth—then closed it. And looked fixedly at the ground. No one said a thing.

Brand nodded, and turned back to Ferrara. "I'll ask around— but I wouldn't count on it. And don't ask me to call you Mayor, again. You're not a mayor. You're just a local bully who's got a screw loose. You're out of control, Lon."

"Now look—"

Brand turned his back on Ferrara and gestured, drawing Russ's father, Jill, Russ, and Dale to one side. "I think we should go and discuss this blockade. Privately."

Dad nodded slowly. Russ could see he was relieved to have a good reason to back away from the confrontation.

Russ didn't blame him. It must be just now sinking in for dad how close he came to being shot.

"Sure," Ferrara called out, as they turned away, heading back to the high school. "You . . . you think it over! I'll post those notices in the morning!"

No one responded. They just kept going. They walked away from the fire, faces turned to the clammy, fetid wind. The other townspeople followed in a separate bunch, whispering as they all went back down the hill.

Russ and Jill and Pendra and Dale and Dad and Brand stuck together in a tight group. When they got partway down the hill, Russ heard his dad mutter, "I think Ferrara's lost his mind. I mean—literally. Snapped."

"Totally," Pendra said glumly. "That dude is fucking nuts. Maybe not all the way there but . . . He's on his fucking way . . . "

"I was thinking that too," Russ said. "And I think that Dickie guy knows it."

Dad nodded. "Dickie's playing some kind of game with Ferrara. And Dickie's a truly dangerous man. If we push them—someone's going to get shot. But we can't stand for this either."

Jill said, "Lon had very little cash left before the tsunami. He was way overextended. Anyway—that was the rumor. And you could tell it was true when I asked him about it. Now he's had his businesses destroyed. He's in debt. He's panicking. And—maybe the whole experience broke something in him. He was always kind of borderline . . . nutty."

"That stuff about the FEMA detention camps," Russ said. "What was that all about?"

Russ's dad chuckled grimly. "It's this urban myth that these anti-big-government fanatics like to bandy about on the Internet. I never heard that one from him before, but—seems like he's ready to believe it now."

"It looked to me," Russ said, "like his brother wasn't happy about the whole thing. Like he was going along because he didn't know what else to do."

Jill looked at him and nodded. "Or maybe Mario's got his own reasons. Like maybe he's wondering what happened to his son . . . "

Dad looked sharply at her. "You think Dickie did something to those kids . . . ?"

"Could be. He didn't like the subject." After a moment she added, "I know Lon Ferrara pretty well. There's no way that he really believes deep down any of this stuff about his new company, his corporation, making us do all this—about anything he said really. It's a crazy scam to get back what he's lost. I don't say crazy lightly. He's basically gone out of his sad little mind. I mean, when I fell off that roof, he never even glanced at me. Didn't say a word. He was like a zombie. In his right mind, even Lon Ferrara would never believe that what they're doing is going to work."

"You know," Brand said thoughtfully, as they paused in a group at the bottom of the hill, "what we have here is *two kinds of crazy*, coming together. You have a couple of toxic personalities: a psychopath and a guy simply losing his mind. And when they come together, it's Hell. It's like the ingredients of gunpowder. And yeah—seemed to me that Dickie's playing with Ferrara's mental state." He started for their apartment building. They followed, and after a moment he added, "Dickie's sick too, in his way. That toxic combination . . . We have to step carefully. Or people are going to get hurt."

ELEVEN

SHIVERING WITH COLD even though she wore a hoody and ski jacket, Nella was trying to make herself small, lying on her side hugging her knees on a sleeping bag in the corner of the living room opposite the front door. They were in the house with the brass crucifix on the wall.

Nella didn't want to be there. But Dickie had chosen it as his base. He wanted some kind of independence from Ferrara. And then there was Songbird. Ferrara might not go for keeping women chained up.

There was no generator here like there was up at that Mario's house. In this moldy living room the only light was from two Coleman lanterns, one hanging over by the door, the other on the floor by the arched entryway to the corridor. The room was even darker tonight than normal, because Dickie and Sten had nailed big pieces of scrap wood over the broken window.

The house smelled like dead things.

Maybe she could slip away, find out how to get past those blocked streets, get over to the emergency camp at the high school gym.

But she felt a despairing inertia gluing her here, on the cold floor. She was tired, and feverish. Wanting the malicious burning in her crotch to stop. She was supposed to be punished, wasn't she, by being here? Wasn't she already dead, really? Maybe that odor of the dead—maybe it was herself she was smelling.

She heard her mother's voice, reading from the Bible: *They are dead, they shall not live; they are deceased, they shall not rise: therefore hast thou visited and destroyed them, and made all their memory to perish.*

There was a mewing sound from the corridor. It was that girl Songbird, so she called herself, sounding more like a cat than a bird.

"Please . . . "

Dickie was standing in the open front door, with a big wad of lunchmeat in his hands. Talking to Sten outside. The Grummons were out there too. Nella was afraid of the Grummons. More now than she used to be.

"Please . . . I can't . . . I'm cold . . . " Almost a shriek now.

Dickie turned his head and glared at Nella. "Make yourself useful, bitch! Go and tell her to shut up, give her a blanket or something." He took a bite out of the wad of lunchmeat and chewed, watching her.

Nella didn't want to go near Songbird. Going near that girl was going to force her to feel things she didn't want to feel and think about things she didn't want to think about.

. . . and made all their memory to perish . . .

"Shut up, Mama," she whispered.

"What'd you say?" Dickie asked, picking his teeth with a thumbnail.

"Nothing. I just . . . "

But she was afraid of what Dickie would do if she refused to do what he wanted. Everything was different now than before the tsunami. Before, she had gotten along with the Sand Scouts better. Felt like she was one of them. Pretty much an equal. Dickie hadn't forced himself on her, in those days. But it was like the wave had wiped away everything that held people back.

She thought about the two shallow graves of those young men

behind the house at the top of the hill. Out in that little woods. Sten had told her about them. Mario Ferrara was guarding the pass out of town now, with some other fellas Ferrara had assigned, but what would happen when he found out about those graves?

She would be buried out there too, if she made Dickie mad enough. At the moment she was feeling like she wanted to live. Maybe because what was happening to Songbird scared her. Anyway, if they were going to kill her, she didn't want to be out there in an unmarked grave, maybe tied into a big plastic bag under six inches of sod and millipedes . . .

So she got up, wincing at all the bruises and, still hugging herself, went back into the corridor, to the bathroom, where Songbird was mewing under a Coleman lantern hung on a shower curtain rod.

Songbird was chained up in the bathtub, a smallish gangly woman with wavy red hair, a hummingbird tattoo on the outside of her right wrist, naked from the waist down. Her only clothing was a sweatshirt so grimy Nella couldn't make out what university it advertised. San Diego State?

The woman looked half delirious, kneeling in the dry tub facing the spigot, her wrists swollen and red in the grip of the silvery-looking hardware store chains, like something you'd use to chain a pit bull. Small padlocks kept the looped chains tight on her wrists, the other end of the chain locked to the spigot. Her shoulders were heaving; she was mewing again, shaking her head from side to side. The streak of mauve in her matted red hair was almost gone; mud clung to the roots.

"You need to wash your hair," Nella said lamely. Something to say. "But of course there's no water . . . I guess . . . "

The smell struck her then—the smell from the toilet, though the woman smelled bad too. She smelled like old semen and blood and sweat. There were streaks of blood on her thighs. The Grummons had been at her.

But the smell from the toilet was pure raw sewage. No one had bothered to flush it, though next to the toilet bowl was a two-gallon paint bucket, one of those big white plastic ones, filled with seawater.

Nella went to the brimming toilet, took the ceramic top off the tank, leaned it against the wall and, grunting, lifted the heavy white bucket, poured the briny water in. When she'd got the tank pretty full, leaving a little in the bucket, she pressed the flush handle, and fortunately the toilet didn't quite over-flow on the floor. After a swirling hesitation it began to drain, and she slowly poured in the rest of the water to encourage it. Then she put the bucket on the floor and opened the window a little bit.

"There, at least it smells better for you in here," she said.

"Please, I'm so cold, take the chains off, let me up . . . "

"They want me to make you be quiet," Nella explained. "You better be quiet or they'll come in here and hurt you again."

She turned and started for the door—and the woman spoke to her, in a different tone, her voice trembling but with some thinking behind it. "Wait—let's talk. Your name is . . . it's Nella, isn't it? Nella?"

"Yes." Nella didn't want to look at her. She leaned against the doorframe, arms crossed, rubbing her shoulders, wanting to go back and burrow into her sleeping bag and hope that the men left her alone. Her privates hurt so bad already. She thought she had some kind of infection down there, from the time Dickie had forced himself on her.

Or maybe the feeling was punishment from God. For being with these people. Sending flame into her groin. Or maybe the infection itself *was* the punishment. That was how God took

His revenge, wasn't it? Disease, bad luck, things like that? And a giant wave . . .

"Well, Nella," Songbird said, "we're two people stuck in—" Her voice broke and she cleared her throat, got control of it again. "—stuck in a bad place and that's when . . . when . . . we should be . . . working for positive energy . . . together . . . I'm a life coach, you know . . . Maybe I'm here . . . maybe I'm here for a reason."

She sounded like she had to make herself say that. *Here for a reason.*

"For a reason?" Nella asked, turning to look at the plaintive, pale creature in the light from the Coleman. Wondering if the woman thought she was being punished by God too.

"Because . . . this might sound funny . . . you might need my help. If you can unlock me . . . I can help you. And I'll tell the police not to . . . tell them you tried to help . . . " Her lips quivered as she tried to stay in command of herself, tried to draw from some spring of persuasion inside her.

But persuasion didn't work here. Nella knew that for sure. When they'd first caught Songbird, skulking around in one of the houses, nearby, eating out of cans, the woman had tried using persuasion on Dickie. Nella had been there. Heard Songbird tell Dickie, "You threaten violence but I feel in my heart that you don't mean it. You're calling out for help."

"Help!" Dickie had said—and knocked her cold.

Sten had smirked at that and said, "Ha! Help!"

"Yeah—now fucking help me carry her!"

Sten had sung that Beatles song "Help" as they carried Songbird over here, Nella trailing along.

"I don't think anything can help us till we have our full punishment," Nella said, now. "Our punishment from God. Then—maybe. Or . . . we just go to Hell."

"Um—God doesn't want to . . . to punish us . . . Nella. Please."

She squeezed her eyes shut. "I'm so cold here. Could you get me a blanket and maybe you could hide the keys in it . . . for these locks . . . if you could put them in the . . . "

"What the fuck is that bitch saying?" Dickie said, appearing like an apparition in the doorway, so that Nella almost fell when she stepped back to get out of his way.

"She's just—we were talking about God," Nella said.

"Oh bullfuckingshit, I heard her talking about getting keys." He turned suddenly to Nella. The light behind her was blocked so that his face was in darkness. "You were talking to her—about getting her out of here?"

"No—! Dickie, we—"

The declaration was snapped off when Dickie backhanded Nella across the mouth, so hard and fast she tasted blood almost immediately as she went staggering back, losing her balance, falling to hit her head on the toilet seat. She sprawled there, stunned, feeling weak and distant from everything, all furry and unreal, as she watched Dickie reach into his pocket, take out keys, unlock the chain.

"Oh thank you, now we can talk," Songbird babbled, "we can help each other, we don't have to have this negative energy—"

"You wanted to get out of there, then come on, bitch. Hey, boys—!" This last a shout to the hall, and the Grummons came to the door, as Dickie pulled the woman out of the tub by her hair, the chains dangling from her wrists, her skinny naked ass all bruised.

"Dickie, she didn't . . . " Nella heard herself say. But it couldn't be heard over Songbird's shrieking. Nella—getting to her feet, feeling sick to her stomach, swaying in the bathroom.

Wondering when Dickie and the men would be punished. Was that ever going to happen? Why were only the women being punished?

Dickie's time would come, she decided. God would pick a time, it would come like an alarm clock ringing . . . shrieking and screaming and ringing . . .

"You want her again or not?" Dickie asked the Grummons.

The Grummons looked at each other, and looked at Songbird. "Naw," Liddy said. "Had her. She's a mess."

Songbird wouldn't stop shrieking, so after awhile they dragged her out to the broken-down part of the house. Nella got up and wandered out that way, thinking maybe she could say something to save the stupid little woman.

But Nella finally just leaned on a wall and watched as they shot Songbird in the back of the head and pitched her off the edge of the chopped-off stairway, down into the pit of mud, slime, and broken concrete and rotting kelp, the falling body disturbing an enormous cloud of sleeping flies, that rose up in a dark swarm to buzz furiously at the sky; to mingle blackly with the stars.

RUSS AND PENDRA stood together in a corner of the gymnasium, leaning against the wall near the door; the gym was now unevenly lit with portable lights powered by the rumbling generator Dale had finally rigged out behind the school.

Several dozen people were gathered in the gym, talking in groups, eating. Someone was smoking a cigarette and someone else was asking them to take it outside. After all they'd been through, it seemed silly to Russ to worry about secondhand smoke.

Russ felt he had to be here, as Dad tried to organize a meeting around the wrestling mats spread out near the door. But in fact he didn't want to be here at all. He wanted to go back to the apartment building. No electricity there—the lanterns were getting dim—but it was cozier, and he could lie on a bed and try to forget about things. He was tired, his eyes still burned from the oily smoke at the bonfire, and he kept seeing that gun in Dickie's hand pointed at his father's head.

"I can't believe that guy was threatening to shoot your dad," Pendra said softly, brushing her hair from her eyes. She shook her head wonderingly. "Dickie and Ferrara are both sick. I just never have gotten people like that. Or like—people who decide to kill themselves but *that's not good enough*, they have to kill their families too. I don't get that. Kill yourself, whatever, that's your business, but shoot your kids? What's that all about?"

"I read somewhere they don't know the difference between themselves and their families—like they're all overlapped in their minds."

"Well, that's sick."

"Sure as fuck is. But I'm getting used to sick." He thought about the woman with the mud stuffed in her torn-open gut; he thought about Dad having to kill that dog. He thought about the child who'd died alone in the farther corner of this very gym. Turn your back a second and the kid dies. *Don't think about that stuff.*

"I haven't even had a funeral for my grandma. When they burned those bodies in that empty lot—that was . . . I mean, just burning them all together like that . . . "

He nodded. "I know what you mean. Seems like, I don't know, like they're saying they weren't individuals. But . . . Lucia and Dad, everyone—they were worried about cholera. They did say some words over them . . . "

"That's not a funeral for any one person. That was for, like, everybody, at once. Not the same. My Gram was . . . She was a real *person*. I mean maybe everyone is but . . . " There were tears in her eyes, and she looked away.

"I know what you mean." It occurred to Russ that here was a chance to do something for Pendra. "We could have a funeral for her. At least you and I could. Like maybe in her apartment, with all her stuff around. Celebrate her life. We could have candles. Have her cats there."

She looked at him, her lips parted, seeming startled. "That's a really *good idea*."

"Those cats are still around, aren't they? You been feeding them?"

"Course I have. She had a big bag of dry cat food. They still have that. I don't know what to feed them when that runs out. I've been scrounging pet food from different houses for all the pets over on Shell Street. It's all dogs barkin' all the time when you go on that street. Lonely little dogs. Most of them probably lost their owners. And the kitties too . . . There's even a turtle . . . "

"When you want to do the funeral?"

"Can we do it tonight after the meeting here?"

"Why not?"

And he got his reward, for starts, when she reached over and almost furtively squeezed his hand.

Just gratitude, he thought. *Nothing to get excited about.* But her touch lingered . . . even after she took her hand away.

Dad came over, then, with Dale and Brand and Jill—squinting without her glasses, picking her steps carefully through the gym mats and people sleeping. Sometimes letting Brand help balance her. Lars wandered over too, in that same marijuana-leaf T-shirt, stroking his beard, scratching in his dreadlocks, his eyes red.

"Spuris wasn't interested in meeting with us," Russ's dad said, in a low voice. "He's not into doing anything except feeling sorry for himself."

"We could get some of the other men, maybe Lucia," Brand said.

Dale shook his head. "Tell you the truth, if we do what Drew's got in mind, the fewer that know it the better. Lord, my back hurts. I need to sit my ass down."

They sat in a circle on a wrestling mat, Russ feeling good about being accepted in this circle of men making a plan, Pendra lying on a mat, face down, just behind him, her chin on her arms, watching and listening. Jill sitting with her long legs drawn up, close to Brand. Russ noticing a sort of bonding between them. Hard to define. But it was there. Dale and Lars and Dad. Dale glancing uncertainly at Lars. Like he was wishing he wasn't here.

"Was me," Lars said, "shit I'd make a deal, we don't need the bad vibes. Just tell 'em what they want. Probably won't mean much later on."

"He's got some plan to make people sign something," Russ's dad said. "Sign property and such over to him. Would it stand up in court? Maybe not. But it's our word against his. And he can argue there was an emergency and he was trying to prevent looting when he stopped us from leaving."

"He's setting up an out-and-out theft," Jill said. "He can forcibly collect things from people—not just signatures and checks. Valuables! He's obviously told the authorities at Deer Creek we don't need their help any further. So when *do* we get any help? If we put up with this, we're at their mercy. And with people like Dickie Rockwell and those others—who knows what could happen? I mean—Christ, I don't know if he'd have shot Drew tonight, if Ferrara hadn't stopped them—but it sure looked that way to me."

Dad made a growling sound in his throat. "I think he probably would've done it." He glanced at Russ, as if afraid of worrying him. "Well, who knows. Maybe it was a bluff. But I sure as hell could have done without it." He hesitated, musing. Then added, "I saw him and those other punks over on the north side of town, when we were checking houses, me and Dale, looking for trapped people. Saw them on a street that only had a couple houses, down the hill, slammed. Dickie said they'd already checked, no one alive there. 'Just us fuckin' roosters' he said." Dad glanced at Dale. "You remember . . . "

Dale nodded. "They wouldn't let us search the houses on that street. Said they were keeping an eye on things. They had guns on them even then. I had that pistol sticking out of my coat pocket—if I hadn't had that, I don't know if they'd have let us go."

Dad looked at him, startled. "Really? You think they'd have shot us that time?"

"Maybe. Except they didn't want a firefight in the middle of the day there out in the street. Dickie had a good thing, looting those houses. Didn't want attention drawn to it."

Russ noticed Lars leaning forward, listening to all this carefully. It gave him a pinched feeling in his stomach. But the guy was just a flake. No way he could be a problem.

"So what do we do? He's going to start trying to enforce his stupid little ultimatum," Jill said. "We can't let them do that. Once they get started that way . . . "

She shook her head.

Brand nodded. "I agree. We can't play that game. It's extortion and it's dangerous to let them get any power over us. But who do we turn to? There's no working phones, to speak of. There're no cell phones, no wi-fi, no Internet. All the boats in the area have been trashed . . . There's debris all up and down the coast . . . "

"There must be a boat that could be fixed up," Pendra pointed out.

"I was thinking about that," Russ said. Feeling kind of uncomfortable, speaking up. But the idea had been growing on him. "There *are* some boats that are, like, intact, on the beach. Overturned but they don't look like they have holes in them. Some with engines. We could fix them up, find some fuel. Use trucks to pull the boats to the ocean. Go down the coast to get help. It'd take time . . . "

"So much debris out there, doesn't look like a boat could get through," Dad said. "Even if you could, it's so far down the coast. And which way do you go to find people who are any better off than us? I mean—if they were on the coast, they were swamped too. I've been thinking about it and . . . it's just probably faster to get through the hills, and get to Deer Creek, where we know we can get help. Talk to the sheriff there—call FEMA. Get the National Guard out here. It shouldn't be that hard. I think several of us should go, so we can back up each other's story—I mean, one guy tells them the mayor is keeping us from leaving, he might not be believed. And . . . " He grimaced. "Whoever goes might need the other kind of backup . . . "

"So—who'd be going?" Russ asked. Afraid to be asked. And afraid they wouldn't ask him.

Fuck, he told himself. *Man up, dude.* But those men with guns at the roaring bonfire—something primeval in that had shaken him up.

"I'll go," Dale said. "I'm a veteran. I've got some weapons and I know how to use them. My eyes aren't so good anymore but . . . "

Jill looked at him. "You really think it'll come to that?"

"Probably not. What we want to do is—a few of us go, me and Drew and Brand say, and we go around on the trails in the hills, we slip past them, we head down the highway for Deer Creek. We can't use any kind of motorcycle, any quads—they'd hear that. But—keepin' it real—we'll need to be armed, though. Just in case."

Dad nodded. "I agree. We'll need guns. We'll need to be ready to defend ourselves against Dickie and that bunch. We just might have to fight our way out of Freedom."

TWELVE

FOUR CANDLES were set up around the cluttered little living room. Each one was making its own pool of quivering yellow light. Russ and Pendra sat in the center of the room on the braided rug, facing one another, blankets over their shoulders—it was cold. No heat in the apartment building. Pendra had a small flashlight, pointed at a piece of notebook paper. She leaned self-consciously over it, her hair drooping down, embarrassed but intent. The two cats slipped around in the shadows, behind her, meowing sadly, as if consciously taking part in the funeral ceremony.

Russ had brought something else: the shoebox. He'd set it down on an end table by the sofa Pendra's grandmother had covered with a somewhat-psychedelic patterned blanket she'd knit herself.

"I wrote something about my Gram," Pendra said, rustling the paper. "Kind of a . . . not a poem but sort of. I feel stupid now but . . . this is the only ceremony she's going to get any time soon . . . "

"No, it's cool, go on, read it," Russ said.

She cleared her throat, and read aloud: "You created her and she created me and then you lost her. The connection of blood and DNA between you and me, through my mother, is still there. She is like an echo in me and that's you echoing, you made the sound, with Granddad, and I'm a bell it's ringing. So you're still here. And when I remember how you always looked for something good in me, something good and smart and talented and worth keeping in me, I feel like I kept going because of you. And if I'm still going on it's because you wanted me to because you said I was precious."

Russ wondered if Pendra was saying she'd considered suicide, before coming to Freedom. He suspected she had. Because sometimes when they talked she seemed, in some indefinable way, like she was only tentatively committed to being here in the world. Like someone at a party trying to decide if they wanted to leave before it broke up. Because it wasn't a very good party and it was making them depressed.

"But I was always caught up in my own thing, what about me, why can't I do this, why did this happen to me, and I didn't think very often about what had happened to you, losing your husband and your daughter, you were like the last person on a battlefield waving a flag, and you're saying 'You can all go to hell, I'm here, this is me!' And the flag was your house and your cats and the little things you did for people . . . "

As she read through it, Russ looked at her and felt like he was seeing her for the first time: a person alone in the world, trying to find a reason to be there, trying to be someone she liked, trying to express herself. Trying but sometimes wanting to stop trying. He felt a rush of sympathy that made him feel almost mingled with her.

He'd felt bad for himself when his parents had broken up. But he'd kept them more than Pendra had kept her family. Pendra had no siblings, no parents, now she'd even lost her grandmother.

When Pendra finished reading she looked at him—and her eyebrows went up in reaction to what she saw in him. Something in his face surprised her. Then she looked quickly away.

Russ cleared his throat. "Your grandma was—an amazing person."

Her mouth buckled and she nodded, her head dropping, eyes hidden by her hair.

Russ reached for the shoebox, set it between them, took out the whiskey bottle. "I don't know if you feel like having a drink to her. But it's about all I have to offer."

"Yeah. That'd be good. She liked to drink rum and Coke sometimes."

"Haven't got rum or Coke but . . . " He poured out two small glasses of whiskey. They were juice glasses he'd cadged from a deserted house. His was a Disneyland glass with a picture of Goofy on it, hers had Princess Leia. "I'll take the Goofy glass. I'm totally that Goofy thing, whatever he is."

"I saw him at Disneyland when I was a little kid, some guy in a big foam-rubber suit. Big foam-rubber ass wobbling around. Couldn't tell if he was a dog or what . . . "

"Yeah, see, that's totally me, foam-rubber ass, can't tell if I'm a dog . . . I feel just like him . . . "

She laughed—it was hoarse laughter with tears mixed in it—and took the Princess Leia glass. "I *never* fucking felt like Princess Leia. But I was sort of into her when I was seven. My mom loved *Star Wars* and she made me watch the DVDs. Princess Leia's cool actually. I mean, she kills Stormtroopers. I always thought I'd want to kill some Stormtroopers . . . "

She came and sat close beside him. They drank the whiskey in several short sips, talking of her grandmother. He told her a little more about his mom and dad.

"That sucks," she said.

"At least I had them—longer. I can appreciate my dad a lot more now. I feel like . . . we're sort of not always staring at each other going 'What the fuck' anymore. More like we're standing next to each other staring at other people . . . ."

"And going, 'What the fuck?' "

His turn to laugh. "Totally. You want some more?"

"No. I sort of have a headache. Can I . . . " She stretched out across the rug and he had a wild notion she was going to initiate sex with him, but instead she crooked an arm across his lap, and lay her head on it, the back of her head pressed against his stomach. "Just lay down a second . . . "

He didn't say anything, but it seemed okay to stroke her hair, and she let him, and in a few minutes he was surprised to hear the sound of her soft snoring.

He smiled to himself. Knowing he was going to be really uncomfortable, pretty soon, sitting here on the floor with her head on his lap, but there was no way he was going to move, not till he was sure she was way deep asleep. He was going to be sitting there a long time.

Fortunately there was still a little whiskey in the bottle, and he could just reach it.

NELLA SAT on a canvas chair, in the corner, in Mario's house. Glad to be away from the house with the brass Jesus on the wall; glad to be away from those watching brass eyes; glad to be away from the smell of the dead.

The men had taken off their firemen coats in the warm room. Mario and Lon at the other end of the room, in two dark-green leather easy chairs, drinking and talking in low tones. Lon trying to convince Mario of something. Looking like he was talking to himself, more than his brother. Trying to convince himself maybe. She had the feeling he knew he had gotten himself into something and didn't know how to get out. Had that kind of scared-animal look in his eyes.

Dickie and Sten were half sprawled on the big wide brown leather sofa under the seascape—a room that denied there'd been a tsunami, a normal-looking room, warmed by the generator chugging away outside, all the lights on, electric heat coming from the fireplace with fake concrete logs.

Nella was interested to see the old Rasta-hair white dude come into the living room. The old stoner blinking in the electric lights. Looking at the fake fireplace.

Lars. That was his name, wasn't it? He was coming to stand before Dickie, though this was supposedly Lon Ferrara was in charge. And Ferrara frowned, seeing that.

Skinny old guy in a long raggy-assed coat, pot-leaf T-shirt, mismatched socks in sandals. Nella thought socks in sandals looked stupid anytime. Lars looked stupid himself, standing there, gawping around at them. "Where's the others?" he asked.

"What, Cholo and the Grummons, them? They're guarding the pass," Sten said. "They're—"

"Shut up, Mike," Dickie said, in an amiable tone. "He doesn't need an intelligence report from us. We need one from him."

Nella had seen the old, smelly guy with the dreadlocks around town. Sten knew him. Sold dope to him. Pot and 'shrooms. Didn't seem like a customer for crystal meth.

She knew Dickie had some crystal meth on him. He wasn't taking it, not yet. He seemed to be all about the booze they found in the houses, lately, and some of that angel-dust pot, now and then. Maybe thinking that bringing out the methedrine was about timing, what with most of these guys having guns handy. Plus having to be "political" with these Ferrara guys. But Nella wished he would give her some speed. She wished she could get hold of even some lame crank and spark up her energy and maybe think of a plan. Jumpstart her mind, figure out how to run away. Of course, if she took enough of it, she'd get all paranoid and probably end up tweaking under a bed or something. Again. Ronnie Burke had told her to stay away from crystal.

"Make your teeth drop out, girl. Don't want to lose those pretty teeth do you?"

"What you got for us, Lars?" Sten asked.

Lars tugged at his beard. "Yeah, but listen—we do have a deal about this? Some . . . I got to know there's . . . "

"I got a nice bag of pot for you. What'd you find out?"

"They're going to try to slip away, outta town, get past you guys, go to Deer Creek," Lars said, talking fast. "Take one of those little trails out to the south. Two or three of them, armed. Get Deer Creek to send the National Guard."

"Back-stabbing sons of bitches!" That was Lon Ferrara, jumping up, stalking over to them. "When is this dishonest sleaziness going to happen?"

Lars looked startled. "Um—tonight, Mr. Ferrara. Like after midnight. Two in the morning I think is what they're thinking. Being really sneaky and all that. On the down-low."

"Tonight!" Ferrara's hands were shaking. Dickie was looking at Ferrara almost fondly, smiling a little to himself. Nella was pretty sure Dickie knew Ferrara had gone out of his head and he was enjoying that, somehow. He had a crazy mayor on a leash.

Sten reached into his shirt pocket, took out a quarter-ounce baggie of weed, tossed it over to Lars. "Whatever. Keep your ear to the ground and your mouth shut."

"Hey, pothead—" Mario Ferrara getting up, strolling over, hands thrust in coat pockets, head tilted bullishly forward. Looking at Lars with real dislike. "You hear anything about my kid? My son? He went to get them some help. Didn't seem like he got through . . . "

"Nah." Lars was opening the baggie, smelling the dope as he spoke. "I don't know what he . . . " Sniff. " . . . just that he went with that other college boy. Up here somewhere. Heading up this way. But after that . . . Maybe—"

"We'll let you know, Lars," Dickie interrupted, suddenly, "if we need anything else."

Nella noticed Mario staring at Dickie. Suspecting. He didn't really belong here, she decided. He was watching. Waiting for something . . . "Here," Dickie said, tossing Lars a Bic lighter. "Go toke up outside. Knock yourself out."

Lars licked his lips, nodded, backed away, half stumbled over an ottoman—Dickie and Sten laughed at that—and went quickly out the front door.

He's going back to the other camp, she thought. But she couldn't go with him. Dickie watched her close.

But she also knew that Dickie was getting tired of her. She'd heard him in the kitchen, when she was coming down the hall; heard him talking in low tones to Sten about getting some other girls here. Like that Pendra girl. Liddy knew her name from around town. He'd been watching her, before the tsunami. Thinking about her. Now he'd got Dickie thinking about her.

He'd have Pendra up here pretty soon.

Then maybe he'd be done with Nella. That'd be good, if it meant he'd let her go.

But he wouldn't—he'd give her to the Grummons. Or do the simple thing, and kill her to keep her mouth shut.

THIRTEEN

RUSS GLANCED at his watch. It was after midnight. The candles had burned down to guttering stumps, and the whiskey had worn off. Nothing left of it but a throb in Russ's temples and a bad taste in his mouth; a raspy thirst for a long drink of water.

But Russ couldn't bring himself to get up and fetch the bottled water because he didn't want to disturb Pendra. So he just sat there, on the cold floor, with Pendra snoring softly on his lap, his hand on her shoulder. His left leg asleep, his right aching from staying in one position all that time.

He was listening to someone in the apartment upstairs bitching. He couldn't make out most the words, just the cadence, and the tone: bitching for sure. A few words came through now and then: *Why don't they . . . why can't they . . . They should be . . .*

One of those people who ought to be helping—just bitching instead. Russ felt he was starting to understand Dad better. Something good coming of this. Thinking about that, he was a little embarrassed when the front door of the apartment opened and his dad looked in, a Coleman lantern in his hand. "Oh— Russ, I was just looking for you . . . " He looked at Pendra, her head on his lap. "Didn't mean to . . . uh . . . " Russ saw him look at Pendra, and the empty whiskey bottle; saw him think about warning Russ about drinking. Saw him decide not to. It was all in his sequence of expressions. Finally, he said, "Well, son—I just wanted to tell you we're getting set to go to Deer Creek. You should stay close to Pendra, help Lucia out when you can. I hope to be back late tomorrow sometime. Once we get down the road like twenty miles east of here, there's a hill overlooking the valley that Deer Creek's in. We think we can get a cell phone signal there."

"Dad . . . I'm coming with you." Russ heard himself say it. Felt kind of surprised, when it came out.

"What? No, Russ. Forget it."

"Yeah. I am. I . . . " He reached over to the sofa, took a small paisley-covered pillow from it, disturbing a sleeping cat; he slipped his leg from under Pendra's head, gently tucking the pillow in to replace it. The cat got up and padded stiffly toward the kitchen but Pendra hardly stirred; her soft snoring hesitated, then went steadily on.

"I'm totally going, Dad." Wincing as blood circulation returned, Russ stood, putting his weight on the leg that still had feeling in it—and almost toppled over.

"You look like you can hardly stand, son, I don't think you're ready for twenty mile hikes."

"Dad . . . " He controlled his temper. But his father had irritated him. "I'm not drunk. My leg went to sleep." He leaned against the arm of the sofa, pumped circulation back into his legs. It hurt. "I'm coming with you. Wait for me outside. Please."

Dad shook his head but waited outside as Russ hobbled to the bedroom, found a quilt, returned to put it over Pendra before joining him outside.

He could see Dad's breath in the light from the Coleman. The wind whistled, brought the smell of the sea, and the persistent rot left by the great wave. He felt the wind tingling his nose and fingers. He realized his dad was trying to think of some way to persuade him not to come. "Dad—I just feel like . . . I wasn't quite there, when we were trying to . . . when we were helping people. Organizing things. I walked away from stuff every time it got really ugly. I don't want to look back and think, 'You wimped out when it got hard.' "

"So this is a macho thing? That's not going to help us, Russ. You want to help, stay here and look after things. Keep watch here."

Russ shook his head. He felt a rock-steady sureness about it. He had to go along. He'd thought about it most of the time he'd sat there with Pendra. "It's not a macho thing. I just have to do it, that's all there is. You can let me get your back, for once."

Dad's mouth had been opened to object but that last remark stopped him short. He chewed his lower lip, and Russ noticed that he hadn't shaved in a couple days; that there were deeply etched circles under his eyes.

Finally his father shrugged and said, "You want to go, fine. But, son—you haven't got any training with guns . . . "

"Neither have you."

"That's not exactly true. There were times. I did some target shooting. I went hunting a couple of times."

"You?"

"Just to experience it. Didn't like it. But I got so I could hit something."

"What's your point?"

"What I'm saying is, we're not going to give you a gun. You don't have time to learn to use it. In the middle of the night, for God's sake."

"I'll take along a knife, Dad, whatever. I've got a buck knife in my coat right here. And I'll be an extra pair of eyes. And I'm younger than you guys—I might be able to go on ahead of you when we get past them. Get help sooner. I can sure as hell use a cell phone."

His Dad took a long breath, and let it out with a soft, extended whistle. "Leave a note for Pendra. And—let's go."

HIS WEARINESS WAS GONE, and he didn't feel the cold. A crowd of blue-white stars watched them clamber through the chaparral of the hillside, following Brand, who had a few supplies in a backpack, along a sketchy game trail. Brand, Dale, Russ, with Russ's father at the rear. Dale had provided the firearms: Dale and Brand carried rifles, Brand had a Browning .32, Dale a 30.06, while Drew, Russ's father, carried a big black 12-gauge Remington pump shotgun.

Russ had the buck knife in his pocket. Nothing else. But he could feel it against his right leg, when he took a step in the steeper parts of the hill, and its presence stimulated something in him he hadn't felt since he was about twelve, on a "raid" against Those Kids on the next block over.

They'd all been suburban kids, at the low end of the economic spectrum but not so poor they didn't get bicycles for Christmas. Kids on the next block had thrown a rock at Jerry Pruval and told him to stay away from their street, and Jerry had told his friends, including his best friend Russ, and four of them had gone out in the early evening on their bikes, rocks in their pockets . . .

Somehow, he'd known that none of them wanted anybody to really get hurt. And nobody was. A couple of bruised shoulders, when it played out. A shout from an angry father.

But the simple intensity of looking for adversaries in the darkness on a spring night had burned the memory into his mind. The memory of taking a run at them, of retreating and regrouping, of talking excited strategy, of eluding the cops. The sweat on his palms gripping the handlebars; the scents of blossoms and dinners cooking as he'd ridden through the soft night air. The delight in conspiracy with his cronies; connecting with them in a single purpose. Something primeval, a kind of atavistic high . . .

He was feeling it tonight, for the first time since he was twelve. Feeling primevally alive. And something else: feeling justified and furtive at once. His own group was definitely, most definitely the good guys; Ferrara and his crew were most definitely the bad guys. But did it matter? Russ was of one mind with the three men with whom he threaded the narrow path between boulders, outcroppings of sandstone, star-limned manzanita, the aromatic coastal sage. They had a single purpose—to penetrate the lines of an enemy and bring help to women and children waiting for them, behind. He was connected, in this moment to some dim genetic memory of other men, on similar missions, that seemed to resonate across millennia.

Russ felt his lungs fill with air and seemed to feel its oxygen igniting in his veins, as he climbed, tireless, pumped, through the night.

There was a partial moon, and starlight, and enough space between the shrubs of the chaparral to make out the way, but now and then Brand paused, clicked a pen light on, partly blocking its slight glow with his hand to look at the stringy trail, before going on.

They were skirting the hilltop now, just below a great knob of stone, Russ's left foot slipping on the scree of the slope. Sometimes he had to feel his way a bit with a foot before following Dale.

They didn't speak. They'd agreed to be as quiet as possible, and in the two miles they'd trekked so far, north and east, they were still not sure how far they were from the men at the pass. Maybe a quarter mile northeast of them, Russ guessed . . .

Brand stopped—and turned toward them, waving a hand so they'd see it in the dimness. He pointed—and they saw the flicker of the bonfire at the pass through the hills, seen now from the farther side. It seemed no bigger than a campfire from here.

The down-slope was steep, on the most direct route toward Deer Creek. Too steep. Dale and Brand whispered briefly together, then Brand led the way again, along the trail a ways closer to the bonfire, but trending slowly downward across the eastern face of the hill.

They'd cut in away from the pass pretty soon, Russ figured. But getting closer to it at all was dangerous. The excitement rose in him. Something in him wanted a confrontation, an exchange of gunfire. Thrown rocks.

Something else said, *Quiet, slip past, stay on mission.*

Slowly they worked their winding way, half sliding, angling down the hill, till the next hill south bulked up and blocked their view of the fire—and the view of anyone who might have seen them from there. They slipped down the slope in silence, accompanied only by the sounds of their heavy breathing, the clicking of rocks rolling from their tread, the occasional call of a night bird.

At the bottom of the hill they followed the bed of a faintly trickling creek around a lower knoll to the east. They came out in a wash of moonlight, with the hill between them and the pass, and they all felt a little safer.

"Should be okay to rest here," Dale said. Russ could hear a raggedness in his voice, from breathing hard. He was the oldest, and heaviest of them. "Highway's about a hundred yards on. We're under cover from the west here. Rest a few minutes, then hit the highway and hoof it for Deer Creek. That sound good?"

They sat on two shelves of sandstone, about thirty feet over the trail east. Russ and his father on a higher one, the shotgun slanted across his lap, Dale and Brand on a lower projection, passing a bottle of water. They were half hidden from Russ by a

Monterey pine, growing all alone from a bank of clay in the hill-side. Russ was thirsty but too cold, now, to drink water, sitting on the cold hard rock with his hands jammed in his coat pockets.

"Can you see the safety here on this gun?" his dad said to him, softly. Suddenly. "See where I'm pointing?"

"Um—yeah. I see it."

"Safety's on now. Push it that way—it's off. There's a shell in the chamber. Pretty risky to have a round in there with the ground slanted like this, in the dark. But now I put the safety on, so it should be okay."

"What if you have to fire it, like, real suddenly?"

"Don't expect to have to. But if I do—I know where the safety is. I'll flick it off with my thumb. I just . . . I don't know. I never used guns much. We never talked about them. I thought I ought to . . . "

"That sort of like the birds and the bees? One of those Dad talks?"

"I don't think I ever gave you the birds and bees either."

"Didn't need the sex talk."

"Nowadays I guess not. You kids do a search on the Internet." He paused, exhaled; Russ could just faintly see Dad's out-breath appearing, vanishing in the moonlight. "I wanted to say . . . Russ, I feel like I should've stayed with you back home. I mean—I don't know if I could have stuck with your mom. But I could have stayed *close* to you. In Akron. Just put up with Ohio. I was sure at the time I had to do whatever I could to pay the child support. Even if it meant moving to find a job. But . . . " His dad cleared his throat. His face was hidden; his voice was rich with emotion. "Hell, I should have been a janitor, anything, to stay closer to you."

Russ smiled in the darkness; it was safe to smile there.

"Dad—that's . . . " He wasn't sure how to say it. Then it came to him. He knew what he wanted to say to his father. "Dad . . . "

Then his father jerked back, against the rock, as the hills echoed with a cracking sound, and the shotgun went clattering down the hill from his flapping hands . . .

"Russ . . . ?" His voice hoarse.

His father slipped off the shelf of rock, and rolled, limp, down the stony hillside into the declivity at the base of the hill.

Russ heard himself shout, and was aware that something struck near him, like a steel pick against the rock, and only when he was stumbling down the hill, over the fallen shotgun, making his way to his awkwardly sprawled father—only then did he realize that someone had shot at him.

Dale and Brand were scrambling down beside him, but Russ was already kneeling by Dad, hands pressed against the pumping wound wet with blood from the bullet hole in his father's chest. He couldn't see his dad's face in the deep, cold shadow.

But he knew he was dead. There was no movement, no heartbeat under his hands. Just the diminishing flow of blood, caressing Russ's fingers.

FOURTEEN

"WHAT THE HELL have you done?" Ferrara asked, the words coming with difficulty through his hard breathing as he stumbled up to Dickie in the darkness.

They'd taken up a position below the pass, Ferrara and Mario and Cholo and Steve and Dickie and Sten.

They had lain there shivering on the chilly slanted top of a twenty-foot-high block of stone close to the shoulder of the highway, right where the path between the hills would take the men Lars had said were trying to slip out of town. The stone angled up like a roof, toward the hills, offering natural cover and a good vantage on the trail.

Ferrara had been wondering how he'd gotten here at all. Thinking maybe he had gone too far, but knowing he couldn't go backward. He was committed. And maybe it would work. Maybe he could save the town. Save himself. Stop the destructive forces that wanted to pull apart everything he'd built.

He was thinking that, and then they saw the men coming around on the trail not far above the hill's base—four silhouettes. Three of them had guns. You could see that much.

It was them, all right. The party looking to slip out of town and get help that Lars had told them about. Four of them, resting on some rocks by a Monterey Pine, before heading on toward the highway. Ferrara figured they'd wait them out, catch them from above, get them covered, order them to drop their weapons.

March them right back up the highway to the pass. Have to cut the wire to get through but they could re-string it.

"We'll take them back up the hill," Ferrara had said.

No sooner had he said that then *bang, crack*, the smell of smoke, and one of those men was falling down the hill.

Ferrara, ears ringing with the gunshot, looked at Dickie—who was chortling at Sten.

"I caught that high-handing son of a bitch right in the chest," Dickie said.

"Fuck it," Sten said. "Let's finish 'em all off. It's them or us right about now."

"Yeah. I'm fucking sick of lying on this rock freezing my nuts off. Come on."

"Waitaminnut!" Ferrara hissed—but they'd slipped off the rock, were already heading through the stand of firs next to the road.

Mario was whispering to him. Something about *what are we going to do, what are we going to do, should we really be in this, what was going to happen, this guy Dickie, what do we know about him, for God's sake, Lon . . .*

It was all spinning out of control. But Ferrara had been so sure. It had seemed so clear . . .

He was in it now. "Come on, Mario," he said. "We got to follow through. Try and make this work. Any way we can."

Because that's all that was left to him.

"I CAN'T FIND a pulse, Russ," Brand said, hoarsely.

"My dad . . . " Russ said.

They were crouching in a fissure, about three feet deep, with a rough block of lichen-coated granite between them and the gunmen. Water trickled somewhere nearby. A cold breeze brought, just thinly, the smell of gunpowder from the shots.

Russ took his father's right hand, squeezed it. Felt blood slip between his skin and his father's. No response.

He pressed the wrist, tried to feel a pulse. Nothing . . .

"We can't be sure," Brand said, voice cracking. "I'm no doctor, I haven't got a stethoscope. But . . . "

"We could pump his chest, we could . . . " Russ's own voice sounded strange in his ears. Low, choked, unfamiliar.

"That's where the wound is. Right where . . . "

"They're coming," Dale said. "Two of 'em . . . I think there's more back there . . . I can see a rifle . . . "

"Where?" Brand lifted his head to look.

"In the trees. They're . . . "

A whining *ping*, a smell of something burning, a stinging pain at Russ's scalp—had he been hit?

Heart hammering, Russ ducked lower, wiped his hands on his pants and felt his head, just a slight groove in the scalp, a little oozing. Probably a chip of stone scored off by the ricochet.

"They're shooting at us," Dale said, unnecessarily.

Another round smacked into the hillside just above them, spraying bits of rock.

Russ thought he ought to get dad's shotgun, get his knife out, at least, but he could only crouch there, shivering, trying to take it all in.

What would he do with a knife against men armed with rifles? He was surprised that he didn't seem to feel angry, didn't seem to feel anything, just a kind of stunned paralysis.

A sizzling sound, a crack, the thud of a gun. Smell of gunsmoke heavier now.

"They're about forty yards off," Dale whispered.

Russ realized he was still clasping his father's limp hand. It was already losing warmth. Going cold.

"Now there's four of them shooting at us," Brand said.

Dale lifted up, fired almost randomly over the rocks, the flash startling, the bang making Russ's ears ring.

"They're in the shadows there," Dale said. "I don't know as I can hit any—" He ducked down as two more bullets chopped the air over them. "—body."

"Okay," Brand said, a tremor in his voice. "We didn't come prepared for a gunfight in the darkness. I thought maybe we'd fire at them if we saw them coming but this . . . no. We're gonna run along the crevice here, keep our heads down, and around that boulder. Then book on through the brush back up toward the town."

"One of us maybe cut east for Deer Creek?" Dale suggested.

They were silent then—as another gunshot, sounding louder, cracked into the hill behind them. Russ realized they were waiting for him to volunteer, because he was the youngest and slimmest and probably the fastest. He stood the best chance of getting through to Deer Creek.

But he couldn't speak. He felt unreal and strangely feeble. His father was dead, and he seemed to see all those other dead people after the tsunami, looking like mummies from some ancient bog. His father was becoming one of them.

He was going to become one too. Just another wet dead thing lying on the ground. They'd catch him out there, in the country, and shoot him and maybe leave him to die. Men like that, who knew what they'd do. Beat him to death? If they felt like it.

He couldn't speak. He felt like his mouth wouldn't even work, if he tried to talk. What was the expression? Numb from the neck up.

"Okay . . . " Dale hesitated.

They waited for another gunshot. But instead they heard boots, the labored breathing of men, muttered curses. They were coming.

"We're all going back," Brand said. "They're just too close. Come on."

Russ saw Brand's hunched-over shape move down the crevice, north, and he thought: *My father's body.*

But he let go of it. He left it behind. He followed Brand and Dale and they crept quickly up the declivity, stumbling sometimes, but still holding on to their rifles.

Now and then Russ slipped, skidded, barking his knees on stone. Feeling a pinching sensation in his back where he expected a bullet to hit him.

A thud, something zipping past, a zinging ricochet. Another . . . An angry shout.

Russ thought he caught the word, *bitches.*

Then they'd rounded the big boulder, were climbing a thin path, brush scratching at their faces, stinging.

My father's dead . . .

There were men arguing, behind them, and after awhile, when they'd nearly reached the top of the chain of hills over-looking Freedom, just when Russ was thinking that maybe now he should do it, maybe now that they'd dropped back he could cut across the countryside and head for Deer Creek—another gunshot came and the whine of a ricochet.

Russ and his friends threw themselves flat on the trail, the trail's small broken stones hard on Russ's knees, and palms and elbows.

"They're still back there, goddammit," Dale said. "There's cover up ahead—we got to run for it."

Brand turned, and knelt behind a squat sandstone boulder. The starlight glimmered on his rifle barrel as he propped it across the stone. "Keep going. I'm just going to slow these pricks down a little . . . "

Russ wanted to say something to him but he wasn't sure what it was. So he kept moving between the bushes, up the trail.

Dale led the way. They jumped up, dodged behind little thickets of manzanita, kept their heads low, that familiar pinching in his back, a branch from a manzanita falling to the right as a bullet cut it in two, and then they were atop the hill, going down the other side, sweat clammy on Russ's temples.

Brand's rifle barked and Dale stopped, turned to look past Russ. "What the fuck is he doing?"

"He's . . ." Russ's own voice sounded like a stranger, whispering hoarsely. "Trying to keep them from following . . . "

"Where is he? Goddammit, Brand, get up here!"

An answering bullet whistled past them—Russ crouched behind a bush, seeing, again, those mud-caked bodies in the wreckage of houses. Remembering dead animals he'd seen near the railroad tracks as a boy, carcasses with skin all rubbery and black after a week or so lying on the ground. He and Brand and Dale could end up like that, out here, lying in the brush. Shot dead and turning rubbery and black . . .

Then Brand came gasping up the trail. "I didn't hit 'em but they took cover . . . " He led the way now, Russ behind him.

Russ heard Dale fire another shot to keep their pursuers back and then caught the sound of Dale's heavy boots as he came lumbering up the trail behind, and in minutes they were over the crest, passing through a little woods, going past the town storage shed, to the first row of houses.

Shame rose up in Russ, then. The feeling of shame as definite and strong as the sickness of a hangover.

PART TWO:

The Walls Came Down

. . . And the walls came down.
They just stood there laughing.
They're not laughing anymore.
—The Call
"The Walls Came Down"

FIFTEEN

NELLA WAITED till they were all asleep, about an hour past dawn. She'd been awake most of the night, curled like a sickly fetus in her sleeping bag; clutching herself, trying to ignore the pain in her crotch and the pictures in her head. Now she wormed out of her sleeping bag in the corner of Ferrara's carpeted front room.

She'd been glad of the warmth here, anyway. Glad to be away from the house with the brass Jesus and the dead people in the pit out front. Songbird lying there like a bird run over by a car. But she wanted to get away from here—to see, anyhow, if God would let her go.

She'd thought the men would never go to sleep. They'd come back late, Dickie and Sten and Ferrara and his brother Mario. The other two had gone to relieve the Grummons at the bonfire.

The men had spent two hours in the kitchen, drinking and arguing. Ferrara sounding almost hysterical. The Grummons coming back just as things started to calm down and getting in the argument, starting it up again. Ferrara telling Dickie shooting that man hadn't been necessary, and Dickie saying get real, more than that'll be necessary, hella more, and Ferrara saying we have to get those people to sign, get them to turn over the goods, to start the company, and now those four are witnesses, and they'll testify and I'm part of it, and Dickie said shut up and have a drink, these people needed a scare put in them, that's what'll get them to do what you want . . .

Around and around and around. Then not long before dawn the Grummons had gone off to the other house and Dickie'd gone to sleep on the couch and Sten in the easy chair and the other two in the bedrooms and Nella had lain there still, waiting and waiting to make sure, just to make absolutely sure they were breathing that regular slow loud way that meant they were deep asleep . . .

Now she got up, slipped out to the kitchen, carrying the sleeping bag wadded under her arm. She went out the kitchen door, so she wouldn't call any attention to herself, opening and closing the door real quiet. Then she hurried off, tip-toeing in the sneakers that were a bit too big for her, down the street in the cold gray light.

The damp wind nuzzled her hair, stung her nose. From up here on the hill she could take in the sea, all stretched out, wrinkly, still mucky in places, with some debris still floating in it, including a corner piece of a house looking like a pyramid of wood popping up out of the water. But much of the debris had been drawn out to sea, cleared away—especially soft things, like bodies. The ocean looked steel-colored now, with white tops cresting, farther out. And it talked to her. Whispers of warning.

The sea just hushed and murmured and sent long, low, steady rows of waves toward the wrecked town. It seemed like it was going to do that forever and had never done anything else. But it could suddenly rise up and smack down on you whenever it wanted. They'd all learned that.

She hurried down the hill, throwing the unzipped sleeping bag around her shoulders as a kind of ungainly shawl against the cold. It smelled of mustiness and bodies.

Need to get off this street, she decided. If they looked out the front window of Mario's place they could see her down here.

She cut across the street and down to the left, south along

a side street that was just above the high-water mark of the tsunami.

She walked down the street, seeing no one, thinking maybe they'd all gone over to the school gym camp. Word about the lootings and fires and the gang had gotten out and they were probably all huddled over there. Although most of the houses on her left were intact, the ones on the right had been in the upper reach of the tsunami—some of them were smashed down, and others were partly undermined, half-standing, leaning crazily, as if bowing in servility to the sea. The street went on for a ways . . .

And then she saw the house, on the right, with the big rusty anchor.

She knew it instantly, though she'd never seen it before. Ronnie had described it. Ronnie Burke with his translucent-framed glasses and his weak chin with that little soul patch and his kind words to her. "You'd make someone a great little sweetie," he'd said once, when they were smoking a doob together. She knew what he really meant by that. He meant *him*. He'd been too shy to say. And she didn't feel like she was a good enough person to offer herself to him. That day, she'd come from doing some things with the Sand Scouts that scared her to think about . . .

Ronnie's sister lived in this house. He stayed mostly in Buried Cove but he came up here to spend weekends with his sister sometimes. *She's got a place up on Overlook,* he'd said, *one of those big flat-topped places with a roof deck for sunning, and this hella big giant ol' rusty anchor out front, in the garden. Thing is huge . . .*

That anchor, standing in a growth of ice plant, must be six feet high, must weigh like five hundred pounds. There were lounge chairs on the roof deck. This was Overlook . . .

It had to be the house. Could Ronnie be sheltering in there?

She immediately crossed over, went to the front door. Knocked. An empty sound. No response. She tried the knob, found the door was unlocked. She opened it and stepped cautiously in. Instantly knowing from the smell that there was death in the house.

But that didn't mean he wasn't in here alive too. He could be injured, stuck somewhere with his sister's body, not able to do much for himself . . .

She went a few steps more, hearing the house creak under her steps, wondering if her weight could make the damaged floor collapse. She stopped, several steps in, and gagged at the smell.

Then she held her breath, made herself walk down the hallway—until she came to the edge of the living room and looked down through what had been the floor, into the basement.

The living room was completely gone, along with the whole back wall. A section of roof from another house had been carried by the big wave to fall like a giant axe blade into the back of the house, and the floor of the living room—overlooking the slope—had caved into the lower part of the house, busting through the ground floor at the lower level too, exposing a basement.

The basement, a story and a half below, was choked with dirty water and irregular pieces of debris. The remains of the caved-in floor of the living room, at Nella's feet, angled down sharply to the basement like a big slide down into it, and wedged between two chunks of fallen wood-and-plaster wall, down there, was a man, lying on his back. His right arm seemed to be missing, and his left was just a bone with shreds of flesh. His chest was rent open and half hollowed out. She could see, from where she stood, that there were skewed glasses on his head—with the translucent frame. And that distinctive chin was there, that weed of a beard. Not much more of his face remained, the eyes and nose and lips were mostly gone. The wave had brought a clutch of crabs with it—some of them survived, and they were scrambling in the ocean water left in the rubbled pit of the basement; they were eating his face.

They were eating Ronnie's face.

And as she watched, a crab crawled out of the hollow of his belly, like it had come out of its cave to greet the day, and it was walking sideways up onto Ronnie's yellowing hip bones, and then tilting itself up a little to peer at her, lifting its pincers in greeting . . .

Come on down. Join your lover, Nella. We can take you where he's gone.

Nella backed away, gagging, spitting up a bit as she went. Nothing much came up, she'd eaten so little.

She turned and staggered out onto the street and wandered for a while, sobbing, though no tears would come out of her eyes. They were so dry. So dry they ached.

A block slipped by. Another. She realized that in her daze she'd been going the wrong way. She should find her way to the high school. Get away. Go with her original plan. It was hard to care right now. But she turned—to find Dickie staring at her, standing on the damp, cold street corner in his stocking feet, a pistol held loosely in his hand.

"I knew something was wrong," he said. "It woke me up. I can't trust you out there. I don't know why I keep you around. Except you stuck with me. You did your part with Buff. Seemed like you earned something. But now . . . "

She waited for him to shoot her. But then he surprised her by making a groaning sound she'd never heard before and saying, "Go back up to our house." She started up that way. Not knowing what else to do. And he came padding along behind her. The only thing he said on the way back was, "I'm not letting you out of my sight again."

———

"MAYBE SO," Brand said. "Maybe we lost our nerve. But in those . . . those circumstances . . . " He shrugged. Brand's rifle was leaning on the wall next to where he sat at the sofa.

Pendra and Brand and Russ were sitting around her grandma's living room, all of them bundled up with extra blankets. They'd been listening to a radio about FEMA struggling to help Santa Cruz and big parts of San Francisco. Didn't sound like anyone was thinking about them at all. So they'd switched it off to save the battery and they sat in the slanting afternoon light coming in through the picture window and Pendra kept looking at Russ . . .

Russ couldn't decide if the look was pity because he'd lost his father, or pity because he'd discovered he was a coward, someone inconsequential. One of the limping antelope to be culled from the herd.

She's not like that, he decided. *She wants to tell me again how bad she feels about my dad. But she doesn't know how to start.*

He felt bruised inside. Like someone had cut open the skin of his stomach, and punched his insides, again and again, and then sewed it back up. And what kept going through his mind was his dad's remains, lying in the chaparral.

"My dad's body is still out there," Russ said. Staring at the rug.

He could feel her looking at him.

"We'll get it eventually," Brand said. "But they've probably got people still watching that area. I'm not even sure how many of the sons of bitches there are."

Russ looked at Pendra—but now she had tilted her head to look Brand up and down. "I keep thinking I've seen your face somewhere. Brand. And . . . your name is so distinctive. The only 'Brand' I know of was Brand Grande . . . "

Brand smiled sadly. "That would be me."

Pendra blinked, leaned forward, and looked closer at Brand. Startled, Russ said, *"What?"*

"It's a pen name. When I write kid's books."

Russ stared. "You are not Brand Grande."

"I am, actually. Brand Robinson's my real name, but yeah. I write books. Illustrate them. For kids."

"You're *that* Brand."

"Well, yeah." Brand seemed relieved to be talking about something else besides Russ's father, besides the corpse wedged between boulders.

"My mom loved your books, we used to read them together!"

"That's where I know your face—!" Pendra burst out. "From the book jacket!"

"Yeah. I was sort of like Lemony Snicket but before him and nowhere near as successful. My stuff was a bit more fantasy oriented."

Pendra laughed. "I read *Bleeper In Blueland* to myself when I was lonely. It was kinda goth for a kid's book."

Russ looked at Pendra. Glad himself to be able to think about something besides death. "Can you believe that? We both read him! And here he is!"

"Are you going to do a new book?" Pendra asked.

"I was . . . yeah. I am. I . . . sure."

Russ had the feeling Brand was trying not to disappoint them, so he was talking as if the book was for sure. But he seemed less than enthusiastic.

"Did you write some of it already?"

"I did. I'm illustrating it now. Or I was before all this happened. But my house is still standing. My work should be okay. I'll show you later, if you want." He shrugged, as if it didn't matter much.

"That'd be cool," Russ said, aware that his voice was dull.

Trying to pull away from the bruised feeling. And falling back into it.

"Hey, Brand—that character, Bleeper," Pendra said. "I always wondered about that name. I mean sometimes you'd call him 'The Little Bleeper' . . . "

Brand grinned. "You sure you want to hear this? Might be disillusioning."

"Like anything could disillusion me now."

"You've got a point. Well—I had the story but not the character names. So I said to my wife 'What should I call the little fucker—or should I call him Little Fucker?' "

Pendra chuckled. Russ managed a smile.

Brand went on, "My wife was kidding me—she said, no, you'd have to call him 'Little Bleeper.' So I said what the hell, why not. Marilee never thought my editor would go for it but he did."

"Is your wife . . . ?" Pendra glanced at Russ, looking like she wished she hadn't raised the subject. "Was she in town when it hit?"

"No, she . . . Marilee passed on, some years ago."

There it was, back again. Death was in the room. No one bothered to say, *Sorry for your loss.* Seemed redundant in some way. Had been for days.

Pendra just nodded and sagged back in her chair. *As if the presence of death*, Russ thought, *was a weight dragging her down.*

"I'm so tired now," she said. "I haven't done much today. I ate something. I even took a vitamin. But I'm tired."

"Any fever?" Brand asked. "Maybe you should talk to Dr. Spuris."

"No, I . . . ever since my Gram died I just feel like . . . tired."

Brand nodded. "I felt tired and out of sorts for a long time after my wife died. Grief shows up in different ways."

Russ just nodded.

Brand went on, choosing his words carefully, "We have a right to be angry at life. But we lose something if we blow it all off completely."

Russ snorted. "Sure. We lose our illusions."

"I know how you feel. It's funny to be arguing the other side, considering that just the other day I basically told someone her belief was bullshit . . . but it's a matter of balance. When we were pulling people out . . . hearing a little boy crying with a wall collapsed on him, digging him out—you realize, hell yeah, it *does* matter. Hard to say *why* in the big picture—but it does. There's something there."

Pendra nodded to herself. Russ knew Brand was right. He'd felt it too. But right now he couldn't feel much but the aching void that was the sudden absence of his father in the world.

Someone knocked. Brand got up, picked up the rifle, went to the door. "Who is it?" he called, holding the rifle ready.

Pendra looked at Russ. Whispering, "Whoa. Is it really necessary to carry the gun to the door like that?"

Russ sigh. "My father is dead, Pendra. Someone shot him. What do you think? Yeah. Right now, we need guns."

"It's me!" Dale called, through the door. "Ferrara's asking us to come to the pass. Some kind of ultimatum."

SIXTEEN

"REMEMBER," Dale whispered to Russ as they walked up the highway toward the bonfire. "You don't accuse anybody of killing him—this ain't the place. The time will come. That'll come later. This is just to see where things stand. We don't want to provoke any more killing, we don't have to . . . "

Russ nodded. He didn't know who'd fired the shot anyway. *The time will come.*

The bonfire had mostly burned out. Smoke writhed up from its coals. But the razor wire was still there. And the gunmen.

Eight men stood in front of the antipersonnel wire, when Russ arrived with Brand, Dale, and Pendra. Dale and Brand carrying rifles.

Most of them were the men who'd been here before. There were the Grummons and Dickie and Lon Ferrara and Sten. A big swag-bellied man squatted by the coals, squinting against the smoke; he was red-faced, head shaved bald. He wore a Levi's-and-leather biker's jacket with CHUCKLES sewn across a front pocket—so that'd be Chuckles. An automatic pistol was held loosely in his hand.

There was a man with long, wavy black hair and a full beard. He was carrying a pistol-grip shotgun; he wore leather pants, a grimy trench coat streaked red and black, and dark glasses. A face like Jesus except for the dark glasses. Chuckles asked him for a cigarette, as they came up, calling him Remo.

Lucas would be the rangy, lank-haired man in the army jacket and fatigue pants, carrying a carbine. His lean face stubbly, his sunken eyes flicking back and forth, tongue darting over thin lips. Seemed stoned on something.

Lon Ferrara, stepping up to Brand, carried a shotgun. Sten and Dickie carried rifles.

Russ was aware that Brand and Ferrara were talking, but he wasn't listening. All he could think about was which one had shot his father. There were some guys missing from this bunch, weren't there? That Cholo guy for one. Maybe watching whatever place they holed up. One of the missing ones could have done it. Maybe the guy who'd done it had run away, left the area. Not wanting to be here when the law returned. Or maybe . . .

Dickie was looking right at him. He had a rifle in his hands and he had a look on his face that made Russ think:

He'd like to tell me he shot my dad.

Russ stared at him—letting the accusation show in his face.

Dickie grinned and slapped his rifle.

He did it.

And Dickie kept looking at him . . .

Russ tried to glare right back . . . but finally, he dropped his gaze. Looked away. Couldn't even stare back at the guy. It was like looking into a harsh light.

He felt the shame again. He felt like he was sinking down into his own shoes.

Something Ferrara said made him look up again. "I'm not going to say who fired what shot. Maybe you shot him yourself accidentally, I don't know. But I know you people fired first."

"That is a flat-out lie!" Dale shouted. His rifle, angling at the sky, trembled from the shaking of his hands. Russ had never seen him this angry before.

Brand said, "We never fired at you people till you fired at us."

"I'm not saying I was there—" Ferrara said. "I'm just saying that the way I heard it—"

"Well, shit, I'll say *I* was there," Dickie said.

"Who fired first?" Dale demanded.

"Who's on first?" Sten said.

"What's on second!" Dickie said.

Ferrara threw them a glare. Then he looked back at Brand. "Look—you speaking for those people down at the high school?"

"I'm getting information for them. Not speaking for them."

"What about . . . " Who had spoken? Then Russ realized it was him; he had said it himself. The others looked at him. Waiting. "What about my father's body?"

Ferrara looked him over. "So that was your father. Well. We got a flatbed truck out there and we moved the body. I got it covered with a tarp. It's not just sitting out there."

"In case you need to get rid of the evidence?" Brand asked, his voice taut with emotion.

"Like I said—you people fired first."

"You know that's a lie. Where's Drew's body?"

"It's in an empty house, up across from my brother's place, it's wrapped up and— It doesn't matter, we'll turn it over to the Deer Creek authorities when we've got this all worked out. Between now and then, *we're* the authorities, *we're* the militia, and you can tell those people in that high school gym and wherever, you tell them the time has come. I've got a ream of announcements here about the incorporation of the town and the agreements we're going to sign. We're going to inspect all property to see what's there—"

"So you can rob us?" Dale spat. "You can kiss my black ass! That man you shot—I got to know him real good this week. That was one hell of a good man. You are not a *tenth* of what that man was! You can keep your fucking announcements! Someone else wants to sign it that's their business. But keep it the fuck away from me!"

He backed away from them, his rifle still pointed at the air but now held so he could drop it down and fire easily.

"Yeah. That about sums it up for me," Brand said, backing up a few steps. "Black ass aside. Come on, Russ. Pendra."

"You got till tomorrow morning!" Ferrara shouted as, heart thumping, Russ took Pendra's arm, drew her back down the hill to join Dale—who was waiting for them, a little farther down, rifle now tilted so that it aimed over Ferrara's head. Ferrara yelling after them, "Till tomorrow! Then . . . then we're going to go down there and start searching for looted goods! And nobody better try to get through those hills! This is not going to be a goddamn ghost town! We're sticking together to build this place back up! I'm gonna have people posted, watching! The hills and the cliffs!"

Brand stopped long enough to shout back, "You lost your mind, some time back, and you don't know it, Lon! But those men with you—*they* know it! They know damn well you're out of your gourd and they like it. Means they can mash your buttons."

Ferrara looked startled at that.

"Hey, Pendra," Dickie called suddenly, looking all boyish and wide-eyed at her. "What's up? You picked a side for sure?"

Pendra said nothing. She turned on her heel and hurried down the road. Russ quickened his pace, catching up with her. Wondering if Ferrara's men were going to simply shoot them in the back as they walked away.

At least he'd asked about his father's body. But that wasn't enough. Someone needed to be arrested. There needed to be justice.

They'd picked his dad off, just shot his father like shooting a bird off a fence.

"How old are you, girl?" Dickie called after Pendra. "You old enough? You going to be safe down there? That kid going to protect you? I don't *think* so!"

The men with Dickie laughed at that.

Russ felt like a compass in a roomful of magnets. Where was north?

NELLA WAS WALKING beside Mario Ferrara, wishing Dickie hadn't asked her to do this.

She was cold and feeling feverish and unreal. And she didn't want to be out in the woods this clammy afternoon. Especially not with a man who was mostly a stranger to her. Nella knowing, too, what else was out here.

The pine woods was shady and smelled of sap and the brown needles that crunched underfoot. The wind from the ocean made the trees creak and bend, just a little. Waist-high ferns were cut by trails, marked by bicycle treads. Mist drifted through, trailed from clouds.

Mario was carrying a rifle of some kind. She didn't know one from another. He was walking ahead of her, looking through the ferns. They'd nod their ferny tops in the breeze, as if to acknowledge him, and then he'd move on. A red squirrel rattled around in the branches overhead. A pine cone fell down, thumped in the ground, making Mario spin and stare. She saw from that how nervous he was.

He stared at the rolling pinecone—and then he looked at her. Shook his head. "No reason for you to be here."

"I know," Nella said. "I was just . . . " What was she supposed to say? Dickie had said, *If he starts to go out in those woods, you distract him, talk to him, show your titties, suck his dick. I don't care what the fuck you do, but you do it. Keep him from going out there. I'd just shoot him but we're not through with his brother yet. So keep an eye on him.*

She didn't feel like kneeling on the damp ground to give this old guy a blow job. But what difference did it make? Nothing mattered anyway. Long as he didn't want to fuck. With her infection, that'd hurt too much. It hurt just to walk. She was used to that, though. It was part of the punishment. If that's what it was. Sometimes she thought she was in Hell, and sometimes she thought it just felt that way. She changed her mind about it two or three times an hour.

Lately she'd been thinking that it was both. They were mortal. They could die. *And* they were in Hell. They'd die and then come back and die and then come back . . .

Or it was all real, like a bee sting and sand in your eyes and loneliness. As real as that. And this was her reality. She was sure of one thing, though: nothing mattered anymore.

She started unbuttoning her blouse.

"What the hell are you doing?" he asked, snorting.

"I'm . . . we were alone and . . . Dickie wanted to make sure I was useful to you guys, he said . . . he said I should be useful and I'm not good for much else . . . "

"Button up your fucking blouse, for Christ's sake."

"Okay." She rebuttoned it, relieved. She'd tried. "What you looking for out here?"

She knew, though.

"I'm looking for . . . I'm not sure. I just kept getting this feeling." More talking to himself now, as he looked around. "Like, *Look out there, look out there.* And this is the place near that house . . . I mean, if somebody wanted to hide a body . . . two bodies . . . "

"But . . . if they wanted to hide a body they'd just dump it in one of the busted up houses down below."

"I don't know. It's just a feeling."

But she knew why they'd ended up in the woods. Because Sten didn't want to carry them down in broad daylight into one of those wrecked houses down there. Didn't want the exposure and didn't want the work. She'd heard him and Dickie talking about it.

"You should just go back, girl—" Mario broke off, and his mouth went slack.

Then he turned and stalked into the wet underbrush to one side of the trail. He was up to his waist in dewy fiddleheads, hurrying over to a spot where the carpet of ferns seemed abruptly interrupted. As if something had made a gap in them.

Nella walked slowly up behind him, the feeling of dread growing in her, strong enough to compete with the burning pain between her legs.

She came close and looked over his shoulder. Saw that he was staring down at a piece of black plastic trash bag sticking out from the turf. You could see the ground had been all dug up, here. Someone had buried something. Not very deep.

He took a long, ragged breath, then tossed his rifle aside, and squatted down, took hold of the plastic bag's edge, and pulled, hard. Grunting. Nothing happened for a moment—then he almost fell over backwards, as the sack came loose, tearing in places but staying together enough to pull something heavy partway out. A lot of turf came with it, pine needles and crushed ferns and dirt, and then a head lolled into view, a sunken blue face.

"Antony!" Mario sobbed. "Antony . . . "

She tried to pat him on the shoulder—he twitched her hand away. She wanted to tell him about Ronnie. Say she knew about finding the body of someone loved; say she was sorry this happened to him. But she kept her mouth shut. She looked over his shoulder at the torn up sod, and she could see that there was another black plastic trash bag. You could see a corner of it, sticking up, beyond the one with Mario's son in it. That'd be the other dead boy, Roger, who'd come to visit Freedom with Antony.

Finally Mario got up, and she heard his every breath, wet and rough, sounding like he was having an asthma attack the way her cousin used to have. He bent over, picked up the rifle. Turned toward Antony.

"I'll be back, son." He paused for a long wracking sob. "I'll get you buried right." Face mottled, cheeks wet, he turned away from the body and pushed past Nella, making her stagger with the force of it, and hurried back to the trail. He was starting toward the house . . .

A thought came to her. *She shouldn't have been trying to discourage him from finding this body. This was good. Because he was going to kill Dickie. Maybe Dickie would stay dead and maybe not. But she could see him get killed. That'd be good. She could get some respite, couldn't she? That'd be even better.*

She hurried to catch up with Mario, hardly feeling the pain in her crotch anymore.

He walked ahead in long swift strides, cocking the gun as he went, and pretty soon they were at the backyard lawn of Mario's house, walking through the bark dust strip between the low juniper bushes.

Mario stopped about forty feet from the glass sliding doors to the kitchen where Sten and Lon Ferrara and Dickie were sitting at the wooden kitchen table, with Cholo and Steve standing behind them, the bunch of them smoking pot and drinking, and arguing as usual.

"Lon!" Mario shouted hoarsely. "Lon, get out of there! Run out the front!"

Then he popped the rifle to his shoulder and fired, without

really taking time to aim closely but shooting through the glass door toward Dickie. It was loud, that shot, louder than when they'd shot Buff—

I know, she thought, *I know I helped kill Buff, I know I did, Jesus Lord, I know it.*

Glass in the sliding doors webbed and crashed apart, tinkling down onto the concrete of the patio.

She heard the men shout stuff like, *What the fuck!* And she realized bullets were going to fly the other way, and she thought: *I ought to get out of the way.*

But she didn't move. She realized she was hoping a bullet would hit her, when they fired back. She stood there and waited.

It didn't take long before Mario had another round chambered and read, Sten was firing back with a pistol, but he was unnerved by this sudden attack from Mario and was missing, the bullets kicking up green and brown shreds of lawn behind them. Another bullet—she thought Dickie had fired it—whipped so close to her right ear she heard it buzzing like a bee, and then Mario was firing again and the men on the other side of the glass were scattering, probably thinking they'd shoot at him from the windows.

Mario sobbed, and chambered another round. Nella heard Lon shouting at him from somewhere in the house.

"Mario, stop this bullshit!"

"They killed my son!" Mario wailed. "I *knew* they killed him! I could feel it! I heard him calling out there!"

"Mario, what the fuck are you talking about!"

"Fuck you, man! You're with them!"

He fired another round toward the house and there was a flash at a window and a bullet cut the air between her and Mario.

Sten shouting at someone in the house, "Get away from me, man!"

"He's not going to hit us from there, he's just upset—" Ferrara's voice. "He thinks someone killed his kid, just give him a chance to cool off!" So Lon Ferrara was interfering with their aim.

Mario was struggling with the rifle—something in it seemed stuck. "Fucking jam, fucking jam, fucking *jam!*" He snarled, his eyes streaming, foam at the corners of his lips. He threw the rifle aside, and shouted, "I'm going to get another gun and I'm gonna kill 'em, Lon! You better get away from them!"

He was backing toward the woods now, and his hands were clutching the air. His teeth were clenched.

"And . . . " A bullet splashed at his left shoulder and he grimaced as blood sprayed, but it wasn't deep, and he went on, "I'm fucking coming back!"

Then he turned and strode into the woods. Another bullet chased him—she felt that one go by close too—and then he was gone, hidden in the trees.

She realized her heart was doing a drum roll, and there was a rippling mist over her eyes, She seemed to see the dead hanging out in the shadows of the trees—was that Buff, the man she'd helped kill, right before the wave? Was that him waving at her? Or was it just the fever? But wasn't that her Ronnie, coming up beside him? And there was Songbird, with chains wound around her wrists—and Nella thought: *Maybe a bullet did hit me, maybe I'm dead so I can see them now.*

But pretty soon Lon Ferrara and Dickie and the others were out here with her, looking into the woods, their guns in their hands, arguing about what to do, yet again, and she was sure that, no, she wasn't dead, not in any way that would save her, anyhow.

She was seeing things in a fever, in Freedom, California. She was going to be here for a while.

SEVENTEEN

"Boy? You going to get out of bed?"

It was Dale. Russ knew from his voice. But he didn't want to turn around. He tried to ignore it. He made his breathing louder, and regular, like he was sleeping.

Dale was not fooled. "Come on, goddammit, you're not asleep. It's like four in the afternoon. Come on, kid. Things to do."

Russ wanted to lie there, fully clothed but for his shoes. Just lie there in the bedroom that was supposed to have been his, the bed that his dad had made up for him before he'd gone to pick him up and bring him to Freedom. He wanted to just lie there staring at the wall, with the blankets pulled up to his chin, and the sea moaning in the distance, and try to be blank for a while.

Blankness worked. Blankness felt pretty good. An absence of feeling felt good. That was a strange thing to contemplate. It made no sense but it was true.

"Come on, Russ, you've gotta help us make up our tiny little fucking minds."

"I don't have to do anything," Russ said.

Dale sighed. "Your dad died last night. And you ought to have time to grieve and lay there and just feel bad. But you don't. You got to stand up with us and help us decide . . . That's what you need and that's what he'd want."

"You don't fucking know what my dad would want."

"Pendra's going to be there. She's got more balls than you, man. She lost her grandmother, last relative she had."

Russ winced. Dale had found a chink in the blank wall.

"Fuck. *Fuck!* Okay. Whatever. I'm coming." He made himself sit up. "But . . . you know what? We did a lot already. And Dad is dead for it. And no help is coming from anywhere."

"We did get help. The folks from Deer Creek took our injured out. And that son of a bitch stopped them from getting the word out about the rest of us. But help will be here. We just have to survive with some goddamn dignity till it does. Now come on."

Groaning, Russ moved to the edge of the bed, found his shoes and put them on. He sat there, brushing his hair into something like order with his fingers. Not wanting to stand up. "So—where's Pendra?"

"She's with Brand, some errand for Jill. You coming?"

He lingered on the edge of the bed. Wanting to say, *Sure, the older people tell us to buck up, and get out there and face the world because it makes them feel better when we do. But they know it's meaningless. They know it's always going to be a defeat.*

Then—suddenly, out of nowhere, he had a moment of self-consciousness—seeming to hear his own thoughts, to see himself sitting on the edge of the bed, half-slumped. And he saw that he was ignoble, in that moment. That was the word that came to him. He had seen the word many times, in old books, but he'd never used it himself. Too old-fashioned. But that was the right word. *Ignoble.*

He sat up straighter, took a deep breath, and shook himself. "Okay. We'll go talk about it. I'm not sure what we can do, unless somebody wants to build a boat. Or unless one of us wants . . . "

He almost said, *Wants to get shot.* Then he saw his father, lying there in that crevice.

His mind had to stop, and back up, sometimes, when he thought about that. It still hadn't completely sunk in . . .

"Fine," he said. "Let's just fucking go."

They went outside and downstairs, and saw Jill—who was now staying with Pendra—at the door to Gram's apartment. Jill squinting at the door lock, fumbling as she unlocked it. Having trouble seeing. They heard Brand shout at her, crossing the street, and saw Pendra hurrying to keep up with him. Brand was grinning, nudging Pendra, handing her something. Pendra took it, ran up to Jill, who was turning to squint at them.

Drawn by the look of happiness on Pendra's face. Russ walked up to them, Dale following, in time to see her hand over a pair of glasses.

"My glasses!" Jill gasped, putting them on. "Oh, it's my extra pair! How did you get them? You can't even get through to that house!"

"Brand found a way through! We had to climb a bunch of shit. There was a mean-ass dog running around too. Somebody's pit bull. But we got in!"

"Pendra—thank you!" Jill hugged Pendra and Brand. Lingering on Brand, it seemed to Russ. Then she stepped back, smiling, and said, "I was just going to make a cup of tea on your Coleman stove!"

"That'd be good. There's stuff I need to talk to somebody about. I mean somebody female."

"Good. It'd be such a *relief* to talk about anything but the mayor and FEMA and if we're running out of toilet paper and food for stray dogs and getting to Deer Creek . . . "

"You're not coming to the meeting, Jill?" Dale asked.

"Sure, but you guys will natter around in circles for at least forty-five minutes. We'll come soon enough."

Dale nodded. "We got a meeting, Brand," he said, scratching

his head. "You coming or are you going to drink tea with the ladies?"

"Well, if you put it that way I'd better come."

Russ nodded and followed Brand and Dale toward the gym; Jill and Pendra went into the apartment. It bothered Russ that they'd be in there alone. With all that had happened. But the door locked, after all . . .

"WHAT ARE WE going to do about that asshole Mario?" Liddy Grummon asked.

They were posted all around the living room of Mario's place. The men in their firemen's coats, but the coats not buttoned up. Nella was down in the corner, sitting on her sleeping bag; the others were on the sofa, the easy chairs, Sten glaring out the window, on lookout, the narrow opening where the curtains weren't pulled. Randle Grummon was standing in the door to the kitchen, keeping watch out toward the back door.

Lon Ferrara was standing dourly by the fireplace, head bowed, shotgun in his arms. Nella knew he had come full circle in his mind. The state he'd been in, all that crazy talk about making the town stay and rebuild, the razor wire, all that had drained away. She could see that in his face. Now he was just stuck with what he'd done. And with what had happened with his brother . . .

Cholo and Steve and were there too, sitting on the arms of the sofa like bookends. Chuckles and Lucas and Remo were out guarding the road east.

It was twilight outside. Someone had gone on a run to suction gasoline from a car and the generator was running, the heater in the house going, but cold air wafted from the bullet-busted back door.

Dickie was sitting in the easy chair across from the fireplace, toying with a revolver, not pointing it anywhere in particular, not looking directly at Lon. But Nella knew Dickie and she could tell he was watching Lon Ferrara closely out of the corner of his eyes.

"He's gonna go around, jabbering," Sten said. "That Mario guy."

"That *Mario guy*," Ferrara growled, suddenly, "is my goddamn brother. He thinks you killed his kid. That's wrong information, you tell me, fine. But something he saw in that woods spooked him." He looked coldly at Nella. "Your little bitch was there with him."

She thought, *I shouldn't tell what's out there. But then maybe I should*. Could be it'd start them killing each other.

It was hard to think, with this fever. Her mouth was so dry, lips chapped. She should go and drink some water . . . but it didn't seem important. She felt no thirst . . .

"What about it, uh—" Ferrara paused, trying to remember her name. "Nella. What about it, Nella?"

She licked her lips. "What about *what*?"

Dickie sighed. "Oh, I'm tired of this. I think what we're gonna do is, we're gonna do what General Patton would've done. We're not going to do any kind of money transfers. We're gonna carry the fight to the enemy. We're gonna go down there and just line 'em up and say, turn over your valuables and your keys and we're gonna go through all their shit and all their houses and then we're gonna load all the shit on a couple of big trucks and get the fuck out of Dodge. This contract stuff—it's never gonna happen."

"Ha!" Sten said, grinning at him from the front window. "Now you're talkin', chief!"

Lon Ferrara shook his head, slowly. "No, no, that's not part of the plan. You can forget that. I really think we're going to have to take down that wire and . . . I'll just have to take my losses. I just need to know what went on out in that woods. My brother—I figure he was just freaking out about his kid. Can't find Antony since the tsunami. Going nuts from worry. We got lucky—no one was hurt when he flipped out. So let's let it go and tell him . . . "

He broke off, staring at Dickie. Who had his gun pointed at him.

"I can see from here," Dickie said, "the safety on your shotgun is on. Take you a second to get your thumb there, flick it off. So drop that shit, there. Drop that shotgun, Lon. And you give me your bank account information. Because I don't believe you're broke. You've got an account in Deer Creek."

Ferrara squinted at him, as if trying to see him better. The Grummons looked at each other and hooted.

Sten said, "Ha!"

"See," Dickie said, cheerfully, "I was going to wait on this, use your local authority, but you don't seem to have any, and you're still telling me what I can't do, what I'm supposed to do. So we need to get you done and over with."

Cholo chewed his lip, looking like he was trying to make up his mind. Steve was moving his right hand around behind him—he had a pistol stuck in the back of his belt.

Ferrara swallowed. He stared at the revolver in Dickie's hand.

"That's right," Dickie said. "No safety on this one."

Cholo turned to Steve and shook his head. "Dickie's right. Lon's plan ain't gonna work, bro. Fuck it. Let him go. We'll roll with these boys. Me, I'm gonna, anyhow."

Steve looked at him . . . and at Ferrara. Hesitated.

"Steve," Ferrara said, "You fucking work for me."

Wrong thing to say.

Steve snorted and dropped his hand from his gun. "Oh fuck you."

Dickie said, coldly and sharply, every word carefully enunciated, "Now—Lon?—drop the gun. We're going to talk about your bank account."

Ferrara licked his lips. And dropped the shotgun. It made a surprisingly loud clunk on the floor. He kicked it away. Spread his hands. "Whatever." His face blank. "There's not much in that account."

Nella was disappointed. They weren't killing each other.

Dickie looked toward Randle Grummon. "You get some rope, or chain, from out the garage, and—"

Then he caught the movement from the corner of his eye, Ferrara was reaching under his coat for the pistol Nella knew was in his pants pocket.

The pistol was out in Ferrara's hand and he managed to squeeze off a shot, an ear-aching sound, the bullet going through the front window before Dickie, hissing "Mother*fuck*er!" fired, and Ferrara rocked a step back, dropped his pistol, slid down the side of the fireplace, to sit close beside it, looking startled, mouth open. Ferrara coughed, just once—hard—and spat blood, dark red drops making scarlet teardrop shapes on his shirtfront. Cholo and Steve jumped up from the couch, backed toward the front window. Looking nervously at Sten—who had turned his gun toward the room—and Dickie and the Grummons.

"Goddammit, Ferrara, you fucked up my plan," Dickie said, going to squat by him, shaking his head. Scooping up Ferrara's pistol with his free hand. Looking at Ferrara's dying like a small kid staring curiously at an anthill.

Nella could see blood welling. The shot had crunched right through his breastbone.

Ferrara's respiration was slow and rough and wet and she realized she was hearing his last breaths. What was that like, knowing it was your last breaths? When she'd been caught in the big wave and tossed around, she was scared it was going to kill her, but she never really knew for sure. She'd felt somewhere deep down her time hadn't yet come.

Now she looked at Ferrara in raw envy. *His last breaths.*

Another breath came and went.

Dickie said, "Ferrara—I know you got your bank card. What's your PIN number? Not going to do you any good now. We'll spare your brother if you tell me."

Another long slow wet breath. Blood at his mouth. Ferrara tried to speak and only choked.

"Ferrara—you don't want us to kill Mario, right?"

Another breath. Ferrara looking at Dickie, as if his eyes wouldn't focus.

"Ferrara? What's your PIN number?"

Another breath. Just barely slipping out.

"Ferrara?"

Another breath.

"Ferrara! Hey, bro, listen! Maybe we can fix you up here . . . But first . . . "

Silence. Ferrara's chest stopped moving. His eyelids drooped. His head lolled.

"Fuck," Dickie said. He stood up. "Oh well. Probably didn't have much in that account anyway. I think the prick hid a lot of cash from the IRS in some safe in his bar and that whole building's under the ocean now."

"We could find that Mario, see what he knows about that cash," Sten suggested. "Could be hidden somewhere else."

"That's a thought. But Mario's liable to make me kill him too."

"I got another thought," Sten said, as the Grummon brothers dragged Lon Ferrara's body outside, through the back door. Each taking one of the corpse's arms. Out to the woods.

Everything Is Broken

"You see how red his blood is," Randle Grummon was saying, as they dragged him out. "He took iron pills." Sounded quite serious about it. "Told me so."

"Go on, Sten," Dickie said. "What were you saying?"

Nella was just sitting there on her sleeping bag in the corner, vaguely disappointed, smelling the gunsmoke in the room, and the blood, and watching Ferrara's shoes disappear around the edge of the door as they dragged him out past her.

"What I'm thinking is," Sten said, "we could make them bring the good stuff to us, maybe."

Dickie pursed his lips, tilted his head thoughtfully. "If we take something they want back?"

"Yeah. Maybe some kids. Maybe some . . . women."

"Those planner guys, that Brand—they always seem to keep that Pendra chick and that Jill around," Cholo pointed out. "Like they're real concerned about them."

Dickie looked at him. "I'm not so sure about you, Cholo. Seemed like you might've jumped the other way."

Cholo shook his head, without hesitation. "No. I'm in this now. I like the idea of getting what we can, take it out of town, sell it all somewhere. Jewelry, cash, drugs, maybe a couple real nice cars, whatever they've got. There's a lot of people there and it didn't all wash out to sea."

Sten gave Dickie a wry look, eyebrows raised. "Cholo here's not grieving much for his ol' pal Lon, is he?"

They all had a good laugh at that. Except for Nella.

She just waited, feeling the low fever go through her, in slow waves, like the sullen undulation of the sea.

"ALL WE CAN DO," said the big, white-haired, round-headed man standing by the gym bleachers—someone had said he was

213

the high school principal—"is just wait. I mean they can see the ocean from up on that pass, if you try to get a boat down the coast, they'll see and they'll set up on those cliffs and take potshots at you."

We're all just cowering in here, Russ thought.

At least two hundred people were gathered in the dimming light of the gymnasium—no one had turned on the generator yet. Brand was standing by Dale and Russ on some bleachers to one side; most people were spread out, sitting and standing, on the wrestling mats they used for mattresses. Russ sat on the bleachers a little behind them, near Lucia, who was wearing her white nurse's uniform because, she said, it got people to listen to her when she had to tell them what to do.

Russ looked around for Pendra, didn't see her. Probably still talking to Jill. The women seemed to be bonding. Enjoying their tea probably. But he kept uneasily glancing at the door, looking for Pendra, for either of them.

The principal puffed his cheeks out, passed a hand over his thinning hair, and went on. "That's the kind of people they are. Dickie and his bunch. I've known Dickie since he was a kid and he's no good. I don't suppose it's all his fault. His folks . . . " He shook his head sadly. "Mom in prison, his dad a crack addict. We tried to get him some guidance. I don't know how many of you remember Leonard Courtland—it was some years ago, he was a school counselor—Courtland said the wrong thing to Dickie, that was the story from the other kids. And the guy just vanished. We never saw Lenny Courtland again."

"Hey, Norm," someone said, from the back. "You don't *know* Dickie Rockwell killed that guy."

The principal shrugged. "Practically bragged about it after. But no body was found. Courtland had no family, so . . . "

"What's the relevance of all this?" Dr. Spuris asked.

"The relevance is that Dickie is hopelessly damaged goods," Brand said. "And people have disappeared around him since then. The relevance is that he's a killer."

Norm the Principal nodded. "That's the rumor."

"And," Brand went on, "we have to be willing to accept he might do any damn thing to *any*one. So we have to be willing to fight to protect ourselves. There's also the VVs to think about. And who knows what else is out there?"

"And Ferrara's trying to extort this town," Dale said. "I for one am not going to stand for that bullshit. I fought in the Gulf War. I didn't serve my country so people could order me around just because they got a goddamn rifle in their hand."

There was a grumble of response across the room, agreement and uncertainty overlapping. Russ looked around for Pendra. Didn't see her. Maybe he should go get her, bring her to the meeting.

"Now north and south the highways are blocked," Dale said. "Beaches end in cliffs, sheer cliffs. Dickie's bunch, Ferrara, all those assholes, they're watching the way east. So that leaves sending a boat out of here. Or trying to get through the hills again."

"We can climb the cliffs," said a young man standing near the wall. "Head south along the highway to the next town that way."

"They'll see you climb those cliffs," said Lars. He was lying on his back on the floor near the bleachers, staring spacily at the ceiling. He waggled his bare feet, crossed over his ankles. "Shoot you off the cliffs, day or night. They got a man watching them."

"I think we should repair a boat and send somebody down the coast," Brand said. "We could get it going in a day or two. I can sail. I'll go with someone else. We'll get the law in here. But here's the bottom line. *They murdered someone right in front of me.* They threatened that same man before at their little roadblock up there. And they're threatening us still. So we have to assume . . . "

"Maybe you provoked them," said Norm the Principal, "what with going up there with your guns. They can argue that in court, that they were just camping, watching for looters. It's your word against theirs who fired first. I mean, *I* believe you, but when it comes to a court . . . "

It went on like that, with more people on the wait and see side, and Russ thinking of speaking up and letting them know how he felt, that they needed to do something about his dad being shot down, but feeling kind of weak and sick and tired and just waiting till the moment came when he'd know for sure which way was north.

He found himself listening to the prattle of three young teen boys, sitting nearby on the bleachers. Talking in low voices. The adults, apart from Russ, not listening. Russ knew the boys' names from the gym, the food lines. They'd come here with Mrs. Patterson, who was talking to Reverend Lopez on the other side of the gym—her husband had been killed in the tsunami. Drowned in his car. One of the kids was a squat, pimply, longhaired blond boy with a nose piercing and a faded old Marvel Comics sweatshirt. Wolverine. That was Mrs. Patterson's son, Evan; the other two were neighbor kids staying with her because their house had fallen in. The tall boy, willowy, with a long neck, big Adam's apple, his brown, black-streaked hair in something like a mullet, was Jeremy. He sat bent like a vulture over the other two. "This is actually better than bein' at home," Jeremy said. "So boring there." He wore a black T-shirt with the image flaking off, a blood-splashed cartoony picture of the rapper Necro dressed in Dracula-style hat and cape, with shapely bikini-clad girls draped on his arms; Jeremy's oversized jeans were low on his thin hips, half his boxers showing. On the bleacher below him, beside Evan, sat his half-brother Abe.

"No fuckin' nothin' at home," Abe said. His voice was distinctly nasal. He was not as tall as Jeremy, but equally gangly, with a beaklike nose and jug ears, slack mouth, red-brown hair in a faux hawk. He wore a gray hoody and droopy pants.

"I still think we could bring a TV up here to the gym," Evan said, "and my PlayStation. Use the generator power here . . ."

"We asked, they won't let us, I don't know why," Abe said. "Sucks. So boring. Fucking PSP gone dead now."

"Those guys up on the hill, man," Jeremy said, "they're partying with the chronic up there and they're gonna shoot people . . ."

"It's so boring at home, can't even text, no cells, no Web, no PlayStation, no way to charge my iPod . . ."

Evan said, "Tired of reading my old comics. We could play Beer Pong. If we had some beer. But we don't. I've seen Beer Pong on YouTube. Always wanted to play it. But hey—we could, like, get electricity going, then we could get PlayStation going. We could scrounge a generator somewhere."

"Where?" Abe said. "They're all taken, we looked already."

"Those guys are just killing people if they feel like it . . ." Jeremy went on dreamily, his voice barely audible.

Did he really say that, in that admiring way? Russ shook his head in wonder and sickened fascination.

Abe snorted. "Fucking people are dead all over town and up and down the coast, don't make much difference. My mom—"

He broke off, staring. They were all staring at the door to the gym where Mario Ferrara was walking in, looking glum and pale. Not wearing that fireman's coat any more. Just a plaid shirt. Dried blood discoloring the sleeve of his left arm.

"Some stuff to tell you," he said.

"What happened, Mario?" Brand asked.

Mario leaned against the wall, legs out straight. "I was looking for some liquor, in one of the empty apartments, and, uh, I heard some guys coming. Heard Sten's voice and I wasn't close to my gun." He licked his cracked lips. "So I hid. I heard some women yelling. I looked out the window . . . and I saw them dragging off a couple of your women. My brother wasn't with them. It was Sten and the Grummons and Cholo. They took that Pendra girl and Jill. If anybody's interested."

EIGHTEEN

Russ was pretty sure Mario wasn't lying, but he had to look in Gram's apartment anyway, to see if Pendra was there. Crossing through the gathering gloom to the downstairs apartment, he saw the door was broken in. Feeling a bottomless dropping feeling in his middle, Russ hurried through the door, stepping in over the splintered panels. Inside, a Coleman lantern hanging awkwardly from a curtain rod over the window showed him an overturned coffee table, a broken vase, broken teapot and broken cups, red silk tulips scattered beside Pendra's purse, which was turned inside out like a gutted animal in the middle of the floor.

He felt a stickiness sucking at his shoes as he took another step—and looked down, realizing he'd stepped in a splash of blood, about the size and shape of a hand, on the hardwood floor near the front door.

He looked through the apartment. It seemed to have been searched—drawers emptied onto the floor.

There was no one there. Pendra and Jill were gone.

He returned to the living room, to stare at the blood, as Dale came in and glanced around. Dale patted him on the shoulder, went and looked in the other rooms, and came back.

"I already looked," Russ said. "Mario's not lying."

"I was hoping maybe they were hiding in a closet or something."

Russ shook his head. Feeling like his head was heavy on his neck—as if it suddenly weighed forty pounds.

219

"When are we going?" Russ asked.

Dale looked at him, eyes hooded. "You mean what I think?"

"Just a question of when, today or tonight or tomorrow. I'd like to go right now."

Dale shook his head. "Not yet."

Then Russ saw the piece of paper in his hand. "This was stuck on the refrigerator," Dale said. He passed it over.

It was a note written in blue ballpoint ink, in a neat blocky hand.

They are good for tonight and maybe tomorrow. Then we start to use them up.

Day after that, they're going to die. So by noon the day after tomorrow. OR! You can deliver everything of value to us. Jewelry is good, high quality electronics, pharm painkillers, luxury cars, cash. When we decide that we've gotten enough, you can have these two lady loves back.

On the other side of the piece of paper, in the same hand, was an address and the words:

Bring it to this address. Only one of you can come with each vehicle. Keep hands in sight.

"That address," Dale said, "is where we saw Dickie and that bunch are hanging out. Just above the wave line. House is half stoved in . . . "

"You think this was done by . . . I mean . . . this doesn't sound like Mayor Ferrara. He's an asshole but . . . "

"Mario says his brother wasn't in on this. Says he feels like his brother is dead by now. No—this isn't Lon Ferrara doing this, Russ. This is just Dickie Rockwell's bunch . . . " He took the paper, folded it up, put it in his pocket. "We got the choice of seeing if they're happy with what we give them, whatever that is," Dale said, "or we can try to take the girls back by force. They're giving us a day to get all the valuables their little drug-baked brains can imagine. But . . . "

"They'll never give the women back the easy way, whatever we pay them," Russ said, with a deep inner certainty.

Dale nodded. "That's right. They've given us a little time. And we'll need some preparation."

"Whatever we do—let's keep it to as few people as possible. I don't trust that dipshit Lars."

Dale nodded. "But you know what we have to do, don't you?"

Russ thought about Pendra, how she was feeling right now. He thought about his father, lying sprawled in a crevice, that night.

He thought: *I feel squeezed into this. Pushed into it. But I can't look away anymore. I can't pretend anymore. It is what it fucking is.*

The compass needle spun inside him. He knew which way north was.

"HERE'S WHAT I THINK," Nella said, sitting down on the cold floor next to the older woman, handing her the bottled water. The older one wearing the thick glasses was Jill; Nella knew her from around town. The other was Pendra. "I think we're in the end of the first part of the scary movie."

Pendra and Jill were chained up on the concrete floor of the chilly, mostly empty garage, their legs stretching into a greasy spot, their backs leaning against the washer and dryer. There was a little slack in their chains so they could just manage to lay down in a clumsy way if they wanted. The lady was wearing jeans too short for her and a coat, buttoned up; the girl wore a paisley frock, like something an old hippy would wear, with red leggings.

They both looked angry and Pendra looked like she'd been crying, her eyes red and puffy.

They passed the bottle of water. Pendra scowled suspiciously at Nella. Just because she wasn't chained up like them.

"If you're helping those guys," Pendra said, "you're even stupider than they are."

"I'm not helping them. I'm just *here*. I've *been* here." She couldn't think how to explain. "I think my mom put me here."

The only light was on the wall behind them. The generator chugged from the side yard. Pendra was examining the chrome-coated chains—not the biggest links Nella had ever seen, but hard to break. Loops of chain were tight around their wrists, closed with padlocks through the links, one small padlock under each woman's wrist. The chains ran behind them to wind around the appliances and heavy pipes.

Nella thought Pendra was wasting her time, trying to figure it out. Tools in the garage well out of reach. They had almost no slack. Just enough to raise their hands to their mouths and drink.

Pendra's wrists were already bleeding from where she'd tried to pull out of the chains. Jill's wrists weren't bleeding. Maybe she was thinking about things in a more patient way. Mature people and all.

But her right eye was black, where someone had punched her, and there was blood on her fingernails and under her nose. She'd fought, and they'd beaten her when they'd picked her up.

"I'm sorry I don't have any food for you," Nella said. Glad of someone to talk to. "Maybe they'll let me bring you some food later. They don't let me do too much. We used to be different. But after the wave they just decided I was . . . " She didn't want to say it.

"Why don't you just help us?" Pendra whispered, looking at Nella. "They don't treat you any good. We'll get you out of here."

"Well, now, it's a question of how a person wants to die," Nella said. "If I help you they'll chain me up and make me die slowly. Randle Grummon said he'd set me on fire and watch me burn and flop around. Now, if I wait, I'll just get shot or . . . well, I'm afraid of killing myself." She shifted on the floor, trying to get comfortable. Hard with the burning pain between her legs. "Anyway—"

"Are you sick?" Jill asked. "You look feverish. You should be the one drinking this water."

"I found some ibuprofen. I took that. I'm . . . I've got an infection."

She saw that Pendra was staring at a metal toolbox sitting on a wooden shelf next to a tire rim and an old car battery on the other side of the garage. Completely out of their reach. The girl was probably thinking about using those tools on her chains.

Nella was afraid Pendra would ask her to get the tool kit for her. She was afraid she might do it. And be punished for it. She was also afraid she might not do it. And be punished in another way for that.

So she went hastily on: "But listen, listen, let me explain my idea: I just figured this out today. How in scary movies they usually start out with everything okay for the people who are the heroes of the movie. Usually early in the movie, they are okay, they're with their family and everything's fine. Or they're in a situation where they can, like, pretend it is. But then the monster comes and it kills and kills, right? See, the story wouldn't be any good if it just *started* with the monster killing everyone, you got to set them up. I mean in some movies they give you a *sample killing* out front but not for the hero. And that's what the world is. The world starts out pretty okay for most people, and then they get sick or beat up or tortured or else just trapped somewhere and just they die all disappointed. It's a setup, this whole world, see." She paused, wondering if they would understand her. Figuring they wouldn't. But she had to try, now she'd gone this far with it. "See, this world has to start out okay so the demons can enjoy it when it's all taken away from you . . . but the part where things are good is gone for us, for you guys and me and everyone else in town here, and now we're in the killing and killing part that the demons like. It's just easier to see that and say, that's how it is. Okay? That's how it is. So now the setup part is over . . . "

"Nella!" It was Dickie, in the doorway. "Stop your fucking babbling and get away from those bitches. Come on, get in here and cook us something! Be useful for one fucking minute!"

Nella got up and went in the kitchen. She heard Jill say, "Something like Stockholm Syndrome, maybe."

She sensed the two women, Pendra and Jill, staring after her. She knew they thought she was crazy. That they were disgusted that she couldn't say she'd help them.

She couldn't get the keys to those locks to help those girls anyway. They were all going to be killed by the demons.

It was just a question of how. The part where you pretend you're going to be okay was over.

NINETEEN

Russ couldn't sleep. Alone now, Russ walked back and forth in his dad's living room between candles that fluttered when he passed. Trying to believe that Pendra and Jill were safe, at least for tonight. Telling himself that the message Dickie had left wasn't a lie.

He'd spent six hours with Dale, dry firing a Browning 12-gauge shotgun and the Winchester 92 replica, loading and unloading them. Getting friendly with the weapons as much as he could without firing live ammo. *This Winchester is a working replica of the rifle John Browning made for Winchester in 1892. This one's made by an Italian company—works pretty much the same as the '75 that tamed the frontier, as they say, but it's a little slicker . . .*

Vaguely wondering about his Dad's will. Then embarrassed that he was already wondering about it. Then remembering: *Hell, I should have been a janitor, anything, to stay closer to you.*

And then his father's last spoken syllable. Ever.

Russ . . .

He looked at amateur photos, framed and hanging on the wall. Photos his dad had taken of wild birds, especially sea birds. Looked at his books on birds and sea animals. Stopped at his father's neatly organized collection of CDs and records. Saw Roy Loney and the Phantom Movers, saw Hank Williams, saw Carl Perkins, Johnny Cash, Loretta Lynn, the Holy Modal Rounders, George Jones; saw Country Swing Favorites. The CDs were in a columnar CD rack, the records in unvarnished wooden cabinets beside an old boom box and a dusty record player. On top of the record cabinet was an old mono cassette player. On impulse, he pressed the play button. The batteries still worked: he heard a badly recorded acoustic guitar, just finishing some twangy song, and then a smatter of applause. And his father's voice saying, "Thank you. That was by Johnny Cash. This one's an early number by George Jones . . . "

Russ listened, amazed at hearing his father sing into a microphone, probably at some open mike, doing a pretty fair job with an old country song describing a cause and effect relationship between involvement with women and too much drinking.

"Wish I was doing too much drinking, Dad," Russ said. "But you got not a drop in the house."

He listened to the rest of the tape, savoring his dad's obvious gratification at the patter of applause. He decided that he'd take it with him, if he got out of this town alive.

He shook his head, marveling. He'd known his father could play a few songs on guitar, but he'd had no idea he'd performed anywhere. He felt an ache, vaguely remembering his dad trying to get him to check out some of these records. His dad had sent him a mix of his favorite songs—he'd never listened to it. It had been a chance to know his dad deeper, another side of him. A person's favorite music was a window into them. His dad had shown him the window and he hadn't bothered to look through it.

They were his records now. He'd listen to them, by himself, alone in some room somewhere.

He picked up a plate with two half-melted candles on it, carried it into his dad's bedroom. Not sure what he was looking for.

Pretty late to get to know him now, dumbass, he thought. But it was better than not at all.

Everything Is Broken

He looked through the bedroom. Bed was made, dirty clothes in hamper, everything in its place, Dad was always much neater than he was. Russ had taken after his mom—not the worst housekeeper in Ohio, but in the running.

There were two framed pictures of him as a kid on the dresser, one with Dad, one sitting in a pedal-operated kiddie car on Christmas morning. Beaming.

Another picture of Russ hung on the wall: Russ graduating from high school. A look on his face like he resented having to pose in the green high school grad robe. An adolescent's smug irony. But the photo was framed.

Russ thought he might sleep in here tonight. He carried the candle to the desk in the corner—and saw a letter in the middle of the desk, addressed to his mother. Stamp on it. Unmailed.

Should he? Maybe he should just give it to her, unopened. If he saw her again.

But he sat down and opened it. Squinted in the wobbly pool of light to read his dad's slanted handwriting.

> . . . Sorry about writing this by hand, but you know me and computers, it's enough to have to deal with one for work. Hope you're doing well and Ray too. The boy's coming tomorrow. I can't sleep, thought I'd write you a note about him, put my thoughts in order. If ever there was a silver lining for whatever's happened with you guys, this is it, because he and I have needed to spend some time for a while.
>
> I don't need to repeat my regrets to you. We've each recited our regrets a few times and that's enough. I think Russell knows we both love him and we both care about each other and always will. I want you to know I'm going to say nothing but positive things about

*you to him and that's how I feel, not just putting on a
front. Life can be really hard to live with and I think
we're coming to a place where we know better than to
judge each other harshly.*

*Russell is still a little short of being a man, whatever
his age—I was a slow starter growing up, myself—but
I know he'll get there, he'll find his independence when
he gets a little confidence and he'll be okay with us
when he realizes that people just do the best they can,
with their marriages and their kids, and their lives.
I've got a lot of faith in him and I hope you and I and
Russ and Karen and Ray and your sister and everyone
can have Thanksgiving dinner together this year. I'm
talking like Russ is a little kid who needs those things
but somehow I feel like there's a lot he has to work out
and that will help.*

*I am pretty sure I've got a job arranged for him. I've
got some cash in a drawer I'm going to give him, saved
it up to help him get a car. I think he'll like California.
Freedom has its peculiarities but this is nice country.
You should visit sometime.*

*Well, my hand is cramping up but I knew you were
probably having second thoughts about him coming
out here so I just wanted to tell you I'm sure he'll have
a great new start but he's never going to forget the
people he loves in Ohio . . .*

"Jesus fucking Christ," Russ said, out loud. " 'Short of being
a man.' "

He thought about the phrase, *Life can be hard to live with . . .*
Seemed corny at first, but the more he thought about it, the
more he agreed.

He read the letter through again. *I think Russell knows we both love him and we both care about each other and always will.*

He hadn't known it, not really. For some reason, when his parents let him know that they loved him, he was always skeptical that it was real, that it was more than just obligation. Russ realized he'd stopped trusting them, somehow, when they'd broken up. Like he'd thought that if they'd gotten divorced, they must've been lying about their feelings for each other all along, so they were lying about their feelings for him.

But it occurred to him, now, that something broken was still real. Who knows what they'd gone through, with each other, in private?

He was especially surprised at the tone of tenderness his dad showed toward his mother in the letter. His dad taking care to reassure her that he still had feelings for her. He didn't seem to be trying to get back with her—he acknowledged her current boyfriend, Ray—it was more like he was saying that they'd always have something and somehow that should be important to Russ.

It was important to him, he realized. Some little kid in him wanted his parents to love each other.

He folded the letter up, put it back in the envelope, stuck it in his coat. If he got through tomorrow, he'd take it to her, himself.

He's still a little short of being a man . . .

Russ sighed, and shook his head. That was what he got for reading his father's private letter to his mother.

But it was true.

He went to lie down on the bed. There was an extra comforter at the end of the bed and he pulled it up and over his shoulders.

He found himself imagining what it was like for Pendra now. Dickie, the Grummons, Sten—they could be doing anything to her. Doing it right now. This moment.

It took him another hour and a half to fall asleep.

Russ and Dale and Brand, packs on their backs, weapons strapped to their shoulders, threaded the path through the boulders to the beach.

The sea rumbled; the wind soughed. But the breeze was from the south, the sun was out, and it was warmer than usual for this time of year.

Close to the highway, the beach was like the place at the end of time where flotsam from some swatch of history had washed up. The great wave had deposited cars and trucks of half-a-dozen makes, furniture swathed in seaweed that had dried into green cellophane, several desks from several eras, shelves of disintegrating books, an entire shack turned on its side that might've been from almost any era, a 1960s refrigerator, splintery sections of wooden fences, boxes of all kinds, mattresses, traffic lights, a dead medium-sized yellow dog, the carcasses of seals chewed at by gulls and crabs, a wide selection of rotting fish—and this was after a great deal of debris had washed back out to sea.

Closer to the breakers, the beach was clearer, the fug of decay swept almost clear by the wind. Seabirds wheeled overhead. A pelican balanced on a tilted chunk of house that stood pyramid-like about a hundred yards offshore. Russ wondered if there were bodies in it. Not much left of them by now.

"Maybe we should get a burial detail out here, after all," Brand said, nodding toward a scrabbling, fighting cluster of seagulls a hundred feet down. They could just see the birds tearing at the shreds of flesh remaining on a skeletal human leg that stuck out from under an unidentifiable slab of wooden wreckage.

"Well," Dale said, "if those remains are still there after the next tide, we'll try and get 'em out, but good luck identifying 'em. Unless you want to pull 'em out now."

Brand shook his head. "Let's do what we came to do."

An old, splintery armoire lay face down, half buried in the sand. They took off their backpacks, they had a little food in them but mostly ammo. Dale laid the ammo out on the wood of the armoire, well clear of the sand. Everyone unstrapped their weapons, set them carefully next to the ammo.

The weapons and ammo had been stored at Dale's, locked up in the basement. There was the Winchester 92, the 12-gauge, the 30.06 rifle, and Dale took a .45 caliber semi-automatic handgun out of his backpack and held it up. "This pistol's already loaded, so be careful of it. Now—let's load the others. Keep the safeties on for now and whether or not safety's on or they're loaded you keep them pointed at the ocean, away from one another. You don't turn them toward anyone you're not willing to kill."

Dale picked up the short rifle. "Now, Russ, I'm giving you this Winchester, and when I say giving it, I mean I'm going to sign it over to you, and you'll have to get it registered if you . . . when you leave town. When we were picking out guns at my place, that night, your dad looked at this one, but I was a little reluctant to let it out of the house. I think he liked the old fashioned look. So I want you to have it." He looked out to sea, cleared his throat. "I sure liked your father, Russ, so . . . "

"Thanks." Russ was moved in a way that felt distinctive to the gift. "Thanks a lot, Dale."

"Now we practiced loading it, this one takes a .44 . . . let's put the magazine in . . . Now what do you remember from last night about that lever?"

"That . . . lots of people take the gun from their shoulder to work the lever, but you said not to, keep it there, get used to it that way, keeps it readier to fire . . . "

"Right. First thing you need to work on, of course—like we talked about last night—is a good gun mount. Got to have it just right on your shoulder, and in your hands. Here, nestled like that. Right. Let's try it. Lever a round in. Good. Now you line up the back sights and the front on your target, and aim a little low because—especially with a light rifle like this—it'll rise when you squeeze the trigger. Aim it at that plastic jug floating out there, see it? Don't try to fire it yet. Just practice lowering the front sight onto the target, lining up the sights . . . Okay, let's take the safety off."

Brand looked up toward the houses on the northernmost hill overlooking the beach. "I kind of wonder if we'll tip our hand, shooting down here. For one thing, we might attract 'em to come and fuck with us. For another—we put them on guard."

"Got no choice," Dale said, as he fussed over the guns. "Those dumb pricks have seen us with guns—they didn't seem worried then. They'll just figure we're practicing defensively, same way we're carrying the guns. But just the same, when I'm working with one of you, the other one watch for those sons of bitches. At least there's plenty of cover down here. I doubt they'd rush us across the beach. Let's find a target,"

"Maybe we should shoot those damn gulls eating that person," Russ suggested.

"They're just being gulls. But let's fire near them, to practice, chase 'em off. Then we can dump some sand on the remains. Now, when you fire—do it between breaths."

The first time he fired the Winchester, at a snag of lumber near the feeding gulls, making them rise squawking into the air, the rifle's recoil wasn't too bad. But as he continued firing, it soon bruised his shoulder. There was not even a faint chance he was going to complain about that to these two men.

"You got to work with that recoil," Dale said. "Let it pop up a little, lever a round in, bring it back down. Now the best way to shoot is to be as relaxed as possible while still controlling the gun. Hard to do at first because you're going to tense up in anticipation of the gun going off, and the bang and all. But fire it enough and you can do it. We got a lot of ammo here. I got more at the house. Now, when you've got a moving target, like that jug, you want to pick the front of the target, whichever way it's going, aim toward that. You got to move the gun with the target. Now that jug's moving quite a bit in the wave, that'll be good. Stay with it. Track it smoothly. *Squeeze* that trigger, don't pull it . . . See, that's too high . . . Focus on the target, not on the end of the gun.

"You've got to line up but trust yourself to aim. Let your hands follow your eyes. It takes a lot of tries. If it feels like your shoulder is swelling up and coming out of joint you've only fired half enough rounds. You need to fire a lot of rounds to get a feel for it . . . Now while he's reloading we'll start you on that thirty-ought-six . . . Brand and you're both going to get a feel for the shotgun and the revolver . . . "

Hours passed. As the day wore on, Dale could see Russ wincing when the gun cracked into his shoulder, so he declared a rest. "Best let the swelling go down some."

They sat on the edge of the armoire, their backs to the wind, eating cold chili out of cans with plastic spoons, drinking bottled water, watching the hilly streets coming down to the debris-strewn highway. Half expecting Dickie's bunch. Seeing no one.

"I almost hate to turn my back on the sea," Brand said. "I don't trust it any more than I trust Dickie. It's not fair. It was kind to me all my life till a few days ago. But that's how I feel. Gonna take awhile to get over it."

Russ nodded. "I know what you mean." He gazed down the beach, thinking it surreal. Seeing someone's old trunk on a sewing dummy next to a rotting mattress. "Like every attic in the world emptied out here." After a moment he said, "You know—this time tomorrow—they could be dumping our bodies right here on this beach. We could all three be dead. Right here." He felt a pang of embarrassment, thinking he shouldn't have said that. It didn't sound manly.

"I was thinking along the same lines," Brand said, chuckling. "But . . . " He closed his eyes. His voice was solemn. "We have to do this. Or not. There's no in-between. Not with things the way they are. Not with Dickie Rockwell. It's all or nothing."

Dale glanced at Russ, then away. Something on his mind. Finally he said, "You going to be up for this, Russ? I mean—we got to face two big things. The good chance we might get killed. Shot dead, if we're lucky. That's one. And two—if we don't get killed, *we got to kill other people.* We got to end their lives. It's easy to *say* you'll do that. But unless you're some kind of . . . psychopath, or something—it's not that easy to do when you're right there in the moment. To just . . . shoot a man dead. In boot camp they train you up in the idea. Doesn't help that much. But it's something. We haven't got time for that."

Russ's mouth felt dry. "Yeah. I've been sort of putting that off to the side. Not thinking about it—just trying to do what I have to."

"But it's there," Brand said. "I worry about it too—I've never killed anyone. I'm not sure I can do it. Except—we can't let them keep Jill and Pendra. We can't let them get away with shooting your dad down. Penning us in like sheep. I feel like—they're just going to slip away if we don't confront them. And they'll take the women with them—or kill them. I just—" He squeezed his eyes shut. Shook his head, then chuckled ruefully. "Not sure I can kill anyone."

"No point in going up there if you aren't willing to kill 'em," Dale said. "All you can do is think of it, like . . . it has to be done and it's going to *save* lives, really. And—you have to get mad enough to do it. You have to get in that state of mind. You have to get mad enough to send that bullet *right through* another man. Do anything to get past him. That man's in the way of what you really, truly got to do. He's hurting your people. Got to keep it that simple in your mind. And as for dying . . . " He exhaled noisily. Cleared his throat, grimaced at some memory. "We all die. I watched a bunch of people die. In war and at home. My folks—I was with them when they died. Comes to all of us."

" 'All beings are invisible before birth and after death are once more invisible,' " Brand said softly.

Dale looked at him with raised eyebrows. "That a quote?"

"The Bhagavad Gita," Brand said, scooping a handful of sand, letting it spill back down through his fingers. "Somebody wrote that down around 500 BC."

Dale turned to Russ again. "Tell you what, man, I hate to talk a young man into risking himself. That's been done way too much. So you decide. If you're going with us—you have to take that attitude the Indians had: It's a good day to die. You want to do this thing, be ready to face that, *Today I might die.* If you're not ready to die—you're more likely to. If you're right in the fight, I mean." He paused to think about it. "How we got through it, when I was in a firefight, was like this: You don't take stupid risks—but you got to go for it, and say, *Maybe today I die. So be it.*" He paused, and nodded. "Just: *So be it.*"

Russ nodded. It was like there'd been a space in him, waiting for that: *Maybe today I die. So be it.* And that space was filled now. He felt a new orientation around it.

Dale rubbed his forehead. "But if you take stupid risks—you're not going to get the job done. You need the willingness to die if you have to, but if you throw it away—it's all a goddamn waste."

Brand said, "The hard part for me is killing another man. That expression, 'taking a life.' People use it so casually. It's a burdensome thing to even think about, for me anyway. But I feel like—we don't have a choice. Not this time."

It made simple, visceral sense to Russ. He took it in, and made it part of him. But there was something he had to say anyhow.

Russ put the chili can down in the sand, and shifted to face Dale. Wondering how to say what he had to say. His shoulder ached as he turned. He took a deep breath.

"Dale—here's the thing . . . They're expecting us to bring a load of stuff up there. Like, this evening or tomorrow. Right? It's possible we could bring it. And maybe if they see the stuff . . . "

Brand and Dale exchanged surprised glances.

"You're saying maybe they'll give us the women after all?" Dale looked at him with raised eyebrows. "You're saying—just play their game? Just . . . give them the stuff? Well, I never thought you'd want to go that way . . . "

The gulls shrieked mournfully, sounding disappointed in him.

TWENTY

NELLA KNEW for certain-sure that the demons were whispering, when Dickie brought crystal meth out, that morning in Mario's house. Dickie woke up after just four hours—the men had gone to sleep at dawn, drunk, getting plastered when the Grummons came back from their watch on the pass. Relieved when Lucas and Chuckles and Remo went grumbling back out to take their place. They were all drunk except Sten, who seemed nervous, wary. He stayed mostly sober. Watching at the windows for Mario.

She'd gotten blankets and pillows for the two women in the garage, but she doubted they'd slept much. She felt them judging her every time they saw her.

God will judge me, she'd told them. She'd heard her Mama's voice: *For we must all be manifested before the judgment seat of Christ, that every one may receive the proper things of the body, according as he hath done . . .*

Sten had a hard time keeping the Grummons and Steve away from the women. "We need the hostages intact," he said.

Dickie supported him. But Nella figured Dickie was just keeping Pendra for himself. "Soften her up, keeping her out there, that way she'll be ready to play nice," he said once.

Nella couldn't sleep much. She was lying there listening to the gulls yelling. She tried to work out the messages in their squawk. Closed her eyes and pretended to be asleep when Dickie'd come

237

out of the back bedroom around ten; she'd heard him drag the ladder around the side of the house, climb up onto the roof; heard him stomping around up there talking to himself. She figured he was looking out to sea, up there.

Then he came down and went stalking through the house, yelling, "Okay, that's it, we're getting ready to fucking rock, no more ball-scratching! Get your fucking lazy pink-pussy asses up!"

And he pulled out the baggy of yellow-white crystal meth and waved it under the Grummons's noses, and in front of Mike Sten, who rolled his eyes. Cholo had a look like he wanted to tell Dickie to forget it but then he stared at the meth and said, "What the fuck. Maybe I won't feel this hangover anymore." And Steve, waking up, ran to the bathroom, vomited loudly, came back, clapped his hands together once and said, "Okay, let's do it."

"We got a shitload of stuff happening today," Dickie said, leading them into the kitchen. "Either they bring us the goods or we go get 'em."

"Look at how yellow this shit is, only half processed," Liddy Grummon said.

"Shut up," Dickie said, chopping it up with a buck knife, "it'll work just fine."

"Lot of shooting down on the beach yesterday," Sten said, as they gathered around the kitchen table where Dickie laid out the crystal meth. Nella stayed in the next room, huddled in her sleeping bag, but she watched and listened through the door to the kitchen.

"So what, some assholes target shooting," Dickie said. "Not going to do those snaky little bitches any good."

"Which snaky little bitches, the ones in the garage or the ones over at that high school gym?" Randle Grummon asked, laughing and then wincing because his hangover made it hurt to laugh, right then.

"Not none of them," Dickie said, rolling up a ten-dollar bill. " 'Cause I got the word from out past the edge of the world."

"That what you were doing on the roof?" Sten asked. "Woke up and heard you stomping around."

Dickie gave him a hard look. "You got some kind of issue with that?"

Sten shook his head, and yawned. Always smart enough not to let any friction with Dickie escalate. "No. Served us well."

"I got word that today we take action," Dickie said, and snorted up a long line of the shitty yellow crystal meth, right off the dirty table top. "*Fuck* but that burns! What *shit!*" He laughed shrilly and snorted up some more. "Here. We're gonna wake up on this shit and be ready. Because when it comes from the edge of the world, it picks me up—that's what that wave was, that was me calling it from the edge of the world, that was *me* kicking this town's ass, that's what that fucking tidal wave was, strong as a bar of steel, fucking skull-ring-certain, bro, we're getting lifted up and carried on to the next place but we're going in the best cars in this fucking hole of a town—"

Going on like that, speed rapping for a while. The others shaking off their hangovers with speed. Complaining of the burn but whoofing up more and more of the shit. *The Shit, in fact, was what meth was called, in a lot of places; people liked to snort up The Shit and wasn't that kind of funny?* Nella thought.

But when they offered her some she just mumbled, "No. Not feeling too good. Have to rest." She'd figured on getting some, before—but now she didn't want any. She thought it might kill her, the way she felt now, all sick and dragged out, and she didn't want to die that way. She was counting on a bullet in the head. Or maybe she'd drown herself, if she got up the nerve.

"Better get your ass up and wash or something," Dickie told her. "You look like shit. It's kind of makin' me queasy."

She got up, wincing at the pain, then paused at the door—thinking maybe she should have some meth after all. And at the same time not wanting it. Wavering.

"What we oughta fuckin' do," Steve was saying, real fast, a quiet guy gone all bold on speed, "is we should go check out the houses like two blocks north of here, you know some of those houses, shit man, some of those fancy-ass fucking houses look like they've been hardly touched—"

"We went through most of the empty houses, and some not so empty, before you got here," Dickie said, snorting up a lot less meth than the others. He grimaced at the burn. "Ow. Shit. Yeah, we checked that block out, we got a lot of stuff from there, I don't think anyone's there—lot of the residents are sort of hiding out at the high school—"

"Tell you something," Cholo said, rubbing his nose after a line. "Tell you something. Tell you what, I scouted over there a bit, yesterday, when we were looking for that Mario asshole, and I came down out of the woods a little too far north, and I seen some people look out their windows on some fucking street over there—uhhhhh, *Breezy*, Breezy Street it was called." They were all looking at him with fascination because he didn't talk much normally, even less than Steve.

"Ha," Sten said. "Breezy Street." What was funny about that wasn't clear.

"So I figure, tell you what," Cholo went on, rubbing a shaky hand on his bleeding nose, "they're in there, they got all their stuff in there. What stuff I don't know—but they got a Jaguar out front, nice looking Jag . . . "

"Now that's a real possibility, there, Cholo," Dickie said. "It could be that we'll send a coupla official representatives of the militia over there—"

"Ha," Sten said. "Militia."

"It *is* a fucking militia," Dickie said, slapping the table. "Not because Ferrara called it that—he was an asshole."

"Yeah, I'm glad we're not going to see that guy again," Sten said. "Hypocrite. I don't do high-fives. But if I did, I'd high-five you for shooting that fuck."

"Consider yourself non-high-fived," Dickie said, and they laughed. "But I'm just sayin', why *shouldn't* we be a militia? Militia for our own little nation-state. Let me take another hit of this toxic nose-rot and think this through a little . . . "

Cholo jumped to his feet, reaching for his gun. "Fuck!"

The others tensed, seeing what he'd seen—the face at the window of the back door. Two of the panes had been shot through, were patched with plywood, and he looked through the third: It was Lars, the old stoner with the dreads. Yelling, "Hey! I gotta . . . !" Something, something, she couldn't make it out from here.

"Sten," Dickie said, fractionally relaxing.

"Yeah." Sten got up, pulling his gun out, looked out the window to either side past Lars, then out toward the woods. Didn't seem to see anyone back there either. Then he opened the door a crack. "What?"

"They're up to some shit," Lars said. "What you got? You got any opium? I've got this craving on for opium. I used to go down to Santa Cruz, there was a guy down there, he had a connection came in from Vietnam—"

"Stop fucking babbling," Sten said. "Opium! Ha! What do you think this is, a fucking opium den? We're all sitting around in a haze listening to Chinese gongs?"

This was a lot of gassing for Sten, and the others laughed at it. They were all pretty fucked up, seemed to Nella.

"Ask him what he's got for us," Dickie said, toying with the meth, sniffling. A little blood ran from one of his nostrils.

Lars heard and shoved his head a little way in the door to answer. "Um, not sure, but they're like shooting at target shit and they won't talk to me and I know you gotta deal with them and I dunno but . . . it's all, like, kinda, fucked up, but . . . maybe they're cool but, uh, dunno . . . "

He went rattling on like that, not really coherent.

"I want him out of here," Dickie said. "First, close the door."

Sten closed the door sharply, almost catching Lars's nose in it. The men laughed.

Dickie gestured for Sten to come close. She couldn't make out all of what he whispered. Something about the woods. Don't trust the fucker. Knows stuff. Runs his mouth too much. Walk him out. Don't be long.

Sten nodded, sticking his pistol in his waistband. He went to the door, opened it, gently pushed Lars away from it as he stepped through. "Gonna show you some big pot plants we got in the woods, you can, like, cultivate that shit for us," Sten said. "You can . . . "

Couldn't hear the rest as he closed the door and, one hand on the old stoner's arm, escorted him into the woods. They were hidden behind the trees.

"Open the back door so I can hear it," Dickie said.

Cholo, still standing, went to the door, opened it, and came back to his chair. Seemed to have to think about it, before sitting down. Sit or stand, sit or stand, could go either way. Finally he sat.

They didn't say anything for a minute—and then they heard the shot. A second shot. Not that far off. Just inside the woods. Another minute or two and Sten was walking back toward them, waving, all cheerful, grinning. Chore done.

"That was quick," Randle said. "Didn't bother to even stick 'im in a hole." He chuckled. "I hate those fake Rasta fuckers like that Lars."

Sten came in, gun back in his waistband. He closed the door, seeming thoughtful.

Dickie whoofed up another line, and then the doorbell rang.

They whipped their heads around with paranoid speed toward the front door. This was too many visitors in too short a time. Guaranteed to spin anyone whoofing meth.

"What the fuck!" Randle Grummon said, for everyone.

"We should've had a watch on the doors," Sten said, pulling the pistol from his belt.

"Maybe it's the high school gym people," Steve suggested. "With the stuff."

"Better not be," Dickie said, standing, pulling his own pistol and cocking it. "This isn't the address we gave 'em. That fucker Mario—might be him . . . "

"You think the cops are back in town?" Steve asked nervously.

"No. No way," Dickie said. "I'd know. It's not them. Authorities are dealing with like millions of people smashed by the wave in other towns, man. No. Nella—go see who it is."

She thought, *Maybe it's Mario and he'll shoot me.*

So she immediately got up and went, in her underwear and bare feet, and just unlocked the door and opened it, and stood right there in the doorway almost undressed, ready to be shot dead.

But no shotgun blast came. Instead, just the cool air on her feverish body and a rank sweaty smell off three pimply early-teen boys. They stood there blinking at her, their mouths hanging open. The pimpliest one had long blond hair and a Wolverine T-shirt; the tall gawky vulpine one wore a Necro T-shirt; the big-nosed one wore a dirty hoody. "Is Dickie here?" he asked.

"Who are you?" Nella asked.

It was the tall one who said, "I'm Jeremy. This is, uh, my brother Abe and this is, uh, Evan? And, uh, we're looking for

Dickie because we want to join up. With him. And . . . his thing. Just—join up with you guys. I mean, if this is the right place, if Dickie's here . . . "

"Who told you to come here?" she asked.

They all gawped at one another. "Uh—nobody."

"I mean—how'd you know about this place?" she asked.

"Oh that Mario guy was saying where it was. I mean—he used to live here, right?"

"Mario?" She'd been wondering about him. "What's he doing now?"

"Talking about killing you guys. But he just drinks a lot. He got some vodka somewhere and he's drinking it. He's not sharing it with no*body*."

"Okay." Nella saw they were staring at her body. She wasn't sure it was because it looked good to them. She knew she was emaciated now and she had some scabs. "Hold on."

She turned around and saw that Dickie was standing, his face twitching, gun in his hand, in the doorway to the kitchen. Gesturing for her to get out of the way.

She nodded and backed away, turning to see out the open front door, feeling bad for the short one in the Wolverine T-shirt. Nella wasn't sure why she felt bad for him and not the others but that's just the way it was.

She saw Sten walking up behind the three teenaged boys on the front porch, pistol in his hands stretched out at the end of his arms, pointing at them. "Who the fuck sent you here?" Sten demanded.

The boys spun around at that, jumping on the porch, all three of them, almost like they were doing The Wave. She almost laughed. Except she felt bad for that Evan kid.

"Uh—nobody sent us," Jeremy said.

"Nuh, dude, nobody." Evan said. "That a real gun?"

"What the fuck you think?" Abe said, "Course that's a real gun."

"Should we raise our hands?" Evan said.

"Yeah," Sten said. "You should. What do you mean nobody sent you?"

"That's what I'm wondering," Dickie said, making them spin around again, their hands raised. Spinning with their hands raised, it looked like a Broadway dance routine.

Maybe I should eat something, I'm getting all ditzy, Nella thought.

"Nobody told us," Jeremy insisted, shrugging. "We just . . . decided. But we can, you know—go away."

He was staring at the gun held loosely in Dickie's hand. It was not even pointed right at them. Dickie's confidence was scary enough.

Evan licked his thick lips and spoke up. "The thing is, we were . . . these guys thought . . . well, we were hella bored. Our fucking games *totally* don't work. We thought . . . "

Sten walked up behind them—snorting. "You wanted to join us. Because . . . you're *bored?*"

They whirled around in tandem again. "Yeah!" Jeremy said.

"Totally!" Evan said.

"For reals!" Abe said.

Dickie laughed, lowering his gun. "Makes perfect sense to me, Sten! No way these idiots were sent here by anyone. The Three Fucking Stooges here."

"Ha," Sten said. "Three Stooges!"

"Okay, Stooges," Dickie said. "Come in the house. *Entrez* your *vous* right the fuck in here."

He stood aside and waved them in and if it hadn't been for the gun it would have been like a butler making a welcoming gesture.

They came filing into the living room, gawking at Nella and at the Grummons and Steve and Cholo coming in from the kitchen.

"Nella!" Dickie snapped. "Put some fucking clothes on and clean yourself up, like I fucking told you to already. I never expected you to open the door *wide* and stand there in your fucking panties. Christ, what a whore."

She went to the hall closet where she kept a few things and got dressed and went to the bathroom, ignoring the smell of unflushed vomit in the toilet, and used the bucket of water to bathe and clean up a little. She found some ibuprofen and took three of them.

When she came out she found them all crowded into the kitchen, the grinning men standing around the owlish boys, who were sitting at the table—Jeremy trying to get the hang of snorting speed up his nose, the other two watching him, big lines of meth laid out on the table in front of them.

"Ow, shit! It hurts!"

"Ha," Sten said.

"What are you laughing at, Sten, that's what you said just a few minutes ago," Dickie observed. "Now you three—" His face was tightened into something between a wolfish grin and a stoned rictus as he regarded the teen boys. "You want to be part of it, you got to take the initiation!"

"Yeah!" Randle chimed in. "You said you were bored, right? Well, you're gonna be too fucked up to be bored!"

"Initiation!" Sten said. "Ha!"

Dickie caught the tip of his tongue between his teeth, tittering to himself. Even from here, Nella could feel the meth-energy vibes leaking out of the room, squiggling out across the floor like spastically dying eels. Dickie looking from one boy to the other, saying: "And the initiation starts with sucking up the really nasty bad shit right into your brain. It's going to fuck your brain all up just precisely the way we like it to be!"

Dickie grabbed Abe and Evan by the hair, from behind, one kid's head in each hand, and he shook their heads around by their hair, and high-beamed at Jeremy. "You look like you're getting there. Now these two!" Then he shoved Abe and Evan's heads down so their faces went right into the meth powder. The other men hooted with laughter and Dickie yelled, "Snort it up, get it, get it, get it!"

"Get it get it get it get it get!" the other men chanted.

Faces mashed in the caustic meth, the boys started coughing and struggling. Dickie held them a few more long moments, then let them go—they straightened up, wheezing, cheap yellow meth—like urine crystals—stuck to their faces, their hands shaking.

"Now you can be just as fucked up as your pal here," Randle said.

"Jeremy was already pretty fucked up in the head, before we got here," Abe said, his teeth chattering, nose running red from the shit, wiping at his eyes. "Without any . . . Oh, this *stuff* . . . oh, my fucking *God* . . . "

"Ho ho ho!" Cholo said, barking it out, his teeth clacking from his own speed hit. " 'Oh, my fucking God' he says! It's hitting him now."

"And, and," Jeremy said, breathing hard, looking around with a kind of translucent sweat-sheen of desperation, "and, and we just came from our house, checking out our mom's body again, and we showed it to Evan here."

"Yuh, their mom's body is hanging in the rafter of their house," Evan said, through chattering teeth. "The wave left it there and it's all twisted up, up, up and they were just, like, all like, like 'Dude, that's our moms up there, check it out, ha ha.'

You know, all fucking 'ha ha!' " His upper body heaved; he made a gagging sound. "Hey, I think I might throw up now."

"Throw up in the sink there if you got to!" Sten said.

Evan lurched up from the table and vomited in the kitchen sink and everyone in the room howled with laughter and applauded and he laughed and choked on it as more vomit came up and they hooted and clapped their hands again.

"Important to get that done," Steve said, laughing softly. "I did mine this morning."

"Liddy," Dickie said suddenly, "you stay here and watch the house. Sten, you're gonna take some of this shit to the boys at the bonfire, on the road east. Here . . . Here's another baggy for 'em. And take that walkie-talkie thing of Ferrara's, in case I got to call you. I want everybody on the same wavelength, more fucking ways than one. You others, we're taking these boys to check out that house on Breezy Street, Cholo's gonna show us where it is and the Three Stooges here are gonna have some more initiation . . . Nella, you come with us, you're gonna initiate these teeny-boys a different way."

She winced. They were probably going to make her have sex with these boys. That was going to be unpleasant—and it would hurt too. She hoped she could just do blow jobs.

TWENTY-ONE

PENDRA FELT like she was going to go lose her mind in this clammy, dim, dingy garage; that her mind was going to be stuck in here, maybe up in that spidery dusty dark corner of the garage ceiling, stuck there forever. She felt a blunt amazement that no one had come to rescue them. She was starting to believe they never would come. Her wrists burned and ached.

For about the sixth time, she said, "Jill, there has to be a way to get out of these chains. If we both pull on the pipes long enough we can wrench something loose!"

"Last time we tried to pull out the pipes, they heard us," said Jill, with maddening reasonableness. "When they were drunk last night, Dickie came in and kicked you in the stomach. So if they can hear a noise and check on us when they're drunk . . . I mean, it'd take awhile, and by the time we got the pipes halfway pulled out, they'd be in here. Maybe if they'd all leave the house but I don't think they'll go all together. Some of them left for a while but there's others . . . "

Pendra felt like hitting the older woman. "Jill—there *has* to be a way to get *out of these fucking chains!*"

"Pendra, girl, listen to me—" Jill's voice soft, though Pendra could see the strain in Jill's face. "We are going to do this a different way. I think. I have an idea that if we wait for our moment—"

She broke off when the door from the kitchen into the garage opened and Liddy Grummon came in.

Pendra shrank back. She was afraid of him. A long flexible face, that seemed all tensed up on one side, like he was squinting all his sight through that eye and squeezing something in his mouth on that side. He wore a tattered San Jose Sharks jersey, long over his jeans. His arms looked too long for the sleeves. Arms a few inches too long for his torso as well; they hung motionlessly at his sides when he moved, never swinging like a normal person's. Black fingernails, yellow teeth, dishwater hair pushed back to drip to his shoulders, lank and greasy from not being washed.

But it was the look on his face that scared her. Grinding teeth, pupils dilated, hands trembling, heat coming off his body as he came to stand over them. Powder around his nostrils. She thought: *He's stoned, fucked up on meth. He might do anything.*

Liddy rubbed at his nose, blew bloody snot onto the back of his hand, wiped it on his pants. "Nobody else here, girls, but us kids, and we're gonna have a—what do they call it now—a playdate!" He said it fast, with something he imagined to be a grin. "So here's the deal." He held his long-fingered hands up palms toward them and flicked his hands in the air like a surgeon shaking water off his fingers, with the end of every statement. "We get busy, first one, then the other." Flick. "Then whoever I want." Flick. "And you get fixed up and you say nothing to Dickie or I will have to kill him and then you." Flick. "See, he'd be really mad so I'd have to shoot him before he could do anything and I am fucking sick of him anyway so I'm tempted. So then I'm going to for sure kill you after that happens." Flick. "Maybe my brother can have you when he comes back too. But for once, it's me first." Flick.

He licked his lips and, hands trembling, pulled up his shirtfront, fumbled with a San Jose Sharks belt buckle.

Pendra thought maybe she could strangle him with her chains, like Princess Leia in *Star Wars* did with that big fat outer-space fucker, but then Liddy got his pants down to his ankles on his pallid, hairy legs, squatted down, grabbed her ankles, and jerked her flat on her back with a painful thud. That took up the slack on her chains. She kicked at him, but her legs felt weak in his grip.

She was aware that Jill had edged away, gotten her knees under her. Seemed to working to get as much slack in her chain as possible. Maybe to keep as far back as possible from Liddy. Saying nothing. Doing nothing, really.

She's just going to sit there and watch while he rapes me . . .

Then Liddy was kneeling on Pendra's ankles and the weight hurt. She yelled and spat at him and he laughed and clawed under her paisley frock and tore her underwear like tissue, and then he took his limp purplish little member in one hand and flopped on her, knocking the breath out of her, spraying her face with halitosis, licking her right ear. Trying to jam his limp dick in her. But it wasn't working because he was on speed and most people, if they took enough, she'd heard, it made them impotent, and that was one thing, anyway. *But then again*, she thought, trying to get a breath, *maybe it's bad because he'll get frustrated and start beating me instead; might end up killing me.*

"Bitch!" he snarled, "rub up on me, show me them tits, you're like a fucking rag, now open up . . . "

The rage boiled up in her and overwhelmed her fear and she was shouting, *"You can't get it up because you're a fucking meth head, a smelly, ugly—"*

The rest of it was cut short as he gripped her throat with the long calloused fingers of his right hand and started to squeeze—

Then there was a sickening *thunk*. And he yelped like a whipped cur. And then another *thunk*, with a bit of a wet *crunch* at the end of it. Then another. Then two more quick. Each one wetter than the last. Blood streamed off him onto her face . . .

She heard Jill growling and grunting, and she pushed from beneath Liddy—and together they rolled his twitching body off her, so he was wedged on his left side, on the concrete floor. Staring, mouth open, between her and Jill.

Pendra turned and, panting, her neck aching, stared at Jill—who had a gun in her hand, a big automatic pistol held by the barrel. She'd reversed it, and there was blood and bits of bone and hair all over the gun butt. And some other gray stuff—maybe brains.

"Jesus, Jill!"

"I saw earlier, when he looked in on us—he had this sticking out of a back pocket. He had it in there when he laid down on you and . . . " She held up her arms to show what she'd done. Wincing with the pain of the motion.

Then Pendra saw that a lot of skin was pared off of Jill's left arm and it was bleeding badly. She'd forced it between tight lengths of chain to reach the gun.

"Oh God! You have guts!"

"I was afraid if I shot him the bullet might hit you too. So . . . ." Jill put the gun down on her lap, easing her chains back a bit on her wounded arms, sucking air between her clenched teeth. "Shit. Ow."

"Oh God," Pendra muttered, looking at Liddy. One of his eyes was open, the other closed; bloody drool dripped from his slack mouth. He wasn't even twitching now. Dead. "I feel like I need to take three baths. He was so . . . I feel sick."

"First thing is, how are we going to get these chains off? I'm sort of afraid of that thing you see in movies where you shoot a lock. I don't think that works in real life . . . I mean, the ricochets—one of us could get killed trying it. It might not even work."

"Uh—he said no one's here. We can pull on the pipes, not worry about the noise. Wait . . . maybe he has the keys to these stupid padlocks . . . "

They had to pull his body up closer between them to search it. Hard to do with so little slack. They managed, getting his blood all over them and not caring.

Pendra, feeling in his pockets, felt something metallic. "There's something . . . not keys. Shit. Oh. It's a big old pocket knife. That's a pretty big knife. We could use the butt of the gun, slam the knife between the links, hammer it and pry it apart . . . "

"Good idea. We have to pick the right links . . . "

"Wipe the blood off that gun, Jill. Anybody comes in before we're done, I am so totally shooting them right in the fucking balls."

ALL THE MEN were wearing their firemen's coats, unbuttoned, and carrying guns. Dickie had a pistol and a 10-gauge shotgun that had belonged to Mario. Steven had an AR-15 rifle, but only fixed for semiautomatic—also rustled from Mario's gun rack.

Nella looked the place over, as the Sand Scouts walked up, hoping the people weren't home. But there was a generator running somewhere behind the house and an older silvery Jaguar in the driveway, so probably they were there. It was a three-story split-level redwood house, built down the hillside, with a pool in its backyard, covered over with a tarp. Driftwood and rosebushes decorated a professionally-gardened front yard edged with crushed seashells; an expensive-looking wrought iron mailbox out front. The blinds were all pulled. The gray lid of the sky seemed to suck color from everything. A little rain drizzled; a cold breeze made her skin bumpy.

"What the fuck we gonna do here?" Jeremy asked, his jaws making a couple of extra clacks at the end of the question, because of the meth. His eyes were big, his hands shaky. Abe and Evan looked even more nervous, dancing from foot to foot, looking around like foxes cornered by hounds. But Jeremy seemed ready to leap into anything.

"Shit, look at those two," Randle jeered. "Look like they're gonna piss their pants! What's a matter, I thought you were gonna join us?"

"We are!" Jeremy said.

"Um—well—" Evan said.

Cholo and Steve and Dickie were standing between him and any place he could run to. Dickie was bringing out a pint bottle. "You see what this is? This is tequila. It says bourbon on the label here but I keep tequila in it. We found a shitload of this in Mario's rec room. Now you're gonna drink some of this, take the edge off the speed. Puke if you have to. And then in we go . . . "

"In?" Abe asked, almost hyperventilating. "In where? In this place? Are the people there? They got a generator, I see a gen, a gen, a generator. We could steal the generator, if they're not home."

"Here—take a few hits." Dickie handed him the pint bottle.

"Sure. I've had tequila. Not like we haven't had tequila."

"Stole it from your folks?"

"Hells—yeah!"

The men laughed. The boys drank. Nella waited in the background, hoping they'd forget about her so she wouldn't have to do anything. Vaguely thinking maybe she should, after all, get away now, if they were distracted in the house.

But she followed them up to it like a plastic bag in the slipstream of a truck, as they strode up to the house, Dickie leading the way, the boys just behind him; the other men and Nella bringing up the rear.

"I saw somebody peek out the window upstairs," Cholo said.

"Peekaboo in there!" Randle said. "Peek-uh-*boo*-ooooh!"

"Shut up, Randle," Dickie said blandly.

"We're not seeing any visitors!" shouted a reedy voice from the other side of the front door. "No visitors at all! We don't have any supplies! We don't have any medical stuff! We've been telling people that for days!"

"Fucking lying to them too!" Dickie said, laughing, pumping the shotgun. And he fired the 10-gauge through the middle of the walnut door. A fist-sized chunk of door vanished inward.

There was a pealing scream from inside, wavering up and down in pitch.

"Whoa!" Evan said.

"Tight!" Jeremy said.

"Fuck!" Abe said.

Dickie looked at them and chuckled fondly. "You kids. Adorable." He tried the door. "Still locked though."

"Let me get this," Cholo said.

Dickie and the boys stepped aside, Cholo rushed the door, slammed it where the lock connected to the frame, and it popped inward.

Looking past them, Nella could just make out someone crawling up carpeted stairs in a high-ceilinged front hallway, trying to get to the second floor. An old man, looked like, leaving a trail of blood. Groaning.

Nella backed away—but Dickie seemed to sense it, and turned, gave her a look made out of chilled metal. "Get over here. Now. I can feel you sneaking away. Don't even fucking think about that."

She walked automatically forward into the foyer, suddenly feeling the pain at her crotch again, and walked past the shattered door, waited by the red smear on the floor as the men and the three boys came in.

The old man, dressed in tan slacks and loafers and a yellow golf shirt, was almost to the second floor. He was face down, climbing, they couldn't see the wound. A woman appeared on the stairs, a white-haired, pasty-faced woman with a wobbling head. Her thin hair was dyed blond; she wore a fuzzy yellow bathrobe and slippers. "Oh God. Morris. Oh no. Where are the police, where are the police?"

"Oh well, the *police!*" Dickie said, strolling around the bloody smear. "Now they want the police! Our ol' pal Mayor Ferrara got rid of them! And, you know he got rid of anything connected with 'big government,' so that means no one's here helping, which means, guess what—*real freedom in Freedom!* You people are free! *We're* free! You're free to defend your shit and we're free to *take* your shit! It's like the pioneer days when they crossed a fucking mountain range and found some people living on the other side and they killed them dead *and took their shit away!* Now *we* get to do that! We came over the mountain—so, we can *just take your shit!* It's the inspiration of history! Breathtakin' as the Grand Canyon! Ain't freedom grand?"

Jeremy laughed. Abe snorted. Evan groaned. *Definitely*, Nella figured, *having second thoughts.*

"Steve," Dickie said, "drag that old prick down here and the biddy too. Cholo, have a look around, see if anybody else is here, see what looks good."

Steve climbed the stairs, looking a bit stiff and mechanical, his face drawn; Cholo went industriously to the living room, down another set of stairs, searching through the house . . .

A fleshy thumping, anguished sobs—Steve pulling the old man down the stairs by his ankles.

"Sorry, old dude," he said, with a trace of real regret. "May as well get this bullshit over with." Another trail of blood down the stairs. The old woman vanished at the top of the stairs, wailing.

Steve ran up the stairs after her. There was a crashing sound, breaking crockery.

"Hey, she's throwin' shit at him!" Jeremy crowed.

Dickie laughed. "Sounds like it."

The elderly man lay groaning on the tile floor of the foyer. Then Steven appeared at the head of the stairs, shoving the old woman ahead of him. She came staggering down the stairs, blood seeping from a split in a swelling below her left eye.

Nella heard a muffled roaring, coming from somewhere between her ears and her brain. Demons, roaring. Her mother hissing.

Judgment, you servant of the great whore . . .

Cholo got there as the woman was pushed to her knees in front of Dickie. "Nobody here," Cholo said. "Just them. And there's some good stuff. Nice wine, cheeses, medical shit, extra gasoline. They've been holing up good here."

"Selfish old fuckers, aren't they?" Dickie said. "I can't fucking abide people who don't share."

"You're cowards!" the woman sobbed. "Shooting people through closed doors! Pushing old women around!"

"No, lady—we're just *free!*" Randle said with exaggerated innocence. "The mayor said so!"

The men laughed and Dickie took a gun and handed it to Evan.

"You shoot that old lady in the head, kid, and you are thereby initiated. Go on—right in the head. Get 'er done."

The kid looked at the big revolver in his hand and then at the shocked old woman.

"Mister," the woman said, her voice tremulous, "don't do that to that boy. Don't make him do it. Do it yourself. But don't force that boy to do it."

"Got to! He's got to initiate hisself! Go on, kid! Shoot her! Then you get first pick of her stuff!"

Evan looked at the shotgun in Dickie's hand. Pointed at no

one in particular. Then he looked at the old lady. Nella could imagine him thinking: *What if I refuse?*

He lifted the pistol, pointed it at the old woman's head . . . his hand shaking . . . the gun wavering . . .

He licked his lips . . . and lowered the gun. "I can't," he said. "I don't want to."

"Then drop the gun on the floor," Dickie said.

He dropped the gun, with a clatter. Dickie turned to Jeremy, who was following all this with snake fascination. "Pick up the gun, kid."

Jeremy nodded, picked up the gun. Held it just like he'd seen in movies and videogames.

"Now point it at Evan's head."

"Evan?"

"Yeah." And he pointed the shotgun at Jeremy. "Or I shoot you."

Jeremy hesitated, and then he shrugged, and—the words coming between excited gasps—said, "This is kind of a cool situation. Like in a John Woo movie." He pointed the gun at Evan's head. "You ever see John Woo movies, Evan?"

Evan didn't answer.

Dickie propped the shotgun on one hip, held it pointed with his right hand at Jeremy, with his left took a buck knife from his pocket. Opened it with the fingers of his left hand with a single, practiced motion, never looking at it. "Now . . . Evan—take this knife."

Evan mutely took it.

"Jeezus, Evan," Abe said.

"Evan," Dickie went on, "Just stick it in her neck. That ought to be easier than a gun. You do that and Jeremy doesn't have to shoot you."

"I can't," Evan said, his voice breaking. Lips quivering.

"'I can't!'" Randle said, in a little girl voice.

Steve and Cholo didn't laugh. They just glanced at each other. And watched. Nella realized they didn't like this either. But they were scared of Dickie. And greedy for things. They weren't going to do anything to stop it from happening.

"Jeremy, if he doesn't stab her, count to three and then shoot him in the head."

"Whoa, dude!" Abe said.

Jeremy had the gun pointed right at Evan's head from the side, about six inches away. "Uh, okay, um—Evan? Better stab her."

"I can't."

"Whatever, dude. One . . . Two . . . "

"I *can't!*"

"Three—"

Evan dropped the knife and ran for the farther door into the back of the house.

"Well, shoot him, you dumbass!" Dickie bellowed.

Jeremy squeezed the trigger, the barrel jerked, the roar of the gun echoed in the foyer, but the shot went way wide of Evan. Dickie swung the shotgun around and fired after the boy but he was already through the door—part of the frame vanished in buckshot.

"Go on!" Dickie shouted. "You too—what's your name?—Abe! Go get him! He'll tell the cops what you been part of! Go! Chase him down! Kill him!"

Still clumsily carrying the gun, Jeremy ran after Evan. Abe came after him, yelling, "Wait! Let me shoot it! You missed him! It's my turn!"

There was a gunshot from the farther room, and then some confused yelling. "I think he got outside!" Jeremy yelled, from back there.

Dickie shook his head and sighed. "Fuckwads."

"Good for you, kid!" the old lady said hoarsely. "You get away! You tell someone! You—"

Dickie turned the shotgun and blew the upper half of her head back onto her marble floor tiles. It took a moment for her body to flop back, follow her head. Then he shot the old man in the back, and Nella could tell Dickie wasn't thinking about it as he killed the guy, his mind already on something else.

Dickie lowered the shotgun and turned to Steve. "You got a watch. What time is it?"

Steve stared at him, swallowed—then looked at his watch. "Oh—shit! It's fifteen to noon! Didn't we say noon for the delivery of our shit at that other house?"

"Yeah, we sure as fuck did. Dammit, we gotta get back there." He pumped a round into the shotgun's chamber as Jeremy and Abe returned. Gawping at the remains of the dead woman. Dickie snorted in disgust. "You little shits lost him. Didn't you?"

"The back gate wasn't completely closed," Abe explained. "Jeremy shot at him but he missed. He wouldn't let me shoot!"

"Shut up, Abe, Christ," Jeremy said. "I know where he lives . . ."

"No time for that bullshit," Dickie said. "Toss that gun over."

He pointed the shotgun at them. From five feet away.

"Jeremy," Abe said, softly. "Don't do that . . . Don't give up the gun."

"We have to. It'll be okay. He's gonna figure out we're cool and shit."

Jeremy tossed the gun on the floor. Dickie said, "Fun's over. You seen too much and you ain't coming with us."

Nella turned away. She didn't want to watch as Dickie shot the two boys. She walked out the front door. But she heard the gunshots—and heard them scream.

It took four shots in all.

She was partway back to the street Mario's place was on when Dickie and Cholo and Steve and Randle caught up with her.

"Where you going?" Dickie asked, grabbing her arm and spinning her around.

"Nowhere. Home. Whatever you call it. Where we stay."

He stared at her, breathing hard, eyes dilated. "Go on. But not Mario's. We're going to the other house."

The house with the brass Jesus. "'Kay."

She walked down the street and after a moment they followed, surprisingly quiet. Except after awhile, Randle started babbling about the old people's house, maybe it should be their new headquarters, they could clean it up, it was a really cool place, it even had a pool.

"We have to fucking leave town, you retard," Dickie said, "Once we get the stuff."

"Yeah," Steve said. Sounding a bit shaken. "Sooner or later the National Guard—they'll be here. Someone anyway."

"I'm not a retard, Dickie," Randle said in a flat voice.

Dickie chuckled. "Sure as fuck are. You and your brother. When cousins marry."

Cholo laughed.

"Our parents weren't cousins," Randle said. Seemed like he wasn't completely sure.

"Couple of you guys need to get that kid that ran off," Dickie said, as they got to their street. "I figure he's hiding in one of these empty houses around here."

They got to the corner, just about thirty yards from the house with the brass Jesus. And there was a little sky-blue pickup truck coming up the street, with some stuff piled in the back, mostly hidden under a tarp which was only tied down close to the cab.

The little pickup was coming slowly, and there was an older black man driving it. Nella had seen that man. His name was Dale something. She couldn't see anyone with him.

"You think that's the stuff?" Cholo asked. "Shouldn't they have cars with them, for us too? Those luxury cars?"

"Maybe this is the first delivery," Dickie said.

He stared at the small blue pickup, which was a battered Nissan Frontier, as it pulled up at the curb a little bit west of the house with the brass Jesus. The chunky middle-aged black driver, wearing a San Francisco Giants jacket, sat there with the engine idling. Looking tense. Scared? She wasn't sure. Then he nodded at Dickie, and gestured, hooking a thumb over his shoulder at the rear of the truck. So that was the delivery in exchange for the two women.

Dickie started toward the truck . . . then stopped.

"Randle, Steve," Dickie said. "See what they got in the back of the truck. Better be valuable shit. Go on—I'll cover you from here."

Randle looked at him, brow furrowed. Then he shrugged and walked with Steve over to the little blue pickup, around to its tailgate, and lifted off the untied dark blue-plastic tarp to see what loot they'd gotten.

Russ Haver sat up in the back of the truck. He'd been hiding under the tarp, and he shot them both, at close range, with a.45 pistol. One, two. Just like that.

Randle was hit in the stomach, and fell over backwards, writhing; Steve was hit in the left shoulder and staggered back shouting.

Cholo and Dickie started yelling and Nella instinctively threw herself flat on the ground.

TWENTY-TWO

IT WORKED, Brand thought. *Russ's Trojan horse worked.*

Brand tasted metal, felt his pulse pounding in his temples as he stepped out from between the houses across the street from the pickup. Rifle in his hands. He was half-hidden by a tall thin Italian cypress as he took up a position at the corner of the dark-brown ranch-style house. Watching Russ and Dale and the men in the unbuttoned orange and black fireman's coats.

Everyone seemed to be moving in slow motion, as Brand's adrenaline telescoped time. His hands shook as he clicked off the safety and raised the 30.06 to his shoulder, the barrel projecting between the house and the tree; he set it into a proper mount with his left hand steadying the rifle, his elbow crooked almost ninety degrees the way Dale had showed him.

Thinking, *Shoot him, shoot Dickie Rockwell right fucking now!*

He settled the sights on Dickie, who was swiveling a shotgun to fire at the driver. But Brand didn't squeeze the trigger. *Shoot him.*

His trigger finger didn't want to work.

Dickie and Cholo were standing in front of the appointed house, focused on the little pickup where Steve, backing up, was trying to set the AR-15 into a shoulder mount, having trouble with the pain. Randle was clutching himself on the ground, dying behind the Nissan pickup.

Brand glanced at Russ, saw him hunkered in the back of the

truck between the wooden crates of heavy garden rocks they'd set up around his hiding place. As he watched, Russ dropped the pistol, snatched up the Winchester, popped it to his shoulder. There was a stony, settled rage in Russ's face. He was having no trouble pulling triggers.

Dale was getting out of the pickup, pushing the driver's side door wide open, using the door for some protection, propping the 12-gauge through the rolled-down window.

Shoot them in the center of their mass, boy! Dale had said. And Russ had done just that with Randle Grummon, who was contorting on the asphalt like a worm dropped on coals. But Steve, about twenty-five feet from the truck now, was firing the semiautomatic at Russ. The bullets were hitting the wooden, stone-filled crates, and pinging off the steel of the truck bed. A shotgun blast from Dickie took out part of the Nissan's windshield.

Brand tried to squeeze the trigger—and lost the bead, the sights wavering off his target as Dickie stepped back, pumping the shotgun with one hand, the shotgun propped against his middle, the other hand holding up a little walkie-talkie. Shouting into the walkie-talkie. Calling Sten?

Dale stepped out from the truck, turning toward Steve to take the heat off Russ, exposing himself—Dale fired the shotgun and the blast caught Steve under the ribcage, he spun and went down, caterwauling in pain, the AR-15 clattering away. Cholo fired at Dale, who was still turned toward Steve—and the shot caught Dale in the back of his right shoulder, seemed to fling him against the truck, as if an invisible cop and shoved him into "the position." Dale grimaced and ducked back behind the faulty protection of the driver's side door—

Brand made himself take a breath, let it out slow as he tracked Dickie with the rifle sights. Dickie and Cholo hadn't seen him— they were tunnel-visioned on the threat close by, as he'd hoped they'd be. He almost had a shot . . . but a motion from the back of the truck distracted him, he saw Russ leaning over the back of the rear gate—coldly shooting Randle Grummon in the back of the head with the Winchester. Taking cover again, levering another round into the Winchester.

And Brand thought, *Jesus Fucking Christ, Russ.*

Brand saw Cholo was backing up, face taut, firing a pistol—the bullet striking sparks off the roof of the pickup by Dale's head.

Dickie Rockwell was swinging the shotgun, firing sloppily toward Russ. Russ rose up, fired the Winchester, taking only a split second to aim, and seemed to catch Dickie in the right hip. Dickie staggered, dropped the shotgun—as Brand tried to track him with the front sights of his rifle—and pulled a pistol from his waistband, firing it toward Russ and Dale both, several shots. Dale was trying to control his own weapon but was too injured to do much with it, just managed to fire through the pickup's driver's side window. The shotgun blast missed Dickie, punching a hole in the wall of the house behind him as he ran for the front door of the closest house—the house they'd arranged to meet at. Now the pickup was between Brand and his target.

They'd assumed the women were in the house because that's where the delivery was to be, where they were supposed to make the exchange for them. If Dickie got in there with the women, he'd use them for hostages. Unless they were up at Mario's . . .

A bullet from Dickie's pistol clanged into the truck's left rear tire rim and the loud ringing sound seemed to wake Brand up. Dickie was coming out into view beyond the bed of the pickup. Russ was ducking down, under fire from Dickie and Cholo. Dickie ducked toward the front door, Cholo trying to follow.

I have to shoot! Brand thought, tracking Dickie. Before he was spotted and shot down. Before he died here for nothing.

But he'd never killed anyone before. To just end a man's life . . . to take that responsibility . . .

Lines from the Bhagavad Gita came to him, suddenly, flashing by in a moment: *If we kill these evil men, evil will come on us?* And Krishna's answer: *Think of your duty and do not waver—there is no greater good for a warrior than to fight in a righteous war.*

And Brand fired the rifle at Dickie—who was dodging into the house.

He missed Dickie—the shot knocked away an upper left corner of the door as Dickie ducked indoors. Brand worked the rifle's bolt, reloaded, swung the muzzle toward Cholo who was running toward Dale, firing. More windshield glass shattered. Brand tracked Cholo who was aiming carefully at Dale. Brand squeezed the trigger—the rifle bucked—

Cholo jerked in mid-step, his body twisted. He fell on his face. Shot through the chest.

The Spirit that is in all beings is immortal in them all . . .

Brand reloaded the rifle.

. . . for the death of what cannot die, cease to sorrow . . .

RUSS FIRED another round from the Winchester toward the front door, suppressive fire. He levered another round into the chamber, hearing the ejected brass ring on the truck bed, then jumped out of the truck near the curb. Aware—exquisitely aware, in this moment of heightened perception, slowed time—of the drizzle from the lowering clouds, the smell of his own sweat, the feel of the asphalt under his sneakers as he struck the ground, rock dust in his mouth from the bullet-smacked stones, the mirroring crimson puddle forming around Cholo's awkwardly sprawled body close to the house's front door . . .

Russ hurried to Dale, who was leaning against the side of

the truck, breathing hard, the butt of the shotgun against his left hip turned toward the house. His right arm dangling, his left controlling the gun. Keeping an eye on that front door as he leaned there, gasping.

"You hit, Dale?"

"Some. Not too bad. Not going to do any heavy lifting any time soon."

Russ nodded, feeling his hands quivering against the Winchester. He hadn't slept much. He had simmered all night, dozing and trembling inside, and waking up and wishing for day. For noon. Wanting at first to get it over. And then, as he drank instant coffee that morning, heated on a camp stove, he wanted something more than that.

He'd remembered what Dale had said about having to get mad. He was already there. He was breathing anger, feeling it hot in his nostrils, seething in his veins. He had lain in the back of the truck thinking: *They murdered my father. Right in front of me. They took Pendra . . .*

The rage had boiled out of him the instant he'd heard those footsteps approaching the truck . . .

But in the back of his mind, now, he was appalled at how easily it had come to him. *Fire. Cock the gun, swing it. Fire. Two men down. Find another target . . .*

He turned at a sound behind him—ready to fire again. Almost shot at Brand who was running across the street. Stopping to stare at Cholo's body.

"That your shot, Brand?" Russ asked, watching the front door. What was Dickie up to in there?

"Yeah," Brand said. "I . . . " His voice broke. "Missed Dickie, but . . . "

"You hadn't shot him, Brand," Dale said, reading Brand's face, "he'd have finished me off."

Brand swung his rifle toward the house. "Yeah. But Dickie's in there with the women. He's going to use them for hostages. Or take them out the back way."

"We can't let Dickie get away, no matter what," Russ said. Wondering how far he'd go with that determination if Pendra was in the way.

"Maybe . . . " Dale winced at a stab of pain. "Maybe they're up at the other house—up the hill there. House by the top of the hill is Mario's."

"Usually the Grummons are together—only one here. You'd think he'd have taken a shot at us out of this place, if he was in it. Maybe the other's guarding them some place else."

"Mario's supposed to be . . . " Dale grimaced with pain. "Watching his house, till we get there, but . . . "

Russ pointed out, "But Mario's drunk and half crazy."

A woman's voice, then: "Dickie can't get out the back of that house too easy."

They all turned to look, Russ swinging his rifle that way—he saw it was the woman Nella, at the corner of the house, getting to her feet, hands were raised to show she was unarmed. She wore a ski jacket and jeans. Her head was cocked to one side, making her dirty hair hang lankly; her face was blotchy, and she was unsteady on her feet, incapable of violence. Just a kind of ambulatory despair.

"You can put your hands down," Brand said.

"They boarded up the windows really strong," she said, lowering her hands, "because they stay there part of the time to party. The back door was part of the house that collapsed down into the pit there. So he's still in there. He's going to wait awhile in the brass Jesus house there and then he's going to run out and shoot you."

"How do you know?" Russ asked.

"Because I know him. He won't hide long."

"Where are the girls?" Brand asked.

"Not here. Up the street. At Mario's."

"Shit," Dale said, grimacing with pain. "If we'd known . . . "

I've got to go in there, Russ thought, looking at the "brass Jesus house." *He killed my dad. He's going to come out and kill me if I don't go in after him.*

Then he thought: *Don't be stupid. Watch the door and wait.*

"Look!" Brand said, pointing.

Russ saw Mario staggering down the street toward them, a shotgun in his hands, and behind him came Jill and Pendra. They walked steadily, had chains dangling from their wrists. Didn't seem badly hurt. Jill appeared to be carrying a pistol.

"Thank God," Dale said, weakly.

Brand said, "Dale—How about if you get in the back of the truck, we'll have Jill drive you to Lucia."

"I'm not hurt that bad. Just throbs like a bitch is all . . . Oh fuck!"

They'd all seen it at the same time: a large four-wheel-drive glossy-black extended-cab Ford pickup truck with oversized tires came barreling around the corner about a block up. At the wheel was Mike Sten. In the back were Remo, Lucas, and Chuckles. Russ could see their guns.

Brand shouted, "Jill! You two get down, stay back and flatten down!"

The women ran off the street, at the intersection, as the glossy-black truck roared past them—and past Mario, who was hunkering behind a mailbox. The pickup drove right for the smaller blue Nissan Frontier, half a block away.

"Come on!" Dale hissed, and he lurched toward the house of the "brass Jesus," Brand helping him. The upper corner of the house had broken off and slid down the slope in the wave, but there was a square-yard of ground behind the corner—like a platform of dirt and foundation—before the ragged edge of the wall ended in the fallen wreckage. The girl Nella had ducked back around the other corner of the house, behind Jill and Pendra—gone from sight.

Russ was just behind Brand, turning. Deciding he didn't have time to get under cover, he went down on his left knee, setting the Winchester in a good mount, leaning forward, right elbow propped on his right knee, his hands trembling slightly. One of the infantry man's firing positions Dale had shown him. The big Ford pickup was coming . . .

Russ held his breath, tracked the front of the black truck, fired, and saw sparks from a ricochet off the grill.

Chuckles and Remo, braced against the vehicle's motion, fired out the back of the truck toward him—Chuckles firing a pistol, Remo a carbine, the bullets going wide as the truck veered across the street—and slammed into the front of the smaller pickup, making it crumple and spin around so that Russ—squeezing off an ineffectual shot—had to jump to the left to avoid the whipping front fenders. The big pickup swerved, jolted to a swerving halt, the smaller pickup skidded sideways and then stopped with its engine smoking, flames crackling up. To Russ's left, Brand fired at someone Russ couldn't see from the corner of the house. Probably missed because Brand hissed, "Shit!" to himself. Russ was down in a rifleman's kneeling position again, getting his rifle up, trying to pick out a target.

Sten was getting out of the crookedly stopped truck, Lucas was aiming a shotgun over the top of the cab—but was distracted as a shot came from somewhere to his right, from down the side street. Jill, probably, firing a pistol. Missing but distracting him so that when he turned back, Russ had already centered front and back sights over Lucas's chest. He squeezed the trigger and

Lucas's shotgun boomed uselessly into the air as the man went over backwards, falling against Remo whose shot at Dale and Brand went wild. Dale stepped out from the corner of the house, fired the shotgun. Chuckles shouted as the left side of his face vanished, but he fired back, the bullet *thunk*ing into the rain pipe following the corner of the house where Brand was trying to get a bead to return fire.

A *boom*. Chuckles shouted again and spun, falling, and Russ saw that Mario had run up to the black pickup from behind, fired his shotgun almost point blank into the back of the truck, the lead shot hitting two men, mostly Chuckles. Remo turned, staggering, firing the carbine at Mario who seemed to trip backwards. Wounded.

A bullet cut the air just over Russ's head and he swung the Winchester toward the gunman: Mike Sten, on the street, grinning at him over the top of the truck's hood.

Russ fired but his aim was choked by fear and he missed. As he levered another round into the rifle, he could almost feel Sten's sights centering on his forehead. He figured he was about to die—then Mike Sten jerked around, spat blood, his shot going wild. Sten took two steps and fell, squeezing off another ricocheting round as he went down . . . and Mario stepped up behind him, shotgun smoking. Fired again, finishing Sten off. Blood was streaming from a wound in Mario's upper left arm.

Remo yelling with pain as he vaulted off the truck into the street, back behind Mario, turning . . . Russ trying to get a bead on Remo. Couldn't see him well enough.

Russ stood up and tried to track him. The truck was in the way—

"You fucks!" Mario shouted, at what was left of Sten. "You murdering fucks! You killed my boy! You—"

The rest was choked in blood as Remo shot Mario through

the side of the neck. Mario sidestepped, twice, like a man doing a dance shuffle . . . and then tipped over.

Remo was in the street, near the corner, trying to use the back of the black Ford truck for cover, swinging his carbine toward Russ. A *crack* from left of Russ as Brand fired at Remo—and missed.

Dale was shouting something. Russ couldn't make out what.

Russ made himself stand still, letting out his breath, steadying the Winchester on his right shoulder—firing at almost the same moment as Remo.

Remo's head snapped back on his neck, a small round red hole appearing in his forehead over his left eye. He fell out of sight behind the Ford pickup, and Russ chambered another round into the Winchester, turned toward the house—saw Brand and Dale to his left, Dale sitting with his back to the wall, Brand standing nearby, staring in horror over at Mario, who was dying in the street.

A shot boomed out from the door of the house, shattering the windshield of the black pickup behind Russ. Dickie at the door, steadying the big pistol to fire at Russ again. "Fuck me, fuck me I missed!" Dickie said between clenched teeth. "This time . . . you little prick . . . "

Russ fired from the hip, because he had no choice, and Dickie shut his eyes and gasped, took two steps back—Russ saw that his shot had caught Dickie in the upper right torso just under his collarbone—Dickie was firing but his gun hand was compromised, the shot slapped the air on Russ's left, and Russ raised the Winchester to shoulder, levered the round in.

But Dickie vanished from sight, slipping off to his right inside the doorway.

Russ thought, *If I follow him in there, he'll nail me.*

But some instinct, spiraling up from his ancestors, argued: *He's wounded. He's running. Follow. Finish it.*

Everything Is Broken

Mouth bone dry, blood humming through his veins, he eased the rifle off his shoulder and made himself stalk forward into the house.

"Russ!" Brand shouted, from the corner of the house. "Don't go in there!"

But Russ was already going through the door, following the trail of blood.

He stopped in the living room, swinging the rifle to take it in. Saw a sofa, a Coleman lantern glowing near the ceiling. Light glancing off a brass Jesus crucifix over the sofa. An open door to the left . . . blood speckling the floor that way . . . a fireman's coat on the floor. Dickie had taken it off.

He set the Winchester against his shoulder, got a good mount, sidestepped quietly to his right, keeping the muzzle on that open door toward the sea . . .

Then he saw Dickie, turned away, a coatless silhouette against the gray sky. The door opened onto the broken down western end of the house. Dickie was swaying on the edge of a broken-off section of flooring. Just standing there, swaying, with his back to Russ. Beyond him, the part of the house that had been there was gone, smashed down by the tsunami. There was just sky, clouds streaming by in the wind. Dickie's right hip was dribbling blood, and more red slickness trickled down his right arm. He held the gun in his left hand now. Seemed to be staring downward, trying to figure out how to climb down. Russ aimed . . .

And found he couldn't shoot Dickie in the back. Stupid, but there it was.

"Dickie!" he called out.

Dickie spun around, raising the pistol—and Russ shot him in the chest. Dickie was flung backwards and off the edge of the snapped-off floor overlooking the pit. Falling out of sight.

Russ walked through the doorway, levering another round into the Winchester as he went. He reached the edge of the floor and carefully looked down. He made out several bodies down there. The remains of two women.

And Dickie was there too, lying in muck on his back, all twisted, eyes closed, mouth open. He was completely motionless. A shiny puddle of blood, reflecting the racing clouds overhead, welled up on his chest.

TWENTY-THREE

"DALE GOING to be all right?" Russ asked, as Pendra came into his dad's apartment. She was cleaned up, her wrists bandaged, her eyes dull with weariness. But she smiled at him.

Right shoulder aching from rifle recoil, he was half-lying on the living room sofa, legs stretched out, watching the shadows flicker from the candles. Thinking that he was very tired. That he really wanted to sleep. And wondering if he could.

It was late. His mind had been replaying the gunfight, on and off, for hours. He didn't want to see it anymore. He didn't even want to think about it. But the Winchester was nearby, leaning on the wall. He wasn't letting go of that Winchester.

Pendra sat on the arm of the sofa near him. "Lucia says Dale's going to recover just fine. I think she's got the hots for him. Brand took a bunch of guys and put the bonfire out. Got all that wire down. The pass is open—Lucia's driving Dale into Deer Creek right now. Brand is with her—and Jill. Jill's arm is pretty fucked up. I mean—it'll be okay, I guess, but it's going to be scarred. Hey—thanks for coming over there to get us. *God*, we were glad to see you guys."

"We were looking in the wrong house. Anyway it seemed like you didn't need us. You got out on your own!"

"You had to do what you did, anyhow. They'd have been back." After a moment she added, "Mario almost shot us."

"He almost shot you? What the fuck!"

"He couldn't see us in the garage very good. We opened the garage door and there he was, walking up with the shotgun and he almost shot us—and I almost shot *him!* Then Jill yelled his name and told me to wait. We'd heard them talking about him. He was pretty mad there was nobody there to kill." She chuckled. "Jill took the gun from me."

"Nobody there to kill . . . " His stomach twisted. He was so tired. His arms felt like lead weights. "I almost shot Brand once too, by accident."

Maybe he shouldn't have shot Randle Grummon in the back of the head. But Randle was still alive, still had that gun. Was trying to lift himself up . . .

"Um—what about your dad's body?" Pendra asked gently.

"It was where Ferrara said it was. Dr. Spuris is acting like the great public servant now. He's arranging a burial. Tomorrow morning. We'll have a little service. There's a pretty nice old cemetery on the way to Deer Creek."

"Listen," Pendra said, "I feel like crap. I was wondering . . . "

"Oh shit, yeah—you spent the night in that garage all chained up. You should lay down. Let me get you something to eat."

"I ate something." Pendra hesitated—then went on, not looking right at him. "I was just hoping—could we just, sort of *sleep* together? I mean, under covers, just sort of spooning. For now. I just need to have somebody there. While I'm sleeping."

"That is exactly what I need too. Sure. Let's get some sleep."

They went into his dad's dark bedroom, candles lambent on the desk; kicked off their shoes, got under the covers, still dressed. They lay nestled together, her back to him, his left arm over her, hugging her close. She sighed. He could feel her relaxing. "That is it exactly."

He closed his eyes. Sleep was close. He saw muzzle flashes. He saw gun smoke drifting. He saw the back of Randle Grummon's head coming apart as he shot him. Saw a pool of blood expanding around Cholo. Saw his father rolling down the stony slope. He saw the tsunami, rising up, throwing all into shadow, all into darkness; darkness like sleep. Sleep rolling down on them . . . There would be nightmares, but he'd grown used to them and it wasn't so bad, with her beside him . . .

He was almost asleep when she whispered, "We telling police from Deer Creek about . . . ?"

"Mm, about what happened to Dickie and those guys? No. We're not telling them. Talked it over with Dale and Brand and we're just telling people that bunch killed each other fighting over stuff. We have enough to deal with already, without inquests and shit. People here will back the story up."

"What happened to that girl who was with them?"

"She seems like she ran off, outta town. Nobody can find her."

She yawned. "Where you going next? Staying here in town?"

"Hell no. Taking my dad's car. Taking some of his stuff with me. A letter he wrote, to give my mom. And some money. He had an envelope with two grand cash in a drawer. He was gonna give it to me to buy a car of my own. Probably would've given it to me the day I came, but . . . the wave came."

"Where you going, then?"

"See my mom. In Ohio. Akron."

"Oh."

He thought she was asleep then. Was almost there himself when she said, "Going to *stay* in Ohio?"

"For a while anyhow."

"And do what?"

He hesitated. Then said, "Go back to school. And just live where things work. Where there's electricity. Where people answer if you call nine-one-one. Might be awhile before a lot of California's like that again."

"Study what in school?"

He answered without thinking. Answering the question for himself at that moment. "Law enforcement."

"Seriously?"

He thought about it. He was sure. "Seriously."

She was silent and after a minute he thought she'd gone to sleep. Then she said, "Russ . . . "

"Yeah?"

"Is it nice in Akron?"

"Akron—*nice?* Some of it. Cold in winter. No jobs, hardly. But . . . I'll say this for it. It's a long fucking ways from the ocean. Forty miles from Lake Erie. But—no ocean." He decided to go ahead and ask, right now. "Want to come? Meet my mom?"

"What about Gram's kitties?"

"Oh yeah. Does she have cat carriers?"

"Yes. But they'd yowl all the way there."

"Let 'em yowl." After a moment he added, "My mom likes cats."

"You're a good guy, Russ."

He wondered about that. He hoped she was right. He had his doubts.

After a moment she asked, "Definitely no ocean in Akron?"

"Definitely. None."

"Then I'm in. Let's start tomorrow afternoon."

" 'Kay. We're going to Ohio. Tomorrow." After a minute more, he pulled her a little closer and said, "Good night."

But she was asleep. When he was sure she was deeply asleep, Russ got very quietly up and went to the living room. He locked the front door, got his rifle, brought it into the bedroom. He leaned the Winchester 92 against the wall, with the safety on, where he could roll over and grab it if he had to. Then he got in bed with Pendra again, put his arm around her, and fell into a strangely dreamless sleep.

Everything Is Broken

NELLA KNEW Dickie was still alive. She could feel it.

So she waited and, sometime around dawn, she saw him crawling up out of the pit under the fallen part of the house, climbing up just a little bit at a time. Climbing, resting, climbing. He was weak and filthy with mud and blood and caked slime, coughing blood. Looked like he was going to fall back in, and she didn't want that to happen, so she helped him up onto the broken rim of the smashed western wall.

"Nella . . . " he rasped. "Thanks, girl. Nella. Get me . . . car. Doctor . . . "

"I went to that house with the Jaguar, I found the keys. We're going in style, Dickie. There's a way down to the beach . . . "

She went and got the Jaguar, which she'd parked just a few doors down, backed it up next to him. She put the car in park, got out, helped him into the passenger side. He was heavy. It wasn't easy. He groaned with every movement. He'd been shot through three times. Lot of blood lost. Felt like broken ribs, broken shoulder blade, swollen left shoulder, maybe busted.

"Shouldn't have gotten into the shit," he muttered, eyes closed, when they were almost to the sea. "Can't shoot on meth. Missed the fucker. Missed him."

He slumped there, breath coming slow and scratchy, shuddering on the brown leather seats, as she drove the Jaguar, under the cold gray light of dawn, toward the beach.

She had to drive up on someone's yard, twice, and over a mound of debris in one place. But she'd already scouted the way through.

And then they were at the highway. There was an old concrete boat launch ramp, at the northern end of the beach, hardly ever used. Wooden debris was heaped on the ramp but she was able

279

to drive over it, since she didn't care what it did to the tires. Dickie groaned with the thumping as she drove down the ramp and onto the beach.

Nella drove to the edge of the water—and right into it a little ways. Saw the tide was pretty low and getting lower. He opened his eyes, just cracking them, as the engine died.

"What," he said. "Why here? Someone comin' in a boat?"

"Sure," she said. "That's right. Come on."

She got out, came around to his side. She was barefoot. The sand felt cool and good on the soles of her feet, the water cold on her ankles. She opened the door, got her arms under his shoulders, and dragged him out. Pulled him hard, backwards from the car, so that his feet splashed down into the shallow waves. He yelped in pain and cursed her.

"You fucking bitch! That hurts!"

"Come on. They're coming to take us. Come on . . . "

She dragged him toward the deeper water. He opened his eyes and saw there was no boat, and made a thrashing effort at dislodging her, but he was weak as a kitten, and she was determined. She was going to use all the strength she had left.

She got him full into the water. Its cold embrace was her first release from the feverishness that she'd taken for granted for days. She dragged him out farther, till the sand sloped away under her and they fell back, a wave slopping seawater into her mouth. She gasped and thrashed herself back on the surface, looped her left arm around his neck. A wave from behind pushed them in a little ways but she kicked off the bottom, and pulled him with her, struggling feebly, out to deeper water. The tide was going out and that helped.

Nella was shivering, teeth chattering, and felt sick to her stomach. Her strength was waning, but she felt good too, in a funny way, as she kicked and swam a clumsy sidestroke, pulled him with her out to sea. The waves got bigger and bigger, rhythmically splashing over her head. But she kept on.

He resisted a little, at first. Then he seemed to run out of steam and went limp in her grasp. Made it easier to pull him along. She knew he was still alive only because she heard him gasping and spitting water from time to time.

They swam past a water-smoothed log; she kicked them through a big patch of seaweed. A gull sat on a bobbing, overturned rowboat, eyeing them. They kept going, past the gull, and on out west. Out to sea. Where cold sea met cold sky; where gray-green sea became gray sky.

"Nella . . . fuckin' . . . cold . . . " he rasped. "I'm cold." She didn't answer him, and, taking a long shaky breath, he managed, "Where we . . . goin'?"

"Out past the edge of the world," she said, sputtering a little as a wave slapped over her face. "Out where you get your help from. Out *there*. We're going out to join the ocean out there and ask it to please take us, Dickie."

He spat water. Laughed croakingly. Said, "Not bad." He coughed. "Not bad . . . "

He didn't say anything else. A current caught them, pulled them out farther. Her arms started to go numb, and she lost her grip on him. He floated away, turning face down. He was almost out of sight when she saw him sinking away, down under a wave. Not coming up again. Pretty soon the waves closed over her head too.

Nella was surprised. He was right.

It wasn't bad.

"What is the meaning of it, Watson?" said Holmes, solemnly, as he laid down the paper. "What object is served by this circle of misery and violence and fear? It must tend to some end, or else our universe is ruled by chance, which is unthinkable. But what end? There is the great standing perennial problem to which human reason is as far from an answer as ever."

—"The Adventure of the Cardboard Box"
by Arthur Conan Doyle

ABOUT THE AUTHOR

John Shirley is the author of more than thirty novels. He is considered seminal to the cyberpunk movement in science fiction and has been called the "postmodern Poe" of horror. His numerous short stories have been compiled into eight collections including *Black Butterflies: A Flock on the Darkside*, winner of the Bram Stoker Award, International Horror Guild Award, and named as one of the best one hundred books of the year by *Publishers Weekly*. He has written scripts for television and film, and is best known as co-writer of *The Crow*. As a musician, Shirley has fronted several bands over the years and written lyrics for Blue Öyster Cult and others.

The father of three sons, he lives in the San Francisco Bay area with his wife, Michelina.

To learn more about John Shirley and his work, please visit his website at john-shirley.com.